# HER FATHER'S SECRET

## KATE WILEY

To request permissions, contact the publisher at rights@stormpublishing.co

Ebook ISBN: 978-1-80508-442-6
Paperback ISBN: 978-1-80508-444-0

Cover design: Lisa Brewster
Cover images: Depositphotos

Published by Storm Publishing.
For further information, visit:
www.stormpublishing.co

# ALSO BY KATE WILEY

*The Killer's Daughter*

As Sierra Dean

## The Secret McQueen Series

*Something Secret This Way Comes*

*A Bloody Good Secret*

*Deep Dark Secret*

*Keeping Secret*

*Grave Secret*

*Secret Unleashed*

*Cold Hard Secret*

*A Secret to Die For*

*Secret Lives*

*A Wicked Secret*

*Deadly Little Secret*

*One Last Secret*

## The Genie McQueen Series

*Bayou Blues*

*Black Magic Bayou*

*Black-Hearted Devil*

*Blood in the Bayou*

## The Rain Chaser Series

*Thunder Road*

*Driving Rain*

*Highway to Hail*

## The Boys of Summer Series

*Pitch Perfect*

*Perfect Catch*

*High Heat*

As Gretchen Rue

## The Witches' Brew Mysteries

*Steeped to Death*

*Death by a Thousand Sips*

*The Grim Steeper*

## The Lucky Pie Mysteries

*A Pie to Die For*

*In the summer of 2021 I adopted a cat and named her Margot, hoping it would bring me good luck in getting this series published.*
*This one is for Margot. Proof lucky cat magic is real.*

# ONE

Fat, heavy raindrops spattered across Detective Margot Phalen's windshield, turning the lights beyond into a smeared backdrop of pinpoint glows. The red and blue lights of the squad cars that had been first on the scene continued to illuminate the night, and despite the terrible weather, Margot could see neighbors standing on nearby porches or huddled beneath umbrellas, craning their necks to get a better view of someone else's tragedy.

There was already a news van on site. Must have been a slow night if they were willing to pay attention to a domestic homicide.

Margot took one last sip of her coffee, regretting the choice almost immediately. It was a cup she'd grabbed from the station, and that stuff was sludge at the best of times. Her tongue felt grainy and thickly coated.

She grabbed a pack of gum from her glove compartment and popped a piece in her mouth. The effect was about as enjoyable as drinking orange juice immediately after brushing one's teeth, but at least her breath wouldn't smell like she'd been chewing on coffee grounds.

Margot twisted her long, copper ponytail into a bun at the nape of her neck, a more utilitarian approach since she wasn't sure how bad the scene was. As she ducked out of her car she was immediately pelted with rain. She jogged toward the crime scene, flashing her badge at one of the beat cops unlucky enough to be stuck outside watching the front of the house at 4 a.m.

Inside there was a buzz of activity, but Margot spotted some obvious issues immediately visible. There were muddy shoeprints all over the floor leading into a small kitchen, and Margot had to assume more than a couple of them belonged to the arriving officers.

As she shook rain off her jacket and squeezed the water out of her now messy bun, a familiar figure in a gray suit emerged from the room on her left. He somehow managed to look entirely untouched by rain, as if he'd woken up in the pages of a menswear catalog and simply emerged from them onto the crime scene fully formed.

Wes Fox always looked that good and it was goddamn annoying.

"Margot," he said with a nod of greeting.

"How do you always beat me here?" she grumbled in response. They were partners, had been for years, and during their on-call window they could get notified about a homicide at the most inopportune times. Margot had been fast asleep on the uncomfortable little couch in their shared office space when she got the call.

Wes had been out getting whatever the four in the morning equivalent of lunch was.

"Sometimes a man just gets lucky. This is looking pretty open-and-shut." He had a notepad in his hand, and beyond him in the room he'd just occupied, Margot saw a middle-aged man on the couch, his face buried in his hands, loud sobs filling the otherwise quiet space.

It always amazed her how so many people could be working a crime scene, but it could still sound quiet as a graveyard.

"Husband?" She wasn't sure if she was asking for identification, or if he'd done it.

"Yup."

"All right, walk me through it."

Wes waited for Margot to slip on her protective shoe covers, then guided her into the room across the hall, which she quickly realized was a compact kitchen. The crime scene photographer was busy methodically snapping pictures from every conceivable angle, and every few seconds the space would be boldly lit from the camera flash before returning to the dim glow from some old under-cabinet lighting. It gave the room a macabre disco vibe.

She didn't need Wes to hold her hand with explanations in here. The victim—a white female—was sprawled across the floor, her terrycloth robe partly undone, revealing a plain cotton nightshirt beneath. The woman looked to be about Margot's age, maybe mid-to-late thirties, but the bags under her eyes and ashen complexion spoke of a life that had not, perhaps, always been kind to her.

The victim's eyes were open wide, her mouth formed in a little "o" of surprise. Blood soaked the nightshirt and robe and pooled on the floor beneath her. A weapon was nowhere to be seen, but Margot could see tears in the woman's clothing that suggested a knife as the likely tool.

"Nine-one-one call came from a neighbor who said they had heard fighting for over an hour. Said this wasn't all that unusual, but this time it just sounded worse and they were worried someone was going to get hurt."

"Someone did," Margot said with a sigh. "What's her name?"

"Tracey Clark. Husband is Daryl Clark."

"Has he admitted to doing it?"

Wes shrugged noncommittally. "Hasn't really said much of anything yet except for *oh God oh God is she dead*, but I'm assuming he'll crack pretty quickly once we get him down to the station. The knife was sitting right next to him on the couch when the responding officer came in."

Margot scanned the scene laid out before her, trying not to make assumptions—though it wasn't a stretch to assume the husband was guilty based solely on the scant information Wes had given her. Still, a good cop knew better than to make assumptions. It led to mistakes. It was all well and fine to see where the evidence led, but too often overworked or lazy officers decided who was guilty and only looked for evidence that fit *that* hypothesis, to the detriment of the truth.

She knew Wes wasn't a lazy cop, but she also wanted to see things for herself.

There was broken glass on the floor and a drying spatter of liquid on the fridge that might have been either wine or cola. One of the chairs at the small dinette set was overturned and two plates of spaghetti and meatballs were partially eaten on the table.

A meatball had, at one point, been thrown against the white wall and was settled not far from the victim's foot.

"Is there a history of domestic disturbance from this address? You said the neighbor mentioned fights weren't uncommon." A case filled with empty beer bottles sat next to the fridge, and in the sink were the remnants of dirty dishes from preparing dinner.

The knife block on the counter was missing two knives; one appeared to be a large chef's knife, the other a bread knife. Margot saw the handle of the bread knife sticking out of the sink.

"Call list a mile long. Seems like they were both in the habit of stirring shit up regularly. Few hospital visits, all her. Few times he claimed she threatened him. Looks like they were not exactly a happy couple."

Margot's lips formed a thin line. Something about the scene bothered her. It wasn't that it didn't fit the hypothesis. She could practically see the fight unfolding, him unhappy that the meal wasn't hot enough, or didn't taste the way he liked. Her throwing a meatball at him and missing. Glassware hitting the fridge, then him hitting her.

It all *looked* obvious enough.

Margot cast a quick glance at her watch. "What time did the call come in?"

"Neighbor made the initial call about two thirty, maybe a little earlier. Patrol arrived at two fifty. They knocked and no response, but they did a perimeter check and saw the disturbance in the kitchen, figured there was enough probable cause and came inside. Found the husband. Found the body. Called us."

And they'd arrived around four.

"Do we know anything about his schedule? It seems a bit weird to me they'd be sitting down to dinner at two in the morning?" She gestured to the scene at the table. "And she's in her robe?"

Margot gently tapped the photographer on the shoulder and pointed to the items she had noticed. "Could you make sure to take pictures of all this?"

"You got it," the photographer said. Margot had experienced some crime scene photographers giving her lip for asking for specific things, as if she was telling them how to do their jobs, but when trial came around Margot didn't like hoping the evidence had been properly documented.

"What are you thinking?" She turned to Wes, deferred to him to give his opinion first, since he'd been the first of them on the scene.

"Two possibilities. One, maybe he works late, came home, and got pissed that dinner was cold, took it out on her." Wes moved around the kitchen, avoiding any evidence on the floor and gesturing to the mess around the dinner table. "It's the obvious answer, and a good lawyer could probably get him a reduced sentence, manslaughter maybe, if he can talk it down to a fight over the knife, or imply that she came at him. There's a history."

"Mmhmm. Option two?" She was looking at the body on the floor, trying to imagine what the woman had been doing in the moments before she died.

Wes, a renewed enthusiasm buoying his words, bounded back over to her like a golden retriever. "His woe-is-me act is a cover, fight happened earlier, he waited until later, or left and came back, all with the intention of killing her. So option one." He held up one finger. "It's an act of passion in the moment. Option two." Two fingers. Margot raised an eyebrow. She appreciated him helping her count; math was hard, after all. "Option two, he wanted her dead and he's trying to make us *think* it was spur of the moment when he had plenty of time to plan it."

Margot held up three of her own fingers. "Option three, he left and someone else came in and killed her, then he found her like this when he got back."

"I'm not *suggesting* that to him, but yes, that is an option. We'll have to talk to the neighbors to figure out exactly what they heard, which might help us narrow down the choices."

Margot leaned her body out of the kitchen to look into the living room. "Guess we'll see what he has to say when he can stop sobbing and start putting sentences together."

She rubbed the bridge of her nose, lamenting the crick in her neck and the lack of decent coffee in her body. "Let's have someone take him down to the station and let him sit on ice for a little while we look over the scene. And let's get some of these muddy boots *out of our crime scene*," she declared loudly enough for anyone on site to hear.

A few mumbled apologies filtered into the room and at least two officers left through the front door back out into the rain.

Margot stood in the doorway and stared into the living room where the husband was still crying. She was unmoved.

This was going to be a long day.

# TWO

## SUMMER 1988

Petaluma, California

A piece of newspaper was taped to Ed Finch's dashboard.

*Marissa L, 27, fun, fit, and ready for an adventure with you.*
*Loves line dancing and daiquiris. Looking for Mr. Right, but Mr.*
*Right Now will do.*

Her address was written below it in pen.

Ed was a Petaluma, California native. His family lived only six blocks from Marissa's apartment, and because of that, he knew he had to tread lightly with this one. He'd been learning, evolving. It had been three months since he'd been able to play the way he wanted to, and the craving was becoming too much for him to bear.

There were nights over the dinner table he wanted to take a steak knife and stick it right in his wife's throat as she bitched about some boring parent–teacher drama or asked him if he had paid for Megan's field trip.

He pictured her eyes going wide and the blood spilling from

her mouth as the dead weight of her words dribbled out onto the tablecloth.

Whenever he started to imagine Kim at the point of his knife, he knew it was time to go hunting. But there were dangers about hunting close to home, because he ran the risk of coming under scrutiny.

He was careful, so careful, but after ten dead women, the papers were starting to pay even more attention than the police.

People were noticing his work, and it made a little glow of pride blossom inside his chest.

*Careful*, he chided.

He was parked in front of Marissa's apartment building, the engine off, air cool from the cracked window. Tonight wasn't going to be the night. He needed to pick up Megan from her babysitter soon, which gave him a good reason to be out of the house, but not enough time to linger and enjoy.

It was just enough time to know if Marissa was the right one.

The next one.

He fingered the paper on the dashboard, a bitter taste in his mouth over her frivolous description. *Mr. Right Now.*

Yes, he could be Mr. Right Now.

It was early evening still, the sun just coming down. Kim was at a baby swimming class with Justin. Summer was around the corner and it was apparent in the girls walking out at dusk with their shorts and crocheted halter tops. Their hair, teased and sprayed, was tall and wispy like cotton candy, and their cheeks glowed pink under the warpaint smears of blusher.

He could taste the way their hairspray would smell. It was a scent that lingered in his own bathroom, a chemical baby powder sweetness that coated the back of his throat. He coughed thinking of it.

A girl who was probably only sixteen whipped past his car on roller skates, giant bug-eye sunglasses covering her eyes and a huge pink gum bubble extending from her pouty lips, pink with gloss. He watched her go for a lot longer than he should have; the sway of her hips and the mechanical whirr of her wheels on pavement.

He shook off the hypnotic hold she had over him. Too young. Someone would notice a girl like that gone. Someone was waiting for her to come home for dinner.

Single women living alone were easier. Their independence, something they were so proud of, so snide about, was the exact same thing that made them the ideal victim. If they didn't come around for a day or two, people would write it off.

You had to be careful about your choices, he knew. And he couldn't be stupid just because the hunger inside him was so intense that he wanted to grab the first person who walked by his car door, haul her into the back seat and let his knife drink deep of her blood.

Anyone could be a victim, but not any of them would feel *right*.

It had to be right.

He saw Marissa walking by herself toward the apartment complex. No dog, just a quick jaunt to the corner market. He liked dogs well enough, but dogs were a problem. They didn't like him. He avoided them and was relieved to see she didn't have one.

She was not as *fit* as her profile might lead suitors to believe, with a little pillowy softness around her middle, but it made her breasts fuller, and Ed let out a groan of pleasure imagining his freshly sharpened knife buried to the hilt in that plump belly.

He shifted in his seat, reminding himself not to move, not yet.

She deserved his proper attention.

And soon enough, he'd be back to give it to her.

# THREE

Margot and Wes spent hours going over the Clark house with a fine-tooth comb. There was no evidence to suggest a third party was responsible for what had happened to Tracey, but they investigated as if the question might come up down the road.

At seven in the morning when they returned to the precinct, Daryl was waiting for them in a small interrogation room. Someone had offered him a coffee and a box of tissues. There was a crinkled granola bar wrapper in the garbage can.

Margot's stomach rumbled, reminding her of the meal she and Wes had been forced to skip hours earlier. She took the chair closest to Daryl, ready to play bad cop if needed. She was hungry, wet from the downpour outside, and deeply ready to call this a night.

The overnight shift ended at five and they were officially on overtime. Her bed was calling, and she had no idea when she'd finally get there. All of that was perfect fodder to take out on a weepy bag of shit who had probably stabbed his wife about a dozen times.

"Daryl, what time do you usually get home from work?"

She placed a thick folder on the table between them, looked at something inside, then looked at him again.

The folder was empty, they wouldn't have copies of the crime scene photos until the next day, most likely, and the only reports they had on the case were a collection of vague witness statements, all of which were being collected by the officers at the scene. Margot had stuffed a stack of printer paper into the folder before coming into the room.

Daryl's gaze lifted from his shoes to the table, fixating on the folder, while Margot drummed her fingers on top of it.

Her nail polish, which she had applied herself over a week ago in a Pinot Grigio-inspired fit of *self-care* inspiration was chipping badly, reminding her why she rarely bothered.

"I work nights at a place that makes and repairs boat motors."

"That's busy enough to require a night shift?" she asked.

"Yes, ma'am." The way he added on the *ma'am* did not feel forced. It felt like something that someone with a history of criminal offenses might say though, while trying to toe the line with authority.

This *was* a man accustomed to visits from the police, after all. He was no stranger to appearing contrite.

She wouldn't be surprised if it had worked with some of the older male officers.

It wasn't going to do much for her.

"What time do you usually get home?"

"About one o'clock."

"Care to walk me through getting home tonight?" She glanced inside the folder again, then snapped it shut.

Daryl sat hunched over the table, curling in on himself so he did not appear as big as he was, but Margot figured he was probably well over six feet, maybe close to Wes's height, and had a good twenty pounds on her partner as well. He was a *big* guy, definitely capable of overpowering his wife in a fight.

Margot watched as he looked from her to Wes, maybe to see if he'd find a more generous audience there, but Wes was leaned up against the wall, looking more like a suit mannequin than a sympathetic man's man. Whatever Daryl saw on Wes's face it made him look back at Margot again, resigned.

The pair of them worked well together in interrogations. It wasn't necessarily a good cop/bad cop dynamic so much as it was playing a different kind of game of opposites. If Wes was aloof, Margot was inviting; if Margot was cold, Wes would be warmer. They matched each other in opposite directions, which forced whoever they were grilling to find at least one person in the room to latch onto.

Sometimes they worked apart, in which case Margot defaulted to cold. She wasn't there to make anyone feel better about what they'd done.

She just wanted answers.

And right now, she wanted those answers from Daryl.

"I got home a bit later than usual. Tracey got in on me right away." Despite him attempting to present these facts calmly, Margot could hear the tight venom in his tone that was unmistakable to anyone listening for it. She knew that sound well. It was the sound of a trapped man living with years of toxic loathing polluting his blood. It was all bitterness. There was no warmth whatsoever in the way he spoke his dead wife's name. "She was pissing and moaning about me being late, and how she goes to all this effort and stays up late just to see me and how inconsiderate I am." Daryl hefted a sigh and put his hands on the table, fingers threaded together.

There was blood dried under his fingernails.

"I guess this is the part where I'm supposed to ask you guys for a lawyer." Now, instead of vicious, he just sounded tired. "But look, here's the thing. She came at *me* with that knife. She came at me saying she was sick of my shit, this was right after she threw half my goddamn dinner on the wall and said if I was so hungry after work I could come home on time or eat it off the floor. After she threw a damn *drink* at me. Then she comes swinging, like she's just cracked and has had enough of me or whatever."

"You're saying you acted in self-defense?" Margot asked, leading him right up to the noose with which to hang himself.

"Me and Tracey, we had lots of problems, I'm sure you already know that." He jutted his chin at the folder under her hand. "That was no secret. But we always made it right after. Except this time I don't think Tracey wanted to make it right. I didn't *want* to hurt her, Detective, I swear to you on my life." Tears began to tremble in his lashes again, and for the first time tonight Margot thought there might be some honesty in them.

"Daryl, are you saying you stabbed your wife?"

He nodded, then let out a loud sob that ended in a hiccup. He wiped snot and tears from his face then said simply, "Yeah. Yeah, it was fucking me. God, I'm so sorry, Trace." He fumbled at his cheeks, swiping angrily at the tears that kept coming despite his best efforts to chase them away. "She was so mad at me."

Wes placed a notepad and paper on the table in front of Daryl. "Mr. Clark, to the best of your recollection, I'm going to need you to write us a statement of what happened tonight. For the record."

This was often the point where suspects clammed up and started to take it all back, but Daryl grabbed the pen, along with a wad of tissues, and started scribbling it down, his writing almost childlike in its roughness.

Outside the door, through the tiny window that looked out onto the hallway, someone ran by.

Then two uniformed officers followed.

Leon Telly, one of their fellow detectives who was on day rotation, hustled past, then returned a moment later. He locked eyes with Margot, then Wes, and jerked his head toward the hallway.

Margot quickly glanced at Wes, who took the hint and headed out of the room. When he opened the door a moment later he gestured for her to join him in the hall. She didn't like leaving Daryl Clark alone mid-confession, but he seemed to be focused on his writing and showing no signs of changing his tune. As she came out, she grabbed a passing officer.

"Hey, can you stay in here with him and make sure he finishes that confession. Watch him sign it, and then if I'm not back in five minutes, take him to holding." The uniform, young and enthusiastic, looked like she might argue with Margot's request, but thought better of it at the last minute, slipping into the room as she'd been told.

She caught up with Wes and Leon. "We're in the middle of a confession, what the hell is going on out here?" She glanced toward the war room, a big common area where the detectives worked, and past that into the larger open area of the station. It was absolute chaos. Her heart sank, knowing that few things could provoke such a wild reaction from the police. "What happened?"

Her imagination ran wild, going almost immediately to terrorism, because worst-case scenarios told her that was the most likely thing to cause such a buzz.

Leon, cheeks flushed, shook his head, an expression of disbelief etched on his features. Leon was in his sixties and had seen some of the worst of the worst. He frequently lamented how he had become a detective a mere year after famed San Francisco super-cop Dave Toschi retired, missing his hero like ships passing in the night.

Even Dave Toschi—the inspiration for *Bullitt* and *Dirty Harry*—would have had chills looking at Leon's face in that moment.

It was Wes, not Leon, who answered her question. "There was a shooting down on Pier 39. Five confirmed injuries so far, one dead." When he saw the confusion on her face, just because shootings—even bad ones—didn't warrant this kind of a response, he kept going.

"They think it's a sniper."

# FOUR

*Sniper.*

It was a single word. Two syllables.

All the same, hearing it made Margot's skin go cold and her mouth dry. There wasn't a cop alive who hadn't spent much of 2014 feeling like there was an invisible target on their backs following the weeks-long manhunt for a sniper in Pennsylvania who was targeting the police.

That had been three years ago, but the memory of it, and other recent killing sprees, still felt fresh in the collective consciousness of law enforcement.

There was just something about a sniper, something that loomed larger and more ominously than other kinds of criminals, because they haunted cities like ghosts. They could be anywhere, watching anyone. There was no intimacy to the kills performed by a sniper—probably why the method was popular among assassins—it was all cool efficiency. They could kill you from almost anywhere and you would simply never see it coming.

You'd just be dead.

Pier 39 was one of the busiest tourist attractions in San

Francisco. While it was nothing like it had been when Margot used to come as a kid, it was still one of the biggest draws in town.

The bayside area was littered with overpriced restaurants and rides, plenty of places where a family from Ohio could overspend to get a bite of San Fran's most famous sourdough or tour the Ghirardelli chocolate factory. There were about a thousand kitschy souvenir shops, an aquarium, and dozens of chain restaurants. It wasn't what Margot would call a typical San Francisco experience, but it was a place most tourists felt the need to visit their first time in town, especially with Alcatraz and the Golden Gate Bridge visible as backdrops.

Margot imagined how the pier would normally look at this time of day, with umbrellas bumping into each other and the laughter of children echoing in the air. For a gunman to choose Pier 39 as a target meant he was trying to create the most chaos and terror possible in the shortest period.

Even this early in the morning, when things were barely open for the day, the pier would be packed with foot traffic.

Margot nodded her understanding and returned briefly to the interrogation room and the uniformed officer.

"Did he sign?" she asked.

The uniform nodded.

"OK, can you go ahead and take him back to holding? Daryl, if you want to make a phone call, the officer can help you do that, otherwise you're going to be held here until your arraignment." Margot didn't have it in her to be cruel to him. He had murdered his wife, but she had bigger concerns at the moment, and with his confession, he'd be going away for a good long time.

One case was done, but it seemed the next was just beginning.

She, Wes, and Leon all exited the building together. While she and Wes were officially off duty and free to go home once they'd filed their report on the Clarks, there was no way in hell either of them was going to get any sleep if there was a sniper out putting a target on tourists. That was a level of insidiousness that needed to be stamped out *fast*.

Margot knew a thing or two about the kind of fear that was generated by murder. Gang violence could cause people to avoid parts of town, walk in larger groups, lock their car doors as they drove, but it wouldn't keep them inside their homes or feel like an immediate threat to their everyday lives.

The Bay Area was steeped in a bloody history of serial killers, and Margot knew from personal experience the way a repeat offender spooked people. They would double and triple check their doors at night. Anyone who seemed out of place in a neighborhood was suddenly a suspect. That kind of fear dug into your bones, it ate at you, made you paranoid and vigilant.

But a sniper? A killer who could strike anywhere at any time with a seemingly random agenda and no easy evidence left behind? That was terrorism. It was death for the sake of fear.

And the more scared people got, the better the shooter would feel.

They needed to figure out who this fucker was *fast* because there was no way to keep that level of panic down when it reached a frenzy. They couldn't afford a month-long manhunt.

"We're going to want to get a list of any former military living in the Bay Area, especially anyone with noted weapons training," Margot told Wes while typing a text out as they walked, the cold rain still pelting down on them and making it hard to get the letters right on her phone.

Wes opened the passenger door for her and she got in as he skirted to the other side of his car, slipped the dash light up and secured it in place. He turned it on, red light filling the car. Leon got into his own car, parked just behind Wes, his light going as well. It was morning now, and the lights were of little effect against the rising sun, but they needed something to identify themselves in their unmarked cars, and it was going to be hell getting from the precinct down to the pier.

Siren wails seemed to fill the air from every direction, but Margot knew she was listening for them. Wes and Leon pulled away in unison, both navigating the traffic expertly down to the waterfront, where a huge collection of black-and-white squad cars as well as fire engines and ambulances were assembled.

Normally the area surrounding a crime scene would be thick with onlookers and press, anyone who wanted to get a quick glimpse at a body or make themselves a part of the case in some capacity. People were drawn to violence even as it repelled them. There was a reason true crime podcasts and documentaries were so popular, and it was the same reason people liked to look at sharks as long as there was a thick layer of glass between them and the monster.

People *loved* to be safely afraid.

What made this crime scene feel eerier than most was how empty it was.

Margot didn't come to Pier 39 often. She avoided it whenever she could because being in big crowds made her uneasy, and she liked to be in control of her surroundings. But right now, it was a scene out of a post-apocalyptic horror film. It was completely vacant.

As she got out of the car, Margot took in the scene. There were a scant few employees at various stores and stands obviously rushing to lock them up. They were staying tight to the buildings, avoiding stepping out into any potential line of sight for a gunman's rifle.

In the cluster of ambulances there were paramedics rushing to attend to minor wounds while others loaded up those headed for hospital to get them the hell out of harm's way. They had waited until it seemed the shooting had stopped before letting paramedics anywhere near the scene, and it had been quiet a good fifteen minutes now.

Still, there were efforts being made to avoid standing out. Even the uniformed officers on the scene seemed disinclined to step away from their cruisers. Margot could see more than one witness interview taking place in the back seat of a squad car.

She didn't blame them; she wasn't thrilled about the idea of walking out into an open area minutes after a sniper's bullets had ripped through it. But there was a job to be done. Wes, Margot, and Leon regrouped and headed toward a section of the boardwalk cordoned off with yellow crime scene tape.

Leon's cell phone buzzed, and he checked the message.

"That's Belmont and Lawrence. They went right to the hospital. Sounds like one of the other vics was DOA."

"Jesus," Wes muttered. "What a fucking shitshow." He stayed close to Margot's side, and she saw the way his gaze was directed up and behind them, as if he might be able to spot a glint in the gunman's scope from this distance, something to tell them where he was hiding.

"Detectives." A senior officer on the scene nodded to them as they arrived. Margot was relieved it wasn't some fresh-faced twenty-year-old kid straight from the academy and into his worst nightmare. This guy had the round, taut belly of a man just inches from his pension, and the mustache of a cop who really liked people to know he was a cop. His dark hair was silver around the temples, and he looked harried, in spite of the gruff, serious air he was presenting.

Margot felt a rare spike of anxiety feeding off his obvious unease. When a scene rattled guys like him, that was when you knew you were ankle-deep in the shit and sinking fast.

"Sergeant Galway." He offered his hand to Margot first, which surprised her, since Leon was obviously the elder statesman among them, but she appreciated the acknowledgment, and shook Galway's hand. The rain had lessened slightly, but it was joined with the morning fog rolling in off the Bay to create an atmosphere of wetness that seeped in from every angle. Margot would need to fully change every stitch of clothing she was wearing when she got home if she wanted to feel dry again.

The weather certainly added an interesting element to this. Whoever they were dealing with knew what they were doing, there was no doubt, because gunning someone down on a clear day was very different from hitting your target at a distance in the rain and fog.

"What've we got?" she asked, waving a hand in the direction of the yellow tape.

Galway ushered them forward, lifting the tape so the three detectives could duck under. They found themselves under the awning of a fudge shop, and the sweet smell of chocolate and butter in the air was a shock to the system, given what was lying on the ground in front of them.

"Fifty-two-year-old male. Identified by his wife and by wallet. Name's Dan Wheeler. They were here on an anniversary trip from Utah, and Dan wanted to come down and see the Bridge."

Collectively they all looked toward the Bay, where they knew what they'd see. Nothing. The Golden Gate Bridge, for all its fame and bright red-orange paint, could be a fickle landmark at times. It was positively enormous, and yet it could vanish entirely in the fog.

Dead Dan had wanted to see the Bridge and he hadn't even gotten that wish before someone had put a bullet right through his goddamn eye.

Margot had seen her share of dead bodies, so the sight of Dan didn't turn her stomach, but it did make a pit form there, something in the guilt family. She felt *bad* for him, in a way she normally didn't let herself empathize with victims. Personalizing them often made her job too hard.

But man, what an injustice.

"Poor bastard," Wes muttered, obviously thinking and feeling exactly what she was.

The bullet hole in his eye was very tidy, all things considered. It was the back of his head where the real mess was, something they couldn't actually see, given that he was lying on his back, but the pink-gray pulp of brain matter pasted across the front of the fudge shop's display counter was a bit of a giveaway.

"Jesus," Margot muttered, wiping an errant rivulet of rainwater away from her eyes. Not that she necessarily wanted to see things any better.

Dan Wheeler lay with his head practically against the counter, his arms and legs at his sides, as if he was just splayed out on the beach getting a little sun. From his position, it seemed likely he had fallen backwards from a few feet away, the force of the bullet sending him under the covered awning to where he finally landed.

Margot, staying out of the rain as best she could, peered back in the direction he must have been facing when he was struck. She pictured him standing with his wife, in line for a treat, and then suddenly three feet back and dead.

It would have been quick. If there was one godsend in the whole miserable mess of this, it was knowing that the gunman had aimed true with Dan. Poor guy probably didn't even know something had hit him.

Margot doubted that his wife would take much comfort from that.

What Margot wanted to see as she scanned the uphill climb behind the pier wasn't the glint of a gunman's scope, but rather the most likely place he'd been firing from. There were multiple apartment buildings across from the pier itself, but they seemed an unlikely place to choose, since most of them were mixed-use real estate and businesses were far more likely to notice someone walking in with a duffel bag or rifle case, something big enough to carry the kind of weapon that had done this.

That meant their perp was most likely blocks away, and from where Margot stood that barely narrowed anything down. Pier 39 was a low spot in the city, and there were literally hundreds of vantage points that looked down on it. San Francisco might not be bustling with skyscrapers the way a city like New York or Los Angeles was, but there were plenty of windows Margot could see perfectly from where she was standing, and any one of them could have had a rifle in it aimed right at her.

This was worse than finding a needle in a haystack, because here they couldn't even narrow down the haystacks.

"Any useful witness testimony?" Wes asked Galway. Margot's typically polished partner was dripping wet, his usually perfectly tidy hair had taken on a slight wave from the moisture, and a perfect Clark Kent curl stuck to his forehead. Next to the ruddy-cheeked sergeant, Wes Fox looked like an actor pretending to be a cop rather than a real detective.

Thankfully, him being incredibly good-looking did not impede his abilities.

"We have uniforms out canvassing all the buildings across the street." Galway gestured in the direction of the apartments. "We managed to get some eyewitness testimony from a few folks who didn't immediately leave the scene, but as you can see, the pickings were slim. People said they were just walking around when suddenly bodies were hitting the floor. It was so quiet they didn't realize anyone was shot until this poor son of a bitch lost the back of his head." He gave his round belly a rub, as if it helped him clear his thoughts. "Everyone who talked to us was insistent that there was no one nearby shooting, it was just people hitting the ground. One girl—she's at the hospital now—she told me that she thought something had bit her." He tapped his shoulder, presumably where the girl had been struck. "She didn't know she'd been shot at first."

Wes looked around. "Was there anything happening here

this morning? Special programming, something that might have grabbed our shooter's attention and made the pier an appealing target?"

Sergeant Galway shook his head. "Nothing, just your run-of-the-mill Tuesday morning." He took a long look around the rain-soaked pier and shook his head. "It wouldn't have even been an especially busy day with this. I mean, it's always packed down here, but it would only be the real keeners on a day like this."

Margot looked back down at Dan, whose face showed no signs of fear or surprise.

"He picked a bad day to be the early bird."

# FIVE

It was after eleven when Margot finally made it back to her apartment. Despite her desire to continue working the sniper case in earnest, the captain had been adamant that the night shift get some sleep. There would be hours of witness statements, forensics from the victims, and tip line calls to go through, and half-zombified cops weren't going to help with that. So she and Wes had been sent home.

She had resisted, but Wes reminded her there was no point in driving herself into the ground physically and mentally when the sniper—and inevitable unrelated new homicides—would still need her attention that night.

Locking the series of bolts on her door, she dropped her bag on the floor and kicked off her boots. Her blinds were still shut from when she'd headed to work the previous evening, so the only light was a small lamp next to her couch. It was already the perfect setting for sleep. While she knew her mind wouldn't let her immediately rest, she was going to do her best to get some.

A quick meal of cold leftover pizza was enough to keep her stomach from gnawing itself to bits, and by noon she was in a pair of soft pajamas, nestled under her duvet, with the sound of rain pattering against the window. The clouds outside made it almost dark enough to have the curtains open, but she didn't bother.

She was nearly asleep when the familiar buzz of her phone yanked her right back into the conscious world. Turning it off was a dream for another life. As a detective she had to be available twenty-four-seven, even if it was her scheduled downtime.

The caller ID said SEBASTIAN, and she rolled her eyes, genuinely considering not answering it, but knowing that Seb would remind her a thousand times over how often he was there for her.

Sebastian Klein was a staff reporter for the *San Francisco Sentinel* and from time to time Margot would be an *unnamed source within the police department* so that Sebastian would reciprocate with information he had gleaned through his own sources and research.

It was a mutually parasitic relationship, but it worked for them.

"Seb." She pulled the duvet over her head, letting her eyelids flutter closed again, not particularly trying to stay awake. "I'm on nights."

"Oh, shit. Sorry, dollface, I'll keep it quick and painless, I promise."

"Sure, sure."

"I was just hoping I might be able to get a comment, or some insight about the Pier 39 shooting today."

"You know I can't comment on a case like this, you gotta toe the company line on that one. Sorry. SFPD press liaison will be your new BFF. I bet she's even awake right now."

"Angel, you know I called Yvonne before you. This is not my first rodeo."

"And Yvonne said?"

"*No comment.*"

"That is her favorite phrase. Her life motto, you might say."

Sebastian grumbled. "For someone whose entire job it is to provide comments, you'd think she might come up with some new material after a decade."

"If it ain't broke..." Margot's voice was taking on the thick slowness of sleep, making the call feel more like a dream than a reality.

"All right, well you're fully useless to me right now. But if something changes and you feel like giving your good friend Sebastian something, don't forget me, OK?"

"Never."

She hung up the phone without a proper goodbye and within seconds she was fast asleep.

Her sleep was deep and dreamless, the kind of inky nothing that one never wants to wake from. But wake she did, again to the distinct buzzing from her phone. She was tangled up in her duvet, obviously having adjusted her position somewhat too assertively as she was out cold.

"Sebastian, I promise you I can't make any statements, official or otherwise. I'm sorry." She disentangled herself from the sheets, her phone pressed between her ear and the pillow.

There was a long pause, long enough that she wondered if the caller on the other end had disconnected, until she heard a light, dry crackle of a cough. Someone clearing their throat.

"Ms. Fin... Phalen," came the voice at last, and it was that one distinct mistake, the one errant change of an *fi* for a *pha* that most casual listeners might not hear, that told Margot *immediately* who was on the other end of the line.

"Mr. Rosenthal," she replied coldly.

Her tone might convey a calm and even icy demeanor, but inside Margot was trembling. That one slip of the tongue from a lawyer she barely knew, and it was enough to make her certain that she had just had the last good sleep she was going to get for weeks to come.

"Yes, hello. It's Ford Rosenthal," he announced, as if she

hadn't just used his name a moment earlier. "I'm calling on behalf of your father, Mr. Ed Finch."

"Don't call him that," she said sharply.

"Don't call him *Ed Finch*?" Mr. Rosenthal replied, obviously confused. Margot hadn't interacted with the lawyer much. She actually made a point of avoiding him whenever she could, but what she had learned of him over the few months of their acquaintance was that he did not understand subtlety. He was also blithely unaware of why she might not want to have any association with his client.

"*Father,*" she said slowly. "Don't call him that."

Mr. Rosenthal was quiet again for a long moment, trying to process the request, before finally continuing. "Mr. Finch asked me to pass a message along to you."

Margot had steps she was supposed to follow when these calls came in, there was a new protocol. The FBI had asked her very specifically to make sure that she recorded the messages verbatim so that there would be no mistaking Ed's words when they tried to puzzle them out later.

But Margot was still cocooned in her sheets, and it seemed unlikely that Mr. Rosenthal was going to wait for her.

The FBI was just going to have to trust her memory.

There was a very good reason that Margot's father wasn't calling her herself to pass along this vital message, and that was because he was locked up in a solitary cell in the maximum-security wing of San Quentin, behind so many bars he would never breathe a gulp of air as a free man again in his life.

Ed Finch.

The Classified Killer.

One of the most prolific and infamous serial killers in American history, and he just happened to be her dear old dad.

Mr. Rosenthal didn't wait for Margot to accept the message, he just plowed ahead with it, sharing it like a secret she didn't want to know, a gift she hadn't asked for.

"He wanted me to say he misses you very much, and if you come for a visit, he will tell you a story that Marissa's been dying to share."

Margot's entire body went cold.

"Those were his exact words?" she asked, having a hard time keeping her voice calm.

"Yes. The precise message he wanted me to pass along. Shall I arrange the visit?"

Margot's hand was trembling. "I'm going to have to get back to you on that one, Ford." She hung up the phone without saying goodbye.

Marissa.

There was no one in her family named Marissa, and Margot knew Ed's list of victims like the back of her hand. Seventy-seven named victims and not one of them was a Marissa.

Yet she knew the name as soon as it had been said, knew its significance. She had grown up in Petaluma, California, after all, and *everyone* in Petaluma remembered the Marissa Loewen case. The pretty twenty-something who had vanished one summer and was never seen again.

Margot had been so young when that case hit the news, but she still remembered the picture the media circulated, a black-and-white photo of a beaming, fresh-faced girl, her brown hair feathered and the cute little gap between her teeth.

It was a photo Margot had seen only weeks earlier, pinned to a bulletin board at the FBI field office in downtown San Francisco. A board covered with the faces of cold cases from the eighties and nineties up and down the California coastline.

Marissa's body had never been found; her killer never located. A missing person didn't seem like Ed's style, so no one had seriously considered him a possibility, even years after the fact.

Apparently, they'd been wrong.

# SIX

When Wes got into the office at eight thirty that night, Margot
was already three coffees deep and pacing the small open area
between their desks. She caught the way he was looking at her
when he came in. It was not unlike the way someone watches a
caged predator just to see how they'll react to their
confinement.

"You OK there?" he asked, setting down a new cup of
takeout coffee on her desk and obviously reconsidering it for a
moment before leaving it and throwing out the empties. She
appreciated him disposing of the evidence.

"Can you close the door?"

It was a rare day that their office door was closed, and it was
likely to rouse more suspicions than it deterred, but all the same,
Margot didn't need anyone else at the precinct learning her
dirty little secret.

She hadn't been born Margot Phalen. She was originally
Megan Finch, but that name got a bit too much heat on it once
her father's misdeeds were made public. A name change for her,
her mother, and brother had been the easiest way to avoid
notice by the public. Now, if anyone googled *Ed Finch daughter*

they'd see photos of a chubby-cheeked teenager who didn't bear a ton of resemblance to Margot, and they'd find nothing beyond her middle school graduation.

Margot had done what she could to avoid association with Ed, but sometimes he came back to haunt her at the most inopportune times.

Four months earlier he had requested a transfer from New York back to San Francisco, and he'd begun trying to contact her through his lawyer.

He'd dangled a carrot in front of her then: if she came to visit him, he'd tell her about his previously unknown seventy-seventh victim. Against all her better instincts Margot had gone, and true to his word he had told them where to find the body. He tried to do the same thing only days later, and Margot had agreed to play along with the FBI and continue meeting with Ed.

But Ed had decided he didn't want to participate.

He had rejected weeks' worth of efforts to set up a new meeting. Margot knew it was a power play. He had told them there were more victims, and now he wanted them to beg.

For four months, she had been free, not beholden to Ed or the FBI. It was just enough time for her to think she might never need to go back. Enough time to feel safe again.

How stupid had she been?

She didn't *want* to speak to Ed again, didn't want to be in the same room as him, because every second of her time, every word she spoke to him as an adult, was a little bit of herself that he stole, and she couldn't bear it.

But there were more victims, she knew that much with certainty.

And him using Marissa's name upped the stakes. She had to report it. And that meant she was more than likely going to have to go back.

"I got a call today. A message from Ed," she admitted,

before sinking onto the ratty old couch positioned at the back wall of the room. It smelled of must and decay and about fifty years' worth of police officer sweat, but somehow it was the most comforting place she could think to put herself.

Wes leaned forward in his chair, posture rigid. He ran his hands through his dark blond hair and shook his head sympathetically. "Goddamn, Margot. When it rains it pours, doesn't it?"

She glanced beyond him into the main room of the homicide department. It was busier than usual that evening, with many of the daytime detectives still lingering to work angles on the sniper case. The shooting was the kind of thing that would have a ton of pressure on it from both top brass and the public in general, so even though Margot understood how scant their evidence was, and knew that in all likelihood they wouldn't have much to go on unless he struck again, she also knew why it was so important to these guys to keep working themselves to the bone for it. Anything less would look like apathy, and the police department had a bad enough reputation with the public these days, they didn't need to add an impression of cavalier laziness to the mix.

It was all hands on deck with the sniper, but it was also a bureaucratic nightmare. They didn't need work getting done twice by over-eager detectives who wanted to be heroes. She and Wes had been told to focus on their current workload until the team lead—Leon—gave them something specific they could help with.

Margot turned her attention back to Wes. "You know the Marissa Loewen case?" It was an almost thirty-year-old case, so she wasn't too surprised when he shook his head.

"Name rings a bell but I'm not sure I could give you a brief or anything."

"It was a super-famous missing person's case in the eighties up in Petaluma." The name-drop of her hometown was where she paused, giving him a meaningful look.

"Oh. Shit."

Wes was one of three people in the precinct who knew Ed Finch was her father. The chief knew because they'd needed to perform a background check on her. Leon knew because he was a damn good detective. Everyone else, it seemed, did not think or care enough about Margot's personal life to dig into it, largely because she kept to herself and didn't socialize with anyone else outside work. Wes was the only co-worker she had who had ever set foot inside her apartment, and they'd known each other for almost two years before she'd ever let that happen.

Now she was grateful to have someone she could talk to about this, someone who understood the gravity.

No one could really *get* what her experience was, but at the very least Wes understood why it made her act the way she did sometimes. When he'd learned about her, it had taken a little of the edge off their working relationship, allowing them to become something almost like friends in the process.

For someone who didn't *have* friends, it was a necessary human connection for her.

"Have you talked to the FBI about this?" he asked, sitting on the edge of his desk to create a little bubble between them, but also giving her her own space on the couch. She appreciated the way he sensed that she didn't want to be touched. Perhaps it was the nervous energy vibrating off her.

She shook her head. "No, I'm going to call Andrew, but I just... I guess I hoped Ed had been bluffing? I had hoped he realized he couldn't keep playing us, or he would get bored of the game, and move onto something else. I went four *months* thinking that might be it, and now he's back."

Wes offered her a soft smile, the lines around his eyes crinkling. "I have a few exes like that."

Margot barked out a short laugh, unexpectedly genuine. "I'm surprised it's not *all* your exes, you scoundrel."

"Nah, most of them never want to see me again, if we're being real." He straightened up and took a sip from his coffee. "Look, I can be the sympathetic ear all you want on this, and I'm happy to do it. But I think you need to call Special Agent Rhodes and let him know ASAP. Hiding in your office isn't going to make that call any less real."

Margot hadn't considered what she was doing *hiding* but as she let his words sink in, she knew he was right. In a sense she was at work because she could use it as an excuse not to deal with the call, but she needed to loop Andrew in on this, he deserved to know.

Wes pushed himself up from the desk and settled into his chair. "How about I get started on the final paperwork for the Tracey Clark homicide and we can officially check that off the board. You call Rhodes, and then we can dig into the pile of ex-military names the guys are parsing through so we can try to be useful on this sniper thing."

The bitterness in his tone at the end spoke to a feeling of helplessness she was all too familiar with. Everyone here *wanted* to lock this guy up, but how do you slip cuffs on a shadow? On a ghost?

Being in a room with Wes was about the same level of privacy to being on her own, so she pulled out her phone and called Special Agent Andrew Rhodes. It was evening and he'd likely be long gone from work, but the more she put off the call the more irritated he would be with her for waiting.

In no small way she hoped she would get his voicemail, but the last twenty-four hours had proven that luck was not something she should count on. It had all been downhill after the easy confession from Daryl Clark. Andrew answered on the third ring.

"Margot. I can't honestly say I was expecting you. Is every-thing OK?"

She paused, not wanting to lie, but not sure if she could answer that question in any other way. *Is everything OK?* Everything would never be OK. She was almost always just one bad day from completely collapsing. But she didn't need to *tell* people that.

"Yes and no." She gave him a summary of her phone call with the lawyer, and even let him *tsktsk* at her for not recording it, as she knew he would.

When she was done, Andrew was quiet for a long time, but she knew better than to interrupt. He'd always been a thoughtful man. Even as a teenager when she'd spent time with him he never forced her into conversation, he let her speak in her own time. He was the nicest man she knew, but he was also still a damn fine agent, and had been personally responsible for finding and apprehending some of the scariest murderers in America.

If anyone knew what went on in the heads of killers, it was Andrew Rhodes.

"You think he's being honest?" Andrew asked, finally, inviting her in. "The Marissa Loewen case was incredibly famous at the time, he might just be throwing us a big fish hoping it'll get you invested, make you come back."

"Andrew..."

"Look, Margot, I know how you feel, and I know we've discussed this until we're both blue in the face. I won't *make* you do anything you don't want to do, you're not under my control. And trust me, I was there last time, I could see what it did to you. And I know it was hard for you to say yes to helping us move forward, only to have Ed decide to play coy on us. I think you and I both figured that might be it for us, and it's easy to *feel* ready only to have that feeling completely ripped away. I think that's probably why he did it, because you wanted to do it on your terms, not his. He wanted us to know he was the one in charge. And you know I won't force you to go back there." He left it at that, but they could both hear the *but* he wasn't saying out loud.

*But* we could really use your help.

*But* if you do go see him, we could solve this case.

*But* he won't talk to anyone else no matter how hard we try.

Margot swallowed down the lump in her throat, and said, "I think it's real. I don't think he'd use a name unless he meant it, especially not one so big, because if we catch him in a lie then he knows that's it, there's no more chances, I'm never going back again." She chewed the inside of her cheek and darted a quick glance in Wes's direction. He was busy typing on his laptop, an open file next to him with details of the Clark case. He was very good at pretending he wasn't listening, but she knew he was on her every word.

And she knew how important this case was. Marissa Loewen had been in her late twenties when she vanished, but she was young, pretty, and from a rich family. Her face had been inescapable. The memory of her missing posters haunted Margot even now.

She could give that family the peace they craved.

She knew she was going to do what needed to be done to solve the case. But that didn't mean she needed to do it for free.

"If I agree to this, I want a favor from you. From the FBI."

That certainly piqued Wes's interest enough that he stopped typing and looked right at her, no longer pretending he wasn't eavesdropping.

"I'm listening, but you know I can't promise anything until I hear what it is."

"I'm sure you saw the news this morning."

Wes raised an eyebrow and Margot knew she was stepping

into some dangerous territory. No one *wanted* help from the FBI. They didn't want the feds in on police matters, and as of right now it wasn't a case that would interest the FBI directly. But the Bureau had resources they didn't, and if there was any chance that Margot could pull some strings to utilize those resources, she was sure as hell going to do it, even if it bruised some egos along the way.

If she had to sell a little of her soul by going to visit Ed again, then she was going to make it worth her damn while.

"I'm very aware of the shooting, yes." Andrew's tone was cautious, because he knew whatever she was about to ask was going to require him to take some risks. Margot hoped he'd be able to convince *his* superiors it was worth it to help close a long-festering missing persons' case.

To add another tick to Ed's growing tally.

"If you can help expedite some of our physical evidence, as limited as it is, I would be willing to have a discussion about having a discussion with Ed." While Margot knew perfectly well she had already accepted the inevitability of another meeting with Ed, at least the FBI could help them in return.

Perhaps a better person would have been willing to do it just for the peace of mind it would offer Marissa's family, and that was certainly on Margot's mind, but the FBI had the ability to help run ballistics on the bullets they'd been able to collect from the scene. The overtaxed police lab would take days if not weeks to get anything useful back—and that was the fast version —but a few strings pulled at Quantico, and they might be able to find something a lot sooner.

Time was of the essence in this case.

While she couldn't see Andrew's face she had no problem picturing it. His dark beard, smattered with gray, would be sagging in the cheeks as he frowned, and his thick eyebrows would resemble a fuzzy V in the center of his forehead as he cast a glare at her she couldn't see.

"Let me see what I can do. But Margot, I want you to come by our office first thing in the morning and make an official statement. And if the lawyer calls again..."

"I know."

"I know you *hear* it, but do you understand the importance?" She understood. From Andrew's perspective those phone calls—if recorded—could be used if these cases ever went to trial. They were evidence and Margot knew how vital every scrap of evidence could be.

But she also knew Ed was already serving fifty-two consecutive life sentences and had also willingly moved himself back to a death penalty state. Some of the California trials *had* come with a death sentence attached, something he had avoided by being tried in New York for a handful of his later kills. He'd been arrested in California and stood trial there but was then extradited to New York for sentencing on six more cases, and in New York he had remained right up until that year.

Perhaps Ed was hedging his bets since no one had been executed at San Quentin since 2006, but it wasn't a sure thing by any means.

He was putting himself at risk just to come toy with her.

And *why*? To what end? Sure, he had a game to play and was enjoying that part of it, but he could have just as easily made the offer to Andrew and gone mano a mano with the agent who had locked him up. During her previous visits to see him, Ed had tried to convince her that his interest was purely paternal, and he wanted to get to know his adult daughter.

Margot called bullshit.

There was something more at stake here and she just couldn't quite put her finger on what it was, but she knew when she figured it out she wouldn't be happy about it.

She raked her hand through her hair and sighed. "All right, Andrew. I'll be by in the morning."

As they disconnected, she looked over at Wes. He wasn't

looking at her but there was a faint smirk on his lips as he shook his head.

"Can't wait to see how you're going to explain *that* to the captain."

# SEVEN

Since Leon was the lead on the sniper, Margot went to him first as opposed to happily presenting her insubordination to the captain on a silver platter.

Leon was parked at his desk, and while his computer was open to searches on military personnel and gun ownership checks for anyone who registered a sniper rifle—as if they'd be that lucky—there were other open files on his desk that distracted her.

She sat down at a chair beside his desk before he realized she was there, and he gave a little start of surprise. Leon was one of the senior detectives in their precinct's homicide department. He was in his sixties and probably starting to think about retirement, though he hadn't mentioned anything to them. He'd been doing this job over thirty years now and that had to catch up with you after a while.

He was going gray at his temples and in his beard, the tight curly hair showing signs of aging even while his appearance made him look at least ten years younger than he actually was. His dark skin was smooth aside from laugh lines around his mouth and eyes, more likely acquired spending time with his wife and kids than at the office.

That said, Leon was the first one to offer a joke or a compassionate shoulder if a case just got to be too much. He should have been promoted a hundred times over to a higher rank, but instead he continued to work the shittiest cases there were because he genuinely believed in the value of what he was doing.

If Margot had asked Leon's opinion on what she should do about the Loewen case, he would have told her to go see Ed without hesitation. So, she was hoping he would understand why she had done what she'd done.

She picked up the case file open on his desk; it was one of many from a homicide case the two of them were working on together. Two bodies had been found separately but under suspiciously similar circumstances.

They had spent weeks on the cases looking at every conceivable angle and every scrap of physical evidence. They'd interviewed dozens of people and hiked through Muir Woods park so much that Margot thought she might be able to get a side hustle giving guided tours.

They hadn't gotten any closer to finding the killer.

And while the case got colder and colder, the two of them had to turn their focus elsewhere. Flipping through the file, Margot knew this one bothered Leon more than some of the others.

There were cases that did that to you, got under the skin and festered, not relenting, not letting you sleep at night. She'd had her share of those.

She slipped the file back onto his desk.

"I might have something."

Leon, who had continued to run searches while she took her time saying anything, patient as an old owl, turned in his seat and gave her a long, silent stare. It wasn't an unfriendly expression, just one that said he was on her time.

She explained to him—as best she could since they were out among others—the deal she had struck with the FBI and why. Margot watched his face carefully, trying to judge what he was thinking as she told him about her calls with both the lawyer and Andrew, and when she was done it was her turn to sit back and wait for him to speak.

Leon nodded, not smiling but not frowning. "You know, under normal circumstances I'd probably be pretty fucking annoyed with you for reaching out to the FBI behind my back. But I'm going to give you a pass on this, because quite frankly we are in over our goddamn heads right now, and if the feds want to get us something we can use, then I'm sure as shit not going to look that gift horse in the mouth. But Margot." He pointed a finger at her, and his tone was very much of the *I'm not mad, I'm just disappointed* school of parenting. "I don't ever want you to use your connections like that again without asking me first, am I understood?"

Margot, who was damn near forty, felt like she was ten in that moment. She nodded, feeling both relieved and infantilized at the same time, which had probably been Leon's goal.

"You send your FBI man to me when he gets back to you, and I'll make sure we do a proper transfer of evidence. All aboveboard. We need to be fucking careful on this one."

"Of course." She stood to return to her own office.

"And Margot?"

She paused to look back at him. He was typing again, pretending to ignore her, but she could see the reflection of his eyes on the screen looking back in her direction. "If you have a way to solve that Loewen case, you gotta take it. You know that, right?"

While it had been exactly what she had predicted he would

say to her, hearing the words solidified what she already knew she had to do.

"I know."


Margot and Wes got a fresh homicide call around three that dragged them from the office and back out into the real world.

They'd spent most of their night staring at computer screens and parsing through hundreds of criminal records, military records, and gun registrations. She kept hoping someone would come up on the screen and be obviously their shooter, but so far they were empty-handed and it was wearing on her nerves. The urgency to solve the sniper case was creating a thick atmosphere in the office that had people on edge. Even the skeleton crew working overnight were overcaffeinated and short-tempered.

Everyone wanted to solve this thing, but with limited information available, it was like trying to shackle a rumor. When the homicide call came through Margot was almost relieved to take a break from the oppressive eagerness that was stifling them at the station.

The rain had relented slightly as they arrived at Jefferson Square Park. The road was still wet, streetlights glittering off its reflective surface, and the air around them had a cold dampness that snuck under jackets and into boots and threatened to keep you cold for hours after you got back inside again.

Jefferson Square Park was an open green space that was usually bustling, especially at the peak of summer, with people coming out to have picnics in the sun or play Frisbee with a group of friends. It offered decent views—Margot looked down at the lights of the city and was surprised by how pretty it was despite their gruesome reason for being here.

In all honesty she was grateful to be out in the fresh air rather than cooped up at the office where the stink of stress and desperation was getting thicker by the hour.

They'd had to dodge several eager reporters on their way out the door to get here, ones who didn't care a lick that it was the witching hour, they just wanted to be first to crack the story.

Sadly for them there was no story, though Margot noticed that one of the reporters had trailed after them, figuring any story was good enough at this point. He did keep a professional distance, though, hovering near his battered old sedan as she and Wes headed into the basin of the park where uniformed officers had cordoned off an area with familiar yellow tape.

In a rare treat, no onlookers were huddled together gawking. It was just the police and a pair of EMTs who looked like they were only waiting for permission to leave.

Margot ducked under the crime scene tape, holding it for Wes. She was five foot nine, taller than average, but even so the six-foot-three Wes needed to stoop a little lower to get under it. Margot smirked. It was the simple pleasures.

On the ground at the feet of the two uniformed officers who had called the case in was a woman. It was impossible to guess her age, given that whoever had killed her had aggressively bashed in her face. There were no other signs of trauma that Margot could see on the body at a glance, and a bloody sock lay on the ground near the woman's head, something solid and suspiciously brick-shaped encased within.

The woman's clothing gave Margot pause. Fishnet tights, a too-short miniskirt with a frayed hem that showed off a flash of dark underwear beneath. She sported a bustier top that was two sizes too small, but still managed to keep her covered up despite the obvious struggle she had gone through.

"Sex worker?" she asked, mostly to give voice to the question but also to see if Wes agreed with her assessment.

Wes stood next to her, his big frame radiating welcome heat in the cool night air. "They're not uncommon around here at night. It's usually a pretty safe area, well lit, not the worst part of town." He gestured broadly to the nearby streetlights that kept things from getting too dark.

Again, Margot spotted the reporter lingering by his car, pretending not to pay attention but very obviously scribbling down notes as they worked. He was youngish, maybe late twenties, and so nondescript that even while looking at him she was forgetting his features. Blandly handsome without an ounce of memorability.

Margot looked back to the body at her feet. The woman was short and wearing high heels, but without them Margot estimated she was maybe just over five feet. She was a little plump, but that was mostly accentuated by her tight top and skirt. In other clothing she might look more proportionate.

Her skin was light, not *white* necessarily, but light. With the woman's dark hair Margot didn't want to make any race assumptions, since it might cause them to overlook information about their victim.

Crouching, Margot inspected the woman's damaged face, her studious gaze traveling downward, looking for any signs of manual strangulation around the victim's neck, and any signs of bruising on her exposed skin.

Her neck appeared unadulterated, but there were scrapes and scratches on the woman's hands and forearms to indicate she'd put up a fight before her attacker got her on the ground and finished the job.

Margot glanced over at the bloody sock. "Our guy had to have brought that with him. And you don't bring a brick with you if you just want to get a little head. So, either he knew her personally and was looking to hurt *her* in particular, or he came out here tonight knowing he wanted to hurt *someone* and she was just unlucky enough to cross his path."

Pointing to the woman's damaged face—which it seemed the uniformed officers were perfectly happy to avoid looking at any further—Margot said, "That looks like overkill to me. So, it could be personal."

Wes stood over the victim, looking down at her face from an upside-down perspective. He frowned. "Or it could just be a killer who has never done anything like this before. Things got out of control, he let himself get carried away."

"I like my theory better," Margot said, pushing herself to a standing position and wiping damp grass from her palms.

"Why, because it's yours?" Wes's smirk told her he was just teasing.

"No, because if you're right, then it means the guy is probably just getting started."

# EIGHT

## SUMMER 1988

Petaluma, California

The summer heat had issued a one-night reprieve. The sticky, sweltering barrage of nauseating humidity was enough to drive people from their homes in droves and take to the streets, turning downtown Petaluma into a shockingly happening mecca.

It was almost nine o'clock at night and the sun was starting to dip low on the horizon, but Kim had announced she wanted ice cream. When she did things like that, she reminded Ed of a child, and not in a sweetly charming kind of way. Instead of saying *I want ice cream*, which would have been clear and evidence that she was able to make a decision, she instead sat on their couch and started to stir restlessly.

"Nice night tonight," she said, and Ed's well-honed radar began to ping.

"Mmhmm." He was flipping through some magazine she'd left out on the coffee table, barely paying attention to the stories, using it as an excuse to avoid conversation with his wife. Justin was dozing in a playpen nearby and, although it was bedtime for both their children, Megan was sitting cross-legged on the living room rug, a stack of books in front of her.

She was just starting to enjoy chapter books and Ed was unreasonably proud of her interest. Whenever he would go to yard sales on weekends he would bring her home stacks of Nancy Drew and Trixie Belden books.

Much to his chagrin, she seemed to prefer devouring *Archie* comics when it came to making purchases with her own money, but reading was reading, and his daughter wasn't going to grow up to be some illiterate idiot.

She was going to be like her dad.

Kim glanced out the living room window, where they could still see a few neighborhood children playing outside, the pinky-gold tones of sunset painting the street a pretty watercolor shade.

"Might be nice to get outside for a bit. It's supposed to be a scorcher tomorrow."

"That's what they say," Ed agreed, because agreeing was the easiest course.

"You want to go for a walk? Maybe we could head over to Joe's." She wasn't even looking at him. She was so transfixed by staring out the window it didn't matter whether Ed was here or not. She could have just as easily been having this conversation with herself.

Ed didn't reply.

"Ice cream could really hit the spot, don't you think? Hey Meggy? What do you say, do you want to go get some ice cream?"

Their daughter's head snapped up as if she were a dog who had just received a command. "Yeah, can we? Please?"

"You have to ask your dad." Kim gave him a look that he suspected was meant to be coy and conspiratorial, suggesting they were their own little team of two, the parents. Instead, he felt the burden of that look like a fist to the chest. It was her way of making this all on him. If he said no, he was the villain, he was the bad dad.

Ed sighed. He could point out that Justin was asleep. That Megan should be in bed. That the last fucking thing in this world he wanted to do right then was to walk to Joe's and fork out a wad of *his* money to buy an ice cream cone that Justin would wear all over his clothes—requiring the addition of a bath to their already late nighttime routine—and that Megan would take ten licks off before declaring she was full.

Kim would eat hers and then tomorrow would piss and moan about how fat she was and how Ed never should have let her get the cone to begin with.

He could see all this laid out before him like a movie he'd seen a hundred times, but he also knew that saying no wouldn't be worth it.

"Of course we can get ice cream, Buddy. What flavor do you think you want?" He winked at Kim, joining with her in a two-person unit for one night, because it was easier, because it was kinder, and because Joe's was just a block away from Marissa Loewen's apartment, so perhaps they could walk by.

Just to have a look.

They walked—that was the whole point of this foray after all—and even Ed could admit that getting outside had been smart. The air was ever so slightly cool, and a breeze flitted around them, shimmying the hem of Megan's skirt and making Kim's hair fly around her face.

In moments like that, Ed remembered who she was when they'd met. They'd been nineteen, and she'd been working the concession stand at a drive-in movie theater when he'd come through with his friends one weekend.

She was pretty, freckles over her nose from hours in the sun, and her strawberry blond hair in a high ponytail that swished back and forth when she walked. Her shorts were too short, and she wore an old camp T-shirt that she'd likely dug out of a thrift store bin, but the way she knotted it at her waist made him dizzy for her.

She laughed at his bad jokes and let him put his hand under that knotted shirt after their first date, and back then nineteen felt old enough to play at being an adult, so marrying her just seemed like the thing to do.

Sometimes, when the lights outside hit golden hour, and dulled the fine lines of her face, and she laughed at something he said, he remembered why she used to matter to him, and he could play this game a little longer. Because she had no idea that he hated her. Hated her with every single fiber of his being.

But he also needed her.

Kim pushed Justin's stroller—the boy was still unconscious, so perhaps they might avoid him getting covered in ice cream entirely—and Megan skipped ahead. She was singing "Get Outta My Dreams, Get Into My Car" by Billy Ocean as she jumped onto every sidewalk crack, and blitzed through fading hopscotch games chalked onto the cement.

He didn't think the song was appropriate for her, but he knew better than to mention it. Kim listened to the radio extensively in the car, and she'd be the first to remind him she didn't control what was popular.

Ed picked his battles.

They arrived at Joe's fifteen minutes later, where a crowd of teenagers and families spilled out over the parking lot. People were laughing, and a car nearby had its stereo system up, playing something Ed didn't recognize but was probably much worse than Billy Ocean.

Still, the night was inviting, and being outside meant time he didn't have to sit cooped up at home pretending he wasn't dreaming about knives and what he was going to do with them.

Instinctively, as he thought of honed metal slicing through layers of skin and muscle like they were nothing, he scanned the crowd, wondering if the spur-of-the-moment festivities had brought Marissa out. There were plenty of dark-haired girls, plenty of petite frames, and everywhere he looked there were women who just weren't paying attention. Women walking along with foam Walkman headphones over their ears, women sitting by themselves, women chatting with men it was obvious they had only just met.

None of them were Marissa, but Ed was fascinated by the pure glut of options laid before him. He was not an opportunist. At least not always. He had certainly struck while the iron was hot and he saw a good opportunity. A hitchhiker. A drunk girl stumbling home from a bar.

Sometimes they made it too easy, begging for him with broken heels or thumbs in the air.

What he was realizing tonight as he watched the crowd, eyes dancing from one little doe to the next, was that there were treats for him everywhere. Women were bold now, they were cavalier. They didn't seem to understand or recognize a need for fear, because they believed there was nothing *for* them to fear.

And while Ed did not see Marissa that night, or several more nights to come, even as he walked past her apartment complex with a sleeping Megan draped in his arms and Kim eating her ice cream while telling him some irrelevant cul-de-sac gossip, he understood something.

He was never going to run out of options.

There was always going to be someone new to hunt.

# NINE

A group of sex workers was huddled together around the entrance to a twenty-four-hour liquor store, and the second they saw Margot and Wes headed their direction they started to toss cigarette butts to the ground and head for the hills.

It was Margot who got to them first, waving her hands in what she hoped would be perceived as a gesture of friendly surrender. "Whoa, whoa, ladies, be cool. We're not vice. We don't care if you're working, we just want to talk."

A pretty black girl with blond braids rolled her eyes, but at least she didn't look like she was about to make them chase her. "Pro to pro, you should know talking doesn't come for free in this business, Lady Detective." She, of the whole group of six, had been the only one not to throw her cigarette into a nearby puddle. Taking a long drag, the end embered in the night and she leveled Wes and Margot with a stare that said she didn't give two shits that they were cops, because they were in *her* workplace now.

If Margot were placing bets, she wouldn't have thought the girl was a day older than twenty-one, but she had the world-weary seen-it-all exhaustion that someone could only show on their face if they'd been through hell and back. Margot hated that a girl that young could exude so much cynicism, but she also knew better than to believe there were any magic words or easy solutions to fix things.

Margot felt around in her jacket pocket for an unopened pack of cigarettes. She didn't smoke—couldn't stand it—but nicotine was as good as cash to some people, and it was something she could offer these women without crossing any professional lines.

The girl took the entire pack.

Margot liked her.

"My name is Detective Phalen, this is my partner Detective Fox. You can call me Margot if you want."

"That's a pretty old-fashioned name, don'tcha think?" the girl asked.

"I suppose it is." Margot had thought it was quite pretty when she picked it. There was something grown-up about it in contrast to Megan, and at the time she very badly wanted to feel grown up. She waited a beat and the girl sighed and took one more long drag off her cigarette.

"I'm Dominique." Margot had no idea whether the name was real or not. Dominique didn't offer a last name, and it was the kind of moniker that could go either way.

Most people didn't think Margot was a fake name, and now that she'd grown into it, she felt like it fit her better than Megan ever had.

"We're with the homicide division." Margot handed Dominique her business card.

These appeared to be the magic words to gain a modicum of trust with this group. The five other girls who had been orbiting Dominique like minor moons all gravitated back in against the wall, cooing like doves come home to roost.

"Aw shit, what happened?" asked a girl who looked fifteen and had brightly dyed red hair and a nose ring.

"You *know* what happened if the murder cops are here, JJ, come on." This from a girl whose hair was cut into a short pixie style which made her elfin facial features stick out. If not for the pockmarks marring her skin—Margot knew these were a telltale sign of meth use—there was another universe where that girl could be a model. She had a distinct New York accent, her *come on* sounding more like *come awn.*

The other three girls were interchangeable blondes who were too skinny by far and had some suspect bruising on their arms. Margot wished there was a way she could offer these women an out from their lives, but also knew the best thing she could do was not arrest them, and to warn them that there was obviously someone out there who might be interested in doing them harm.

She couldn't save them, but she could at least tell them to be alert.

"Do you guys know a girl, really petite, maybe only five feet, long dark hair. She was wearing a pretty small bustier today."

"Oh goddamn," whispered one of the blondes.

Dominique waved a hand at them, but the change in her expression was evident even without speaking. She'd been cold and guarded. Now her face belied sadness and the slightest hint of fear.

"Yeah, that's Genesis. Something happen to her?"

Margot noticed the brunette girl with the pixie cut was not in a hurry to snark Dominique the way she had the redhead, though it seemed obvious the reason Margot and Wes were here.

"Was Genesis her real name?" Wes asked. He had hung back for the conversation up until that point, letting Margot be the one to handle the other women. It seemed as if this was the first time the girls had noticed him, and a couple of them gave him appraising once-overs.

"I don't think so," said Dominique.

"Jennifer," mumbled the redhead.

"Sorry, what was that?" Margot inched closer, she could barely hear the whisper of the girl's words, but knew there was something she had missed.

"Her name is Jennifer," the girl said, a little louder this time. "Jennifer Covington, or Coventry or something like that. She told me once she thought Genesis just made her sound more special. And she was a Gemini so she liked that, too."

The girl had barely looked up from her bare toes, peeking out from her too-tall heels. She must have been freezing.

The pixie-cut girl put her arm around the redhead's shoulder and rubbed her arm in a comforting way.

"Did any of you see her tonight?" Margot needed to steer things back to the investigation before she lost these women to their mourning, whatever that was going to look like out here on the street.

She hoped maybe they'd call it a night and head somewhere safe, at least for now. She didn't want to be out here again tomorrow and recognize one of their strappy sandals, or Dominique's distinct braids.

"Yeah, she was here like an hour ago. Complaining it was too quiet and too cold. Then a john came around and saw what he liked, and she headed off with him."

"Was he on foot or driving?" Wes asked, now standing right beside Margot, where his substantial height forced the girls to look up at him.

"He was driving," Dominique said with sharp certainty. "I remember the car, too, because it was really fucking old. Stood out. It was like, an old Caddy, mint green. But not nice, like, no one was taking care of that car. Maybe from all the way back in the seventies or some shit, but it was *old*."

Despite the seriousness of the situation Margot darted a quick look at her partner who had, himself, been born in the seventies, just to see if the unintentional barb had stung him.

Based on the deepening crease in his forehead, he definitely hadn't enjoyed it.

"Do any of you remember what he looked like?" Margot could tell she was starting to lose their attention and they were getting antsy for her and Wes to move on. A car or two had already slowed down and then hustled off when they spotted the two very obvious cops. She and Wes were bad for business.

"White?" one of the blondes offered, but she didn't sound convinced.

"Nah." Dominique shook her head, no question of her certainty. "Latino dude for sure. Mexican."

"How can you be so sure he was Mexican?" Wes asked.

Dominique aggressively slapped her forearm. "Arm was hanging outside the window. Saw a tattoo of a sombrero and a knife." She raised her eyebrow meaningfully at Margot, waiting for it to click.

Margot didn't need time to think about. She'd been on the scene for plenty of gang-related murders. She knew the Nuestra Familia insignia when it was described to her.

"Jesus," Wes whispered, obviously making the same connection. "Did she spend time with guys from that gang often?"

Dominique shrugged and looked over at the redhead. "You two were tight, what do you know?"

The redhead didn't seem too keen on sharing, but finally she said, "She had a boyfriend, I think his name was Eugenio. But he wasn't Nuestra. He was Barrio or Los Zetas or something."

Margot's stomach churned at some of the names the girl was mentioning. If Genesis had found herself in between rival gangs by accident, that would certainly have made her an easy target for disposal. These were no run-of-the-mill street thugs out slashing tires or spray-painting businesses. These were gangs with deep cartel ties.

The Los Zetas would send a message to others with a

beheading, or other grisly violent measures. Beating a sex worker to death with a brick was probably a soft kill by their standards.

Margot handed her card to the redhead. "Look, if you think of anything else that would help me, you give me a call, day or night, OK? We want to find who did this to Genesis and lock them up."

Dominique snorted. "Good luck with that, Lady Detective."

# TEN

Margot didn't bother going home between the end of her shift and her planned meeting with the FBI. There was just no point. Sure, she looked disheveled and rumpled and probably didn't smell like a fresh bouquet of flowers, but she wasn't going to the FBI office to woo or impress anyone.

She'd sleep when she got home, and she would damn well turn her phone off this time.

The exterior of the San Francisco FBI headquarters was cold, gray, and unassuming. Nothing about it screamed *crimes get solved here*. If anything the exterior said *we do taxes here*. It was amazing, Margot had seen at least a dozen different FBI buildings in her life and while none were the same, they all managed to present a uniform blandness that made passersby not want to look at it.

Maybe that was the entire point.

Margot knew she didn't much feel like going in, but she'd made a promise to Andrew, and she couldn't back out now just because she was uncomfortable.

Showing her ID at the front desk, she paced the lobby uncomfortably while she waited for Andrew to come collect her. Was this how people felt when they visited a police station? The lingering vibe that you were guilty of something, or that you were considered guilty of something by everyone who walked past?

Five minutes of overthinking later, Andrew came to get her. He looked almost casual, wearing charcoal trousers and a white button-up top with no tie. His sleeves were rolled up to the elbow, and his brown eyes were protected by a pair of thick tortoiseshell glasses.

Although he was now in his late fifties, Andrew was a fit sort of guy. He was in shape, and his salt-and-pepper beard and largely gray hair suited him. When Margot looked at him, she saw the man who had been so kind to her the night they came to take Ed away.

He'd had no beard then, and had been twenty-three years younger, but she still saw that version of him ghosted underneath the man he had become. She wondered if he still saw a scared fifteen-year-old when he looked at her.

As always, he pulled her in for a hug rather than a handshake, and the same familiar smell of Old Spice lingered on him, the same way it did every single time they were together.

Margot clipped a visitor badge onto her lapel and followed him into the belly of the beast. As they took the elevator up to the designated space for the team working Ed's case, Andrew bumped his shoulder against her.

"You look like shit, kid."

Margot laughed despite her best intentions to remain stoic and unflappable while she was here. "Yeah, well, it's been a long night. Sorry I didn't stop for a beauty nap before coming."

"You're on overnights? Shit, Margot, you should have said something, you could have come by later."

"Nah." She shook her head, staring straight ahead at the elevator doors rather than looking at him. "The longer I put off coming the less likely I'd be to follow through. So here I am. Following through."

"Well, you know we appreciate it."

A soft *ding* preceded the doors sliding open and admitting them both to an open work floor where about a dozen different agents were busy working away at one very specific goal: finding more of Ed's victims.

Knowing that she alone could make their jobs significantly easier caused a pang of guilt to shoot right down to the pit of her stomach.

She tried not to think about it, because she couldn't undo the last four months. Ed had been the one to say no, not her. And if she was honest—like deep down and dirty honest—with herself, she wouldn't have changed anything. The silence had been such a relief. Maybe that was selfish and maybe it made her a shitty person, but she'd had to give up so much of her life and her personal peace because of Ed, why should he get to have a part of her now?

"Come on in, I'll introduce you to a few folks from the team and we'll have a chat, OK? Just a chat. You're not signing a contract in blood or anything like that." Andrew put a warm hand on her back and guided her toward a glass-fronted meeting room.

Margot had been to the unit before, after her first visit to see Ed. She'd marveled then, as she did now, at how the space looked more like it belonged to a dot-com startup than it did the FBI. There was certainly a stark contrast between how this crew worked daily and the disgusting couch that someone had brought into her office probably forty years earlier, where she had spent more nights asleep than she had in the beds of charming lovers. By a long shot.

In fairness there were very few places Margot felt at ease enough to fall asleep, and it spoke volumes about her life that a broken-spring couch with moth-eaten fabric was one of them.

Andrew's presence was the only thing keeping Margot from getting a little squirrelly as she walked through the unit's workspace. The whole area was wide open, and there were so many windows letting natural light stream in that they had dimmed the overhead fluorescents.

Focusing on the small point of heat radiating on her back was a meditation, it was a reminder that he was with her and that this was all going to be OK. Andrew wouldn't make her do anything.

In the meeting room, there were three other agents seated around the table, two men and a woman. One of the men, a tall, lanky guy with unruly red curls and a splatter of freckles across his pale cheeks, got to his feet immediately on their entry and practically tripped over his chair to offer Margot a hand.

Though Andrew didn't say anything, Margot saw the way his cheeks darkened, almost as if embarrassed.

"I'm Special Agent Gregory Howell. BAU. You can call me Greg, if you want. It's a real pleasure to meet you, Detective Phalen. I wrote my dissertation on your father."

Margot allowed him to vigorously shake her hand before he seemed to remember how polite human interaction worked in the real world and released her.

"Oh, shit, that's a weird thing to say, isn't it?"

"As long as it wasn't extolling his virtues, I'd say it's actually a pretty legitimate topic for BAU applicants," Margot said with a soft smile. "You can call me Margot."

She appreciated that even though Greg was very obviously a self-made expert on Ed, he didn't try to call her Megan. A lot of people made that mistake, probably assuming that she still wished she could be Megan rather than who she was now. But Margot didn't like looking backward. It was part of the reason she didn't want to be here.

As Andrew angled her in the direction of the other two agents seated across from Greg, he stooped low and whispered in her ear, "Greg can be a bit much, but he means well. Some of the others call him Gory."

Margot bit back a smirk. She felt bad that he had never quite escaped being bullied, though, and hoped if anyone was calling him Gory it was behind his back and not to his face. He might be a little... odd... but Margot felt a bit of kinship with him that she couldn't quite name.

He made her think of Justin, her brother, who was now David. Justin had never quite grown into that new name, or grown out of who he used to be. Greg reminded Margot of the kid brother she'd had before Ed was arrested. He was kind of who she imagined Justin might have become if he hadn't let his trauma define him.

The woman rose next. She wore her hair in a starkly cut platinum blond bob that looked so razor sharp it should have been classified as a weapon. Her makeup was minimal but expertly applied to make her appear well-rested and about ten years younger than she was. She was dressed almost identically to Andrew in well-tailored trousers and a crisp button-up top, but her top was a deep crimson shade that matched her lipstick —the only obvious bit of color on her face.

On anyone else the color would have been too much, or seemed like a demand for attention, but to Margot it looked just right.

"Special Agent Alana Yarrow." Her handshake was firm, palm dry.

Sometimes when Margot worked alongside other women in the field—and it was a rarity because she was one of five female detectives at her precinct and the only one currently working homicide—she found there was a need to assert dominance. Some women got so used to the boys' club that was law enforcement they took it out on other women around them, as if the opportunities were so finite that it was a fight.

In a sense, the opportunities *were* limited. There weren't a lot of promotions to go around, and often when women got those jobs their male colleagues would whine about affirmative action, as if skill and qualifications had nothing to do with it.

Margot was relieved that she didn't get any of those vibes from Alana, because she was much too anxious to add hostility into the mix right now.

Alana sat and the third man grunted and pushed himself up. He was heavier-set, though Margot wouldn't have used the word *fat* if asked to describe him to a sketch artist later. He was broad across the chest and belly but reminded Margot more of a former football player than anything else. He was just a *big* guy who looked like he'd be able to run someone through a brick wall. Margot figured him to be in his late forties, and not too hard on the eyes.

Between him and Alana it was a bisexual field day of people she shouldn't be allowed to find attractive, given the reason for her being here.

"Special Agent Carter Holmes. Nice to meet you." Margot caught the appraising sweep of his eyes, which he did nothing to hide.

He was, she realized, the exact opposite of Wes, and she thought that might have been what appealed to her most about him. Once the introductions were done, Andrew pulled out a chair for her at the head of the table, before he sat next to Greg, on Margot's left-hand side.

Someone had graciously provided a pitcher of water for the room, and Margot noticed, for the first time since entering, that a PowerPoint document was ready to run on the giant monitor affixed to the wall at the other end of the conference table.

"Margot, first, we just want to thank you for taking the time to come in. Agents Howell, Yarrow, and Holmes are leading various parts of the renewed Ed Finch investigation, and I'm obviously here because of my ties to the original case. Carter is using mapping techniques to try and assess Finch's specific seasonal patterns for known victims to determine which of our most likely cold cases could fit the profile. Alana and her team are creating detailed victimology case files for all known victims so we can cross-reference like cases, see if we can narrow our options down that way when we better understand Finch's victim profile. She and her team have been revisiting all those old letters you got from the Sentinel to see if we can line up any of our victims to the riddles in there, but no luck so far. Greg is our forensics mastermind, and he's in charge of establishing a new profile for Finch based on his kill patterns, especially factoring in the outliers. He might have been a bit enthusiastic during his intro, but if I hadn't already done it, Greg could quite literally write the book on Ed."

Margot nodded to the group, marveling at their hyper-focused areas of expertise, and she felt a little pang of jealousy, amazed that the FBI was able to have people focus on nothing but better understanding the places Ed killed at different times of the year, while she and Wes and Leon were working up to a half-dozen open cases each at any given time, trying to give all they had until there just wasn't anything left.

She hated the bitterness that stung at the back of her throat, but it was hard *not* to feel bitter knowing that all of this was for her father, when these resources could have been applied else-where to much better ends. Ed was already *in* prison. Now they were just trying to figure out how far the trail of bodies went.

And yes, those victims deserved justice, but so did women like Jennifer, whose body was currently being autopsied at the morgue, while some gang member was driving around a free man with her blood on his hands.

It just didn't seem fair, the way the world decided which victims mattered and which ones didn't, when they should *all* matter.

Margot bit her lip and focused on the group in front of her, who didn't get to make those choices and weren't to blame for the lack of equity among victims. At least if Ed killed a sex worker, they'd care about *that* victim.

It was Alana and not Andrew who spoke next, surprising Margot. "Detective Phalen. Margot. We know that this can't be easy for you. Special Agent Rhodes has made it very clear to the whole team that after your father's arrest you originally completely blocked all contact with him, to the point he doesn't even know your new name."

"And I'd very much like to keep it that way," Margot reminded them.

"Of course, yes. There's no question. And, given that after pushing to reconnect he then revoked access, we also understand your apprehension about visiting him again now."

Margot raised a hand, shaking her head. Alana's voice was smoky, like an old-fashioned lounge singer, and listening to her managed to briefly distract Margot's attention from the actual words being spoken, but now they registered, like a well-targeted gut punch. "Respectfully, Agent Yarrow, and I mean this in the kindest way possible, no one in this fucking building *understands* my apprehension. You guys want me to go and have a nice little heart-to-heart because you think *oh, he's her dad, no big deal.* Do you understand that he made me an unwilling accessory to some of his murders? He killed Theresa Milotti after driving me to a sleepover. If not for me, he never would have seen her, would never have been on that road while she was hitchhiking. And Laura Welsh? Do you know what he confessed later, about that crime? Of course you do, because you're the world's foremost experts on Ed Finch. He was taking me for a drive because I couldn't sleep and the car calmed me down. He killed her as I was *sleeping in the back seat.*"

"Margot, you were a baby…" Andrew started an attempt to comfort her, but she shot him a look that silenced him immediately.

The others were all staring at her in startled shock, like they never expected her to express herself, but she just couldn't help it.

To say they *understood* was the biggest lie she could think of.

She barely understood it herself.

Margot resisted the urge to push her chair back from the table and flee from the room. Instead, she fixed her attention back on Alana.

"I'm not the first child of a serial killer to have to grow up with that shadow lingering over me. Believe me, I know that. And I also understand why no one knows where Ted Bundy's daughter even is, anymore. She did it the right way. She changed her name and buried herself so deep in her new life that people almost forget she ever existed. I *wish* I could forget that Ed Finch's daughter existed, but no one will let me. Especially him." Margot let out a shuddering breath, regaining her composure and centering herself, because the only other option was to just lose it, and then what?

Then they ask: does it run in the family?

Is there more to her than she lets on?

Is she just like him?

It was a question that had plagued *her* for decades, whenever her temper bubbled, whenever she wanted to lash out. Was it justified, or was there some kind of twisted malady in her blood?

She took a breath and looked around at their shocked faces. "I'm sorry. But you don't understand."

Alana, who had taken Margot's monologue in her stride, gave her a soft smile and leaned closer, placing a hand delicately on her forearm. Margot let herself look into Alana's eyes, and there was no fear there.

More importantly there was no pity, which might have been the only thing worse than fear.

"I'm sorry. It was a poor choice of words. I hope, if you'll let me rephrase..." She raised an eyebrow, waiting for Margot to give her permission. Margot gave a nod of assent, suddenly very curious about the blonde. If Margot were a betting woman, she would have placed money on Alana having some sort of base degree in psychology.

With Margot's consent, Alana continued. "We are compassionate to the difficult nature of these interviews for you. We understand the efforts you've made in distancing yourself from your fa— from Ed Finch. And as I'm sure Agent Rhodes has made clear—because he made it clear to all of us repeatedly before you came here today—we aren't going to force you to do this interview. It has to be voluntary. We're pretty sure Finch would know the difference if we coerced you or forced your hand somehow."

Margot didn't love the implication that they *had* a way to force her hand, but of course they did. They knew who she really was. If that information got into the wrong hands, her life would become a dozen kinds of unbearable overnight. She didn't *have* any other secrets to barter with. She had no illicit lovers, she was a good cop, and she was so locked up in her own life she didn't make room for anyone else, so there was no drama, no salaciousness.

All of that was in her past, but that was precisely where she wanted to leave it.

"We just wanted to impress upon you how much this interview could mean to our unit," Alana continued. She picked up a small remote control off the table and activated the Power-Point on the monitor.

Margot looked at the four FBI agents gathered around the table, then back to the screen where there were over two dozen different photos of missing women from the eighties and nineties staring back at her.

"You made a slideshow?" For some reason her attention

went right to Greg, and his flushed cheeks confirmed for her that this had, indeed, been his handiwork.

"We thought..."

Margot got to her feet and went to the end of the table where the smiling women all seemed to stare at her. She looked back at them. She knew that in a contest of wills, a ghost was always going to have the upper hand.

She let her gaze rest on Marissa's familiar—now famous—headshot.

"I can't promise them all," she said, mostly to the screen. "But I can do one. I can manage that." Then without looking at any of them, for fear she would change her mind if she saw what their expressions showed, she returned to her seat and snatched her bag out of the chair. "Make the appointment."

# ELEVEN

It was traditional that between shift rotation, officers were given at least a day off. It allowed them an opportunity to reset their internal schedule. In the case of Margot and Wes, they were given a break in between the night shift stretch, to resituate themselves for a return to the world of daylight and the day shift.

With everything going on it was hard for Margot to keep her mind off work, even though her captain had insisted she wasn't allowed back in the building for two days on pain of death.

She woke up too early, barely sleeping two hours, but simply not able to convince her body to shut down. She shucked off her leather ankle boots and pulled a thrift store sweater over her normal T-shirt before she opened up the curtains of her North Beach apartment to a gray, foggy morning, the kind that would melt away before noon and be replaced with a perfect, sunny day.

Normally, she would use her off time to clean the apartment, as general hygiene became the least of her concerns on overnight shifts. But she had barely touched anything in her apartment recently, so the place didn't need any upkeep.

Throwing a load of laundry in as she made herself a pot of coffee, Margot assessed the small space she called home. The building was old and in dire need of modernizing, but Margot hoped that never happened because it would mean losing the beautiful old crown molding and the creaky old hardwood floors. It would also likely increase her rent threefold since North Beach was now a much hotter area to live than it had been when she started renting. The place was small, but not cramped, with a decent living room and a kitchen bigger than she could possibly need. Her bedroom was located on the corner of the building so she had windows on two sides, which was a rare treat on the days she was here to enjoy it.

It was the first apartment Margot had looked at when she decided to move back to the Bay Area, and she'd put a deposit down immediately. At the time it had been owned by an elderly Italian woman who either didn't know or didn't care how much she should be charging for rent, and it was now owned by her son, who just seemed to use it as a hobby whenever he felt the need to fix something.

Margot didn't have a keen eye for décor, almost everything in her apartment had been found at a thrift store or on the stoop outside abandoned by tenants moving out. She didn't order things online, so everything she owned had just found her when she needed it. Nothing matched, and she liked it that way.

She finished her laundry and her coffee, and checked her watch, grateful it was just about time for the meeting she'd arranged with someone who might answer a few questions she had about the Muir Woods cold case.

As much as she needed to rest and reset, she also needed a distraction, and something to occupy herself, otherwise she would just pace around her apartment, waiting for Andrew to call and tell her when her visit with Ed was going to be. They'd planned it for Friday, the next day, but she still didn't know the time, and that uncertainty felt like being in limbo.

She wanted to think about anything else.

Which was how she found herself downtown on her day off, meeting a retired park ranger for coffee.

Wallace Albright was in his mid-seventies, and had the craggy, weather-worn skin of a man who had spent much of his life outdoors. His hair was bright white, and when he saw her come into the café, he immediately headed over in his wheel-chair to greet her.

They exchanged handshakes and greetings, and she followed him back to a table he'd secured for them. After Margot had placed an order for coffee, the pleasant part of the discussion ended.

"I really appreciate you meeting me, Mr. Albright," she said, sipping her much-too-hot coffee and wincing.

Wallace smiled at her, brown eyes twinkling. If Margot had to guess she suspected he was Native American, but the white hair threw her off slightly. "You can call me Wally, I promise it's OK. I know it's a bit of a sinister situation that has you out here, and I also know you gotta be up shit creek with no paddles to your name if you're looking at an old coot like me for help."

His smile was contagious, and while she *was* here to ask for his help in a pretty unpleasant manner, it was a bit of a nice distraction to be spending time with someone so instantly likable.

None of Margot's grandparents were alive—both of Ed's had blessedly passed before he was arrested, and her mother's parents not long after—so Margot had missed out on having that relationship growing up. She imagined Wally would be a genuinely delightful grandfather.

"How long did you work at Muir Woods?" she asked.

"Well it opened in 1908, so probably since right about then." He chuckled at his own joke and sipped his drink, leaving a little mustache of whipped cream on his upper lip briefly before he wiped it away. "I'm just pulling your leg. I was there probably from about 1975 up until this situation changed some things for me." He tapped the arm of his wheelchair. "Much as they've worked on accessibility and all that jazz in recent years, you couldn't really be a ranger in 1999 if you couldn't walk."

Margot had no intention of asking Wally what had happened. It was none of her business why he was in the chair, but it seemed as if he was accustomed to people being curious and immediately said, "Just your run-of-the-mill drunk driver situation. Glad to say I wasn't the drunk driver, though. I've got that going for me." He beamed as if this was a cute one-liner he threw at everyone.

"Did they ever catch the guy?" she asked instead of laughing.

"You gonna offer to do it if I say no?"

"Yes." And she was dead serious. Without a moment of hesitation, she would have pulled out whatever file existed on Wally's incident and thrown herself into finding the person responsible. She'd known him less than twenty minutes and already would have moved mountains for him.

His bravado faltered, and for a moment he appeared genuinely moved rather than just sunshine-and-rainbows happy.

"Well that's awfully kind of you, Detective Phalen, but you're about twenty-five years too late. He died in the accident."

Margot did not say she was sorry.

Neither did Wally.

"You worked in archives for the Parks Department after the accident, is that right?" she asked, steering the conversation back on track before things got too morose.

"Yup, did that until two years ago and then retired. Was surprised to hear from you. Guess you got my name from Ranger Abbott. Good kid, works hard. Loves that damn park, let me tell you."

"Yes, my colleague Leon Telly and I have met him on several occasions, he's been really helpful, but his tenure in the park only goes back about five years. Before that I guess he was up in Washington. But we had questions about any kind of incidents that might have happened in the park before his time, and he said that if there was something that happened there in the last fifty years, you would be the person to talk to. So here I am."

"Ah, yes, my legacy as the officially unofficial historian of Muir Woods. There are worse titles to have. John Muir was a fascinating man, you know. If you ever want a *proper* history of the park and not just some ghost stories, I could talk your ear off about that. But I can see from your face that you don't want me to talk to you about John Muir."

"Not unless he might be recently responsible for a double homicide, no." She gave him a soft smile.

"Probably not your man. But I'm also not sure how I can be of assistance? I obviously want to help, or I wouldn't be here, but what does an old man who sat at a computer for twenty years have that could help you?"

"Knowledge, for one thing. The issue we're running into with doing research for this case is that no one—historically—could agree whose jurisdiction Muir Woods fell under. So there's no way to find any kind of complete listing or even searchable framework to know how many other assaults or possible murders have taken place in the park. And I don't mean like David Carpenter. Obviously, everyone knows about David Carpenter, and none of his victims were in Muir Woods."

David Carpenter—the Trailside Killer—was initially interesting to them in the case study, because he had a habit of stalking and killing his victims in California State Parks. He'd been active in the late seventies and early eighties, and was, in fact, a fellow inmate alongside Ed at San Quentin. He wasn't a particularly well-known serial killer in the true crime circus, but that didn't mean he hadn't potentially inspired a copycat.

But Carpenter used a gun, and neither of the Muir Woods victims had been shot. That pretty quickly ruled out a Carpenter connection, but it had sent Margot on a spiral wondering what other crimes might have taken place in the area that could have inspired the killer or potentially been the signs of some of his earlier work.

That was where she had run into a brick wall attempting to do research in the police database, and Ranger Abbott hadn't been much help, but he had sent her in Wally's direction.

"Leave it to a homicide detective to say *everyone knows about David Carpenter*. But hell's bells, yeah, I remember those days. I was on active duty when he was attacking those folks and every cracking tree branch or leaf that rustled too loud was enough to make me jump out of my skin up until the day they caught him. Those were damn scary times, and I've got to imagine the rangers working there now are feeling a little of that too. It's hard not to be spooked. You get used to one kind of predator, the kind on four paws. You can't ever get yourself used to the kind of predator who walks on two legs."

"See, in my world we *only* work with the latter. I hate to admit it, but it would have been a lot nicer for me to find out my perpetrator was a mountain lion and not some shithead from Modesto with illusions of playing God with people's lives." Margot leaned back in her seat, feeling oddly at ease with Wally. He had an open gentleness to him that immediately made her want to be herself with him.

Or whatever version of herself she allowed others to be privy to.

"That's an awfully grim reality, Detective Phalen, but I think I understand what you mean. I'd also dearly love to know what the city of Modesto ever did to you to get in your bad graces."

"It was just the first place that came to mind." She sipped her coffee, which was now an acceptable temperature to drink without burning her lips. She was about to ask Wally what he remembered happening in the park over the last ten to fifteen years, a timeframe that allowed a sufficient cooling-off period for a serial killer to be somewhat forgotten in between kills.

She didn't get the chance.

A sharp scream from the street outside caught the attention of everyone in the coffee shop, and before Margot was able to see the cause, a dozen different patrons were on their feet, clamoring for a view at the window.

Margot excused herself from Wally and jogged forward, unsure if this was a situation that was going to require police intervention. Every atom in her body was telling her she wasn't going to like what she saw when she got to the window.

"Oh my God," someone muttered.

"Is he *dead*?"

Margot's pulse quickened and she pulled her badge from her inner jacket pocket ready to use it to muscle her way through the crowd if need be.

Then someone next to her screamed, and a bolt of instant panic rippled through the crowd as everyone at the front of the shop moved in a wave, pushing their way back from the window to hide under tables or get to the back of the store.

Margot cast a nervous look at Wally, worried in the crush of bodies he might get knocked around or find himself in harm's way, but he had tucked his wheelchair in next to a shelf of travel mugs, protecting him from the sudden melee and blocking him from the street.

This was a man who knew how to look after himself.

With everyone in hiding, or cowering back near the counter, Margot was the lone figure at the window and finally able to see why they had all panicked.

On the sidewalk in front of the store, a woman who had

been carrying brightly colored shopping bags was lying face down, a halo of blood surrounding her head smeared out around her on the damp street.

A few feet away from her, a sedan sat idle, its door wide open, with a man sagging next to the driver door, his back against the side of the car and a huge bloody bloom on his shirt. He was still alive, wincing in pain, and chaos was rampant around him.

His car had blocked one lane of traffic, and drivers were pulling onto the sidewalk across the road to get around him, but running into pedestrians who were screaming and scattering in multiple directions, unsure of how or where to get to safety.

"Lock the *door*," someone from under a table snapped at her.

Margot couldn't stop staring out the window. It was like witnessing the opening minutes of an apocalyptic thriller. There was no rhyme or reason to the way people behaved when they thought their lives were in danger. She was witnessing a display of fight or flight on a mass scale and it was bone-chilling to see how quickly people abandoned humanity to rely on animal instinct. She was so entranced by the horrors unfolding in front of her, she didn't even think to look for the shooter. Apparently primal instincts suppressed police training.

A woman with a child in her arms was running down the sidewalk and Margot opened the café door and yanked her inside, before shutting and locking the door behind them.

Wild-eyed with panic the woman shrieked and wrenched herself free of Margot's grasp before realizing she had been pulled into safety and not attacked by an armed lunatic.

Outside the door, the window of a parked car, mere feet from where the woman had been, exploded in a confetti of glass shards. This time Margot followed suit with everyone else, grabbing the woman once more and pushing her under a nearby table before scuttling back to crouch near Wally.

"Are you OK?" she asked him. He wasn't a young man by any means, and she worried the intensity of the moment might possibly be a burden on his heart.

Wally took her hand and gave it a squeeze. "Still alive, Detective."

Everyone in the café huddled on the ground, silent as the grave, all eyes on the door. Once someone pounded on the glass, pleading to be let in, but no one moved to help them and before Margot could act, they were gone. It felt like there had been screaming out on the street for hours, but when Margot's eye caught the time on her watch, she was shocked to see it had barely been five minutes since she'd been sitting at the table with Wally.

Five minutes and it felt like the whole world around her had collapsed in on itself like a black hole.

They all waited, the second hand on a clock over the bar ticking so loudly it might have been her own pulse throbbing in her ears. Five more minutes passed, then ten. The street outside fell silent, and she heard the steady, familiar wail of police sirens drawing in.

Her phone buzzed in her pocket, and with her bravery emboldened by the sound of those sirens, she let herself check the text.

It was from Leon.

Sniper hit again. Shopping plaza on Mission Street.

Margot typed out a two-word response.

I know.

# TWELVE
## SUMMER 1988

Petaluma, California

Ed was on an unwelcome mission.

He stood, shoulders slumped, in the overly air-conditioned aisle of the local pet store, trailing behind his young daughter as she made her first foray into the world of adult responsibility.

Megan had been begging them to let her get a pet. She had made intense and relatively well-argued pleas that she was ready to look after it, that she would use her pocket money to pay for its food—evidence she had no concept of what pets cost —and that she would certainly never forget to care for it.

While Ed had been staunchly against it, more for his own reasons than any real concerns about Megan, Kim had finally put her foot down and said it was important to give Megan an outlet to prove she *could* be responsible. It would help her show them that she was prepared to look after Justin when the time came and would be a good learning opportunity.

Ed couldn't explain his reticence to Kim, and making an argument that Megan didn't deserve a pet just because he hated animals didn't seem fair. The truth was he just didn't like the way that animals looked at him. With humans he could fake a level of normalcy and outward friendliness that made him seem charming and approachable. He knew people liked him.

Animals didn't. Animals inched away from him. Dogs got their hackles up, cats hissed. Animals just seemed to understand on a base level—like a warning from nature itself—that Ed was a predator.

It was something humans hadn't figured out yet.

But he loved his daughter. He loved Megan in a way he had never believed he was capable of loving someone, because she was *his*. There was so much of him in her face when she smiled at him, and in her little mannerisms. He loved her, and this was important to her, so at long last he yielded.

She paced the aisles of the store with the kind of studious attention one might expect from someone visiting an art gallery for the first time. Each potential pet was a masterwork that needed her full focus and, under scrutiny, would be given a pass or fail in terms of making the ideal pet.

He watched nervously as she pawed at the Plexiglass windows where wriggly puppies and fluffball kittens were housed. He said nothing, but imagined cleaning up dog shit from his carpets, or being assaulted by the ammonia reek of cat litter in the air when Megan let her responsibility dwindle.

To his relief, she kept moving past those displays. When she spotted him watching her, she stood next to him and looped her chubby little arm through the crook of his elbow, urging him to bend down so she could tell him something. When he complied, she whispered, "I took out a book on pets from the library, and I don't like going on walks, and it said dogs need a lot of walks, and then I know you don't like cats very much." She planted a quick peck on his cheek and then resumed her efforts.

Ed couldn't help but smile to himself.

What a kid.

The process went on for a solid twenty minutes of Megan hemming and hawing over her options, until at long last, when Ed's patience for the whole endeavor had been pushed to the outer limits of where love did not outweigh sanity, Megan declared her choice was made.

They drove home, the windows cracked slightly to ease the heat that had built in the car while they'd been lingering inside the shop. The air conditioning was broken, and Ed was being stubborn about paying to fix it, especially heading into winter. But the late-summer spike in temperatures was making Kim a real bitch about taking care of the AC, and he was hoping the weather gods might give him a reprieve.

Megan peered into the cardboard box on her lap with pure delight. Inside, a ball of fluff smaller than a baseball was making a peeping noise. Periodically it would begin to dig in the shavings that littered the bottom of the box. Ed gritted his teeth.

"Are you happy?" he asked, already seeing the answer written all over her rosy cheeks and gleaming eyes.

"Yes. Thank you, thank you, thank you," she chanted enthusiastically.

"What are you going to name him?" Ed asked, grip tightening on the steering wheel as the scraping noises continued inside the box.

"Phillip," Megan announced without a single moment's hesitation.

Her response took Ed by surprise, briefly chasing away his mounting irritation over how much noise the little shit made. "What kind of name is Phillip for a hamster?"

Megan shrugged, still staring dreamily into the box. "What kind of name is Megan for a girl?"

Ed was silent, unable to name the feeling within him in that moment. He focused on the road, her eerie words continuing to whisper in his head the whole ride back.

That night Megan set up Phillip's cage in her room, where

the hamster spent the entire time running amok on his wheel and chewing at the metal bars of his enclosure. The squealing, grating noises were loudest at night.

A week later Phillip disappeared.

Megan never asked for another pet.

# THIRTEEN

Margot stood next to Leon in the middle of Mission Street, surrounded by SWAT officers with heavy artillery, and more yellow evidence placards littering the ground than Margot had ever seen at a crime scene before.

A bus shelter near the café had been reduced to its metal skeleton, all the windows shattered. Several cars nearby had windows missing, and EMTs were working to treat minor injuries, many of them from flying glass rather than bullet wounds.

The EMTs had time to treat those minor wounds because the four victims with serious injuries were all dead. The medical examiner was en route to remove the bodies, allowing the ambulances the opportunity to treat the living.

It did mean that there were still bodies in the street.

Margot gave her eyewitness account to Leon as they moved through the street. The shooting had long since stopped, and if the guy was going to start again, then so be it. They had a crime to solve.

"As far as I can tell, this was our first victim." She stood next to the woman lying face down on the sidewalk. Many of her wrapped parcels had been kicked halfway down the sidewalk by people running to get to shelter. The contents of her purse were likewise scattered around her, but from what Margot could see it was mostly likely for the same reason and not due to theft. The woman's wallet was still tucked under the strap of her purse, her clearly marked BMW keys were near the curb.

Margot didn't touch anything, not knowing what the crime scene photographers had gotten to yet. She stood and pointed to the car that was still in between lanes in the street. "This guy must have seen her go down and stopped to help." The man who had still been alive when Margot looked out from the café hadn't made it. He remained slumped against the side of his car, his eyes still open and transfixed on nothing, staring straight ahead. There was a large pool of blood around him, his shirt soaked through from bleeding out.

"These two were next." Margot pointed to two men on their backs, one fallen over the other. They had been running to get into their car and never made it. "A few others got clipped getting out of the street, but once these guys were down it was only a minute or two more before he stopped shooting."

Margot was trying to be matter-of-fact about the whole thing. From beginning to end the whole experience had lasted maybe ten minutes tops, but it had taken about fifteen years off her life. She had seen a lot of shit in her time, she'd seen the aftermath of some heinous crimes, but there was a difference between seeing someone's body after death and actually watching them die. Magot had never seen anyone die before, and it was something that was undoubtedly going to haunt her for the rest of her days.

So, to convince herself that wasn't the case, she was out here with Leon, pretending like this was any other day at the office. If she could do her job and *be* just a detective for a little while, then maybe she wouldn't need to fall apart completely.

Leon seemed to sense that need, so rather than sending her

home immediately or forcing her to hit the bench in some other capacity, he was just following her around and taking notes as a dutiful detective ought to do. He nodded. He asked questions.

He did not treat her like a victim.

The hardest part of it all had been convincing the shell-shocked mother that it was safe to leave the café. The woman had clung to Margot long after the other patrons had gone, after Margot had made sure that someone was escorting Wally safely to his home since a Handi-Transit van couldn't get down the street to pick him up. Margot had done everything she could to create an emotional buffer for herself, but the mother hadn't understood.

All she knew was that Margot had been the one to pull her inside, and that meant—as far as she was concerned—that Margot had saved her life. That might have been true, but the gratitude and emotional openness was more than she could handle.

The mother and child had now been taken to a local hospital to ensure that the shock of what had happened wasn't going to be too overwhelming for the young woman.

Margot hadn't even asked her name.

She and Leon finished their circle outside and came back to the front of the café where the body of the woman still rested on the sidewalk. An officer was placing markers where all of her belongings had scattered, and Margot needed to move out of the way as he placed one near a lone shoe.

The woman had been knocked right out of her shoe.

Margot stared at the green velvet ballet flat for a very long time, her gaze briefly drifting back into the café. The lights were out now—the staff and owners had gone home immediately after being given the go-ahead by police—but inside it looked the same. Tables were haphazardly moved into corners; chairs had been knocked onto the floor. Cups of coffee, spoons, napkins, and broken glasses littered the tiles, where they had been knocked during the patrons' desperate attempts to take cover.

She said nothing but took in the rest of the street like she was only just now seeing it for the first time. Boutique clothing shops, a record store, an oddities-themed antique mall, a thrift shop, a cute Thai restaurant, and a dog-friendly bar called The Pound.

This was the kind of place that people came to window-shop, to move from store to store or gather in groups to grab a pint or a cup of coffee. It was the kind of place couples would come for dates, or teenagers might be drawn after school to spend their allowance at the little new age shop next to the bar, where crystals and incense could be bought dirt cheap.

This was an area that made people feel *safe*.

A lot like Pier 39.

It was too early to know what their sniper was doing. They would need to cross-check their victims, see if there was a pattern emerging among them. A victim profile or a specific list of targets would make sense for a killer this highly trained.

But something in Margot's gut told her not to discount locations.

Maybe it wasn't about *who* he killed. Maybe the message was in *where* he killed.

It wasn't quite Christmas season yet, but the presence of the scattered packages around the first victim, and chalkboard signs announcing seasonal drinks at various cafes and restaurants really put a spin on things that Margot hadn't considered at the time of the first shooting.

Of course, Pier 39 had already been festooned with lights and plastic garlands and various too-early Christmas paraphernalia, but that was because it catered so heavily to a tourist crowd.

This area was bustling, and while it would certainly draw in some out-of-towners, it was definitely more of an appealing place for locals to gather at their favorite watering hole or independent coffee bar that wasn't a massive chain.

So it wasn't tourists he was targeting.

"You think maybe this guy just really hates Christmas?" Margot asked, more to herself than anyone in particular.

"What's that?" Leon had been crouched near the victim against the car, just out of earshot. He got to his feet slowly, wincing as if it hadn't been easy, and wandered over to her.

"I'm just saying, the two attacks so far have happened in areas where Christmas seems to have come a little early, you know?" She gestured to a shop window nearby that had holly rimming the interior display and giant decorative Christmas ornaments surrounding pairs of expensive bespoke shoes.

Leon pursed his lips and scratched his beard thoughtfully— a move Margot recognized as something of a nervous tic for him. He scanned the street around them. It was apparent that the season was on its way and many of the shops had bypassed Thanksgiving and headed right to Santa's big day.

"Hmm," was all he said at first.

Margot felt a pang of defensiveness. "It's just a thought. Just something I noticed."

Leon patted her warmly on the arm, obviously hearing something in her tone that implied she was in need of comfort. "I didn't say it was a bad idea, kid. I just said *hmm*."

Chewing the inside of her cheek she gave him a nod, feeling like a rookie for the first time in a long time. Her idea *was* far-fetched, but they had so little to go on that anything felt like an option at this point.

"I think before we start assuming it's the Grinch or Ebenezer Scrooge taking out his bitterness toward capitalism, we need to make sure there are no obvious connections between any of our victims. This looks random to me, but who knows what's motivating this guy." Leon waved his hand over the scene around them.

Margot—having witnessed several of these people die—had a hard time thinking it was anything other than random. Surely, he was taking out whoever was an easy target.

The *why* was a lot less clear.

And the *who* was going to keep her up at night until she had an answer.

# FOURTEEN

"Let's go over it again one more time." Andrew handed Margot a bottle of water, which she took a small sip from, but found her stomach was too tied in knots to even think about drinking.

She tightened the cap and returned the bottle to the drink holder.

A day had passed since she'd witnessed the sniper attack, but every time she closed her eyes, it felt like it was happening all over again.

Andrew's car was disturbingly clean. Margot liked to think of herself as a tidy person, but there were still days where she tossed a fast-food wrapper on her passenger floor, or left an empty cup of coffee in the console for too long. Her back seat was a graveyard of fashion choices she had regretted partway through the day, with sweaters or jackets cast aside hastily.

This white SUV she was currently sitting in looked and smelled as if it had just rolled off a car lot that morning, and she found her gaze drifting to the odometer to confirm it wasn't brand new.

It was not.

"Margot, are you listening to me?"

"No." Her focus snapped back to him, and she met his penetrating gaze. A flash of guilt bubbled in her already churning guts, something she really didn't need at the moment.

Despite the easy opportunity she had just presented him with, Andrew didn't scold her, which she appreciated. He may have been something of a fucked-up father figure for her in her teenage years—and even now, if she was being honest—but he still treated her like an adult contemporary.

He placed a hand on her back, between her shoulder and the seat of the car, and gave a comforting squeeze. From just about anyone else she might have brushed it off, but she let Andrew get away with it, and even tried to let it do what it was intended to: calm her down.

There was no easy or comfortable way to do what she needed to, and while it was nice that Andrew would be with her in there, that didn't help much in terms of providing a buffer between her and Ed.

Because it didn't matter that other people were going to be in the room. It didn't matter that she knew on a fundamental level she was safe.

None of that mattered when she was sitting two feet away from him in shared air, and he started wriggling his fingers into her brain. There was no protection from that.

She was always going to be on her own in there, and that scared her more than any hypothetical monster under the bed ever could.

"We don't need to go over it again, Andrew. Let's get this over with and bring that girl home."

Margot had spent a long time looking at Marissa's photo that morning, the grainy image now burned into her mind's eye so clearly she hoped it was all she'd be able to see when she sat down and looked at Ed. Marissa deserved peace, she deserved to be laid to rest properly, and even though they couldn't put Ed in jail *longer*, he deserved to be held accountable for what he'd done to her.

Andrew kept an eye on Margot for a long while, saying nothing, and then he dropped his hand finally. "You don't have to do this," he said.

Margot gave him a pointed look that probably bordered on severe. "You and I both know that's not true, so stop saying it."

He didn't make the offer again, and together they got out of the car and made their way through security and into the depths of San Quentin. The path was familiar now that she was on her third visit. The sterile corridors were leached of any kind of color or warmth, everything cold and institutional. And while the prison itself was as well-kept as one could suppose, everything Margot looked at seemed just slightly *wet*. It wasn't, but there was a damp discomfort to every inch of the place.

She imagined that it was pretty much impossible to ever feel comfortable or at ease in a place like this, and that was intentional.

Her imagination drifted as she walked and she thought about a dozen different movies or shows that she'd seen over the course of her lifetime where someone goes to meet a violent killer in prison, and they were either behind thick glass with a phone in their hand, or locked up in a tiny cage to keep them at bay while the intrepid cop or reporter tries to figure out their secrets.

The truth was that killers like Ed who had demonstrated no signs of violent behavior in prison were very often afforded in-person meetings with no barriers whatsoever.

Ed had killed seventy-seven women and counting, but he was allowed to sit across from her at a table with uncomfortable plastic seats, and there was nothing between them but the threat of guards standing nearby and a bit of stainless steel and laminate.

Margot was thinking about how much she would prefer the

movie version of things as she took her seat on the round stool that was attached to the table.

A moment later, the jostle of chains drew her attention, and the pit in her stomach became a lump in her throat. Ed, flanked by two guards, shuffled his way into the open meeting area. More guards were stationed at every door, and Andrew sat nearby at one of the other empty tables.

Normally Ed's lawyer would have been with Andrew, but for some reason the frustrating little man wasn't there today.

It had been months since Margot had last seen Ed, and in that time her memories of him had filled up with the man she remembered from her childhood, the tide of remembrance washing away the new reality and replacing it with a younger version of him. Seeing his face was as shocking to her now as it had been four months ago.

Ed's cheeks were gaunt, his jaw peppered with a few days' worth of white beard stubble. His hair was long, pushed behind his ears, and the steel-gray was streaked with grease. Of anything else about him that could have surprised her, that might have been the most shocking. Ed was meticulous about his grooming. He showered daily—sometimes more than once—and would frequently spend his free time filing his nails or focused on his cuticles. He was obsessed with being presentable.

This version of Ed looked disheveled, and Margot's brain was working in hyper-speed desperately trying to figure out why. Was he being mistreated by the guards? Margot didn't feel defensive over him for this, but she would be curious as to what he'd done to deserve the treatment.

Or was he doing this to himself? Intentionally letting himself go to punish her in some capacity for staying away.

The third option was that there was something genuinely wrong with Ed and perhaps these were early warning signs of illness or impending death, and if that was the case there was suddenly an unexpected time limit on how much they'd be able to extract from him about potential victims.

If Margot had to put money on it, she would think he was *hoping* she would believe this third option to be real, while it was actually just one more way for him to manipulate her.

The guards brought Ed to the table and helped him get settled into the stool across from her, his shackles making a dramatic amount of noise.

"You could play a pretty convincing Jacob Marley with all that," she found herself saying without realizing the words were out loud.

Ed stared at her, his expression unchanged, hooded eyes icy and penetrating as they bored into her.

When he finally spoke, his brittle voice grated like sandpaper over skin, making her shudder involuntarily. "Yes, well, let's hope it's a good long while yet before I'm haunting the hallways of those who've done me wrong." His cold stare drifted over to Andrew without any efforts being made to hide the venom within.

Ah yes, all the people who had *wronged* Ed. Margot resisted the urge to laugh in his face as he tried to play the victim.

To Andrew's credit, he met Ed's dead-eyed glare without batting an eyelid.

"Do you want me to leave you two alone?" Margot asked, dragging Ed's attention back to her.

"I'd like that very much, most days, but I don't think my armed friends here would be amenable to the suggestion." He smiled with false warmth at the guards, and while not a single one of them made any move to indicate they'd even heard him, Margot felt a distinct icy chill crawl up the back of her spine.

Coming here had been a mistake.

"Ed, you invited me here for a reason. I'm here. I've met my end of the bargain."

"Oh, was it a bargain, Megan? I wasn't aware there were

parameters we established." He clasped his hands together, the handcuffs on his wrists scraping unpleasantly against the laminate surface of the table.

Margot had already done her song and dance with him about using her old name, there was no point in getting into it again. She wasn't about to tell him her new name, which was precisely what he was hoping to goad her into, so she let it go.

"I'm not going to play games with you. I know you think you've won something already by me coming here, but you haven't." Margot ground the words out through gritted teeth.

"See, that's where I think we disagree, Buddy. Because last time you came to see me you made such a big show of telling me all the power was yours because you could just... walk out. And yet here you are, sitting across from your dear old dad again, because I have something you want."

Margot should have known the bravado of her last visit would come back to haunt her. At the time, she had felt bold, strong, and ever-so-briefly in control of their relationship. He was right, her being back here again simply proved that he was still the one who held all the power, and it didn't matter that he was in prison and she was free, because he knew precisely the thing that would draw her back in every time.

She'd proven that by coming.

She said nothing, because if she disagreed with him, if she got mad at him, if she rose to her feet and walked out, he *still* won. He'd won by her coming here and it didn't matter how the rest of it played out. As far as he was concerned he was already on top.

Margot instead thought back to her first visit with Ed, months earlier, and focused on what it was he had craved from her then. He wanted to feed at scraps of whatever she would offer him of her life, and since she wouldn't give him anything that was personal to her, she thought he would be satisfied with the next best thing.

"Why was it you never targeted sex workers?" she asked, twining her fingers together and setting her hands on the table.

Whatever Ed had been expecting her to say, it was obvious this wasn't it. For the first time he looked genuinely surprised, and it took him a moment to reclaim the collected exterior he'd been presenting.

"Sex workers? Is that the new woke PC bullshit term we're using for whores now?" His lip quirked up in a half smile, and as he waited to see how she'd react to his bait he dipped his neck side to side into his shoulders until a *crack* sound popped from the joints.

Margot tried not to grimace in disgust.

"You understood me just fine."

He hefted a sigh, announcing to everyone in the room that he was bored, and this was beneath him.

"What's the point of this?"

"Trust me, I'm going somewhere with it." She leaned forward, staring hard, and again he looked taken aback for a moment.

"Too easy," he said at last. "You make yourself a victim, then there's no thrill in the hunt. What kind of sportsman goes out and kills a deer that walks up to the rifle? Hmm? There's nothing *fun* about that."

Margot would argue that there wasn't much of a challenge in picking up teenaged hitchhikers and then killing them when there was literally no means for them to escape, but arguing semantics with a psychopath was a pointless effort.

Ed must have read something in her face that suggested she didn't believe him. He shifted uncomfortably in his seat, steely gaze transfixed on her. While his outside appearance might suggest weakness, what Margot saw in his eyes reminded her plainly just how dangerous this man was.

"I didn't kill hookers because I didn't need to. Besides, why have dog food when you can have filet mignon, hmm?"

"Careful, Ed. You keep talking like that and our friend Andrew might think you had a bit of a cannibalistic flair we didn't know about before."

Ed growled. "You don't *ever* speak to me like that, Megan. Not again if you know what's fucking good for you. I am your *father* and you will *respect* me." He didn't move a single inch, but he didn't have to.

The threat was real, and it hung so thickly in the air Margot thought she might choke on it. The guards didn't appear to move, but Margot noticed the way their fingers were just a bit more in line with their triggers now.

There was a bitter teenage girl deep inside of Margot that wanted to keep poking at the open wound she'd made. She *wanted* him angry, wanted to see just how far she could take it.

Thankfully, her developed adult brain didn't take directions from her hormonal inner child.

While his outburst had been little more than a raspy whisper, it had been terrifying. Margot could imagine his threats breathed into ears in the darkness, where he was nothing more than an invisible weight.

Times like this she had no problem imagining Ed as a killer.

Margot leaned in again, making sure he was looking her right in the eyes before she replied. "I'll be polite. But let's be very clear. You will *never* threaten me again. Because you may be my father, and I can't change that, but don't you ever forget that that means I'm *part* of you." She held his gaze unblinking for a long, long time. "So don't you *dare* think I don't know what I'm capable of."

She arched a brow almost in challenge, and Ed's ghost of a smile was all she got in return. There was something very much like pride in his expression now, and knowing she was responsible for that made her feel physically ill.

"Why do you want to know about my preferences?" Ed

asked, his voice steady now, like this was just any other chat between parent and child.

"Thought you might like to hear about the case I'm working on right now."

"The girls in the woods?" His voice was too eager, his answer too quick. Margot knew she had him. She also found it interesting that he still remembered the details of the case she had discussed the last time she'd been here, like he'd been thinking about it during her absence.

"No, different case."

"Busy girl. Always another murder to be solved, hey? Did you solve that one? Find him?"

Margot shook her head, admitting failure. "No. Not yet."

"Don't you worry. He'll be back."

The words chilled her. Why did he sound so sure of the Muir Woods killer's return? His confidence was almost conspiratorial. Margot narrowed her eyes at him warily, before recognizing just how insane her suspicions were. Ed's communications were all closely monitored, as were his guests. There was no reason to believe he could have had any communication with a killer in the outside world.

And it wasn't like he'd done it.

At least, not in that case.

"Unless he's dead, he's not done," Ed said by way of explanation. "Dead or..." He lifted his chained hands and gestured broadly at the room around them. "You know."

"If I tell you about my case will you tell me about Marissa Loewen?" she asked.

"I'm not Hannibal Lecter, Megan. There's no quid pro quo here."

"Isn't there?"

He pouted as if Margot had wounded his honor. "I said if you came to see me I'd tell you about Marissa, didn't I? I'm a man of my word. But I *would* like to hear about your case."

Margot could lie. She could make up a case. Lord knew she had a deep enough history with homicide that she could have dug up some eight-year-old case that was long-solved, but for some reason she was sure he would know.

He always seemed to know when she was lying.

"Two nights ago a sex worker had her face bashed in."

Ed raised an eyebrow and paused to consider this information. "That's an unusual method. Baseball bat?"

"Brick in a sock."

"Utilitarian." He smiled, mostly to himself. "But not a lot of people just carrying bricks around. And they aren't just laying around on street corners. Pre-meditated then. Was she working?"

Margot nodded. "She was."

"What else do you know?"

"She has connections to some local street gangs. Boyfriend."

Ed's posture shifted instantly, his shoulders sagged, and he grimaced. "Ugh. Gang crime. Never mind."

Margot didn't let it drop, though. "Why does that bore you?"

"With murder there are very elemental reasons at play. Power, control, lust, revenge. With gang murders those motives are inherently uninteresting. It's either money or a message. Those things don't interest me. There's nothing interesting about a crime where the victim is incidental."

"What was it about Marissa that made her special?"

Ed chuckled. "Clever. Clever clever."

For a moment Margot wasn't sure Ed would answer, because she had baited him to walk right into the place she wanted him, and Ed was never a huge fan of being played for a fool. But she was hoping his reaction meant he was proud enough of her that he would play along.

This time around, at least, she was right.

"People have a lot of thoughts and theories about how I

picked my victims. I know the big headline was me taking the addresses from the payment slips for classifieds, and that was the *technical* way I found them, but there was more to it than that."

Margot pretended this conversation wasn't making her sick to her stomach. While Ed waxed poetic, his gaze got less focused, and Margot risked a quick look over at Andrew. He gave her a gentle nod that quietly said *Keep going.*

"How so?" Margot asked, goading Ed to continue. Gregory back at the FBI headquarters was probably going to have to write a wholly new dissertation on whatever Ed said next.

"The addresses were just the fastest way to find them. It was what they *wrote* that really appealed to me. Some women were just so willing to expose themselves as being sad and lonely. It was practically an open invitation to let me know they'd be sitting alone most nights, waiting. You could figure out a lot by just a few lines in a newspaper, Buddy. Did they have a pet? *Must love dogs.* Do they potentially have weapons in the house? *Outdoorsy hunter-type preferred.* There were things you wanted to avoid. Single mothers, of course. I may be a monster, but kids were never my thing." He gave her an intense look, making sure she understood him.

Margot would have argued that murdering fifteen-year-olds definitely made kids a *thing* for Ed, but that wasn't the point here. *He* believed he was a better man for not killing toddlers, and she let him go on believing it.

"Were there things you liked to see, instead of avoiding?" she asked.

"I liked it when they thought they were funny." Ed gave a gentle shrug. "I liked it when they used song lyrics, or movie quotes. The complete lack of personality in that—saying literally nothing for themselves—it made me think they wouldn't be too clever, you know? Smart girls are dangerous, you know that."

He smiled at her and when Margot realized this was his way of paying her a compliment she gagged. She had to swallow back the lump in her throat, sharp bile and all, before she was able to speak again. "If you liked them dumb, why did you like the ones who made jokes?"

"Well women aren't funny, but it was nice to see some of them try, you know? Marissa, she was like that. What did hers say? *Looking for Mr. Right but Mr. Right Now will do* or something like that? It's not particularly *clever*, but it did make her stand out. That's another thing you look for. Indications they might be a little slut. I already knew they were single, but if their bedroom is a revolving door, then people aren't surprised to see an unusual car outside, or a man looking for an unfamiliar apartment. They already know she's a whore."

The way Ed doubled down on the vicious phrasing was Margot's punishment for earlier. He hadn't liked her using the term *sex worker* and now she was going to pay the price for it.

She didn't rise to the challenge.

"Was that how you got into her apartment building then? Pretending to be a confused gentleman caller?"

"That's how I got into a lot of apartment buildings, but no. That's not how I got Marissa."

This lined up with the information she had on the case. Marissa hadn't been killed in her home, there was no sign of a struggle, and her missing purse and jacket made more than one cop try to convince her family she had left on her own, rather than there being any foul play.

"So, what was it then?"

"She came to me."

# FIFTEEN

## THREE YEARS AGO

"Margot, I'd like it if we could talk a little today about your fear of commitment."

Margot shifted uneasily on the couch, which was almost certainly very expensive and designed to put people at ease. The problem was that there were very few places in life Margot felt relaxed, and this couch wasn't one of them.

She *liked* her therapist, she would even be willing to say she trusted her therapist, at least as much as someone can trust a person they only see in a single room once a week.

"Are you *allowed* to call it a fear of commitment?" she asked. "I mean, professionally? Shouldn't there be a different phrase for it?"

"Well, I'm not trying to diagnose you with anything, so I want to avoid throwing around terms like *anxious-avoidant attachment style*." Dr. Singh smiled at her.

She had been to at least a dozen different therapists, most of whom she'd found excuses to stop seeing—probably further evidence of her undiagnosed attachment disorder—but Dr. Singh had stuck now for several years. He was patient with her, he let her open up on her own terms, and more than anything when she had told him the truth about her past, she hadn't seen a single hint of pity in his eyes.

"I don't think I have a fear of commitment," Margot said, staring over at the potted succulent on Dr. Singh's desk and wondering—for the hundredth time—if it was real or just a really nice fake. If it was real, he'd done a mighty fine job of keeping it alive for the three years they'd been seeing each other.

Margot's plants were all fake.

Maybe he had a point.

"When was the last time you had a long-term relationship?" Dr. Singh asked.

A pit formed in her stomach, because he wasn't asking her this out of curiosity, he already knew the answer. He was asking so she'd have to say it out loud and hear it for herself.

"Never."

"How do you classify long-term?"

She shrugged, less because she didn't have an answer and more because she didn't *want* to answer. "More than a month?"

Dr. Singh pursed his lips, a rarity for him. He was usually pretty stoic, and it was unusual for him to have a response to her comments that wasn't just a nod.

"Why is it, you think, that you don't want to let people get to know you?"

It was her turn to give him a look, one that was loaded with sarcastic disdain for him asking such a ridiculous question knowing what he did about her. "I think you want me to say I avoid people, so I don't have to let them know the truth about me. But that's not it. I have kept a secret about who I am more than half my life, that's not even hard anymore. I don't *care* about hiding that. The reason I don't let people in isn't about them knowing me, it's about me knowing *them*."

"Can you explain that a little more?"

"My mother met my father when she was a teenager. She

was so blinded by him being charming and funny and whatever her version of handsome was, that she didn't ever bother to look deeper and see who he was as a person. She *never* saw the real him, not until it was way too late." Margot caught herself playing with her ponytail and pushed it back over her shoulder.

"Margot, are you saying that the reason you don't date anyone long term is because you think they might secretly be a serial killer?"

"Look, Dr. Singh, I think you could be incredulous with any other patient if they had that concern. I think you could quote statistics all day long about it—I could provide you numbers of how many active serial killers are suspected to be active in California right now if you'd like, but you are *never* going to be able to play the likelihood card with me on this one. OK?"

"I don't think that's a very healthy outlook to have."

"Yeah, well, there's a lot about my life you probably wouldn't think is very healthy."

"Does your concern over this apply to only the men you see or the women as well?"

Margot couldn't help but smile, though it wasn't a happy one. "I think everyone is equally capable of hiding who they are, Doctor. I do think men are more likely to kill me for rejecting them though. That's just statistics."

"Your job seems to have given you ample ammunition to back up this penchant for distrust."

"I think when you show up to your tenth... twentieth... hundredth domestic homicide, there's a point you start to realize that *till death do us part* isn't a romantic promise, sometimes it's a threat."

"That's very jaded. Don't you think your life could benefit from opening up to someone, sharing yourself with another person? Intimacy is *good* for you."

"I never said I didn't have sex."

"Sex and intimacy are not the same thing, and I think you

know that." He leaned forward, resting his forearms on his knees and pushing his dark-framed glasses up the bridge of his nose. He was younger than she was, and that had initially bothered her, but she had stopped noticing it after a while, unless he moved in such a way she could see how line-free his face was, and it reminded her all over again.

"I can appreciate the value of relationships for other people. But I don't think I'll ever be able to trust another person enough to be with them. I don't trust people enough to be *friends*, I don't think there will ever be a time in my life I can have the kind of connection you're talking about."

"That is a very lonely view to take."

"I might be lonely, but at least I'll be alive."

# SIXTEEN

Margot's brow furrowed and her nose wrinkled in an involuntary reaction of disgust.

"What do you mean, *she came to you?*"

"I mean just what I said. Marissa placed a personal ad, and with her I wanted to try something different. So, I answered it."

It took every ounce of determination Margot had not to turn her head and look at Andrew right then. She was dying to know if he was hearing this, if he was processing what Ed was admitting to. Greg was going to lose his *mind* when he heard about this later.

"You answered her personal ad?"

"Of course, you read enough of them, and you start to realize what people want to hear. The lies they're telling themselves and each other. I left her a message from a payphone, told her a little about myself—or about John, the man she was going to meet—and then told her that there was no point in playing phone tag for weeks. She should just meet me and see if we clicked."

How had this gone undiscovered for this many years?

The classified column that Ed had picked his victims

from used a phone-in service that assigned each single a code. They could then check in remotely for their messages without ever having to give their real phone number to another person.

Ed had played it safe by using a payphone, but surely that message had still existed in the voice logs for the classified services? Or were they deleted by the listener after the fact? Margot was almost forty, but she wasn't old enough to remember how classified singles ads worked in the eighties and nineties.

There wasn't much point in figuring out where the police at the time might have dropped the ball. The investigation was over, she was sitting across from Marissa's killer. Still, it was shocking to know that there might have been a recording out there with her father pretending to be a bachelor who was just right for Marissa. He must have sounded convincing if she had met with him based on one message.

Margot tried to see Ed as he had been three decades earlier. He'd been in his thirties, not too old, and he had never carried a lot of weight, except later on around his midsection. He had always been what one might politely describe as *wiry*. He wasn't ugly—even looking at him now and knowing how rotten his insides were—she wouldn't call him ugly. He was *interesting* looking. His eyes were slightly too far apart, hooded, and his nose was slightly flat. His lips were thin, and when he did smile it was more unnerving than appealing. He had always worn his hair a little too long.

She wondered what a girl like Marissa would have thought, going for a blind date and seeing Ed Finch waiting for her.

Would she be intrigued, delighted, disappointed?

There was, admittedly, a handsomeness to him at certain angles, something that could probably convince a woman to be attracted to him when combined with his seemingly effortless charm. Ed was a chatty guy, from Margot's recollection. He conversed easily with anyone, was a natural flirt, and people gravitated toward him.

That was the gift of the psychopath. He was a chameleon and could be precisely who he needed to be for whatever the audience demanded.

Marissa might not have thought he was much to look at, but Margot had no trouble believing that he could have convinced her to stay with very few words. She'd watched him talk his way out of speeding tickets and de-escalate arguments between drunks. Ed could talk someone into anything.

He'd talked her into coming here.

He was keeping her here by talking.

"Where did you ask to meet her?"

"I invited her to a bar. I don't think you'd remember it; you were too young. A place called The Blue Note." This made him chuckle. "Why is it there's a Blue Note bar in almost every damn city in the world, do you think? Who decided that was *the* name to give to a jazz bar? It's so unoriginal. Is it still there?"

"I don't know. It's been a long, long time since I've lived in Petaluma."

He nodded thoughtfully at this, though whether he acknowledged the role he played in her leaving the town where she'd grown up was unclear. Margot didn't know if Ed actually understood that he was like the specter of death itself, and no matter where he went, he just left behind haunted houses.

She brought herself back to the story at hand. It made sense he'd pick somewhere like that. The booze would be free-flowing, the lights would be dim. He'd have more of a chance to lure her in before she had a chance to realize he was not her Prince Charming; he was the monster that locked her up in the tower.

For one split second Margot horrifically wondered how Ed would have fared now, in the dating app era. Something told her he would have been a natural.

"She met you at the bar," Margot nudged.

"I don't think she liked me very much. Not at first anyway. I think she was probably expecting someone more Richard Gere, you know what I mean? But your old man did OK for himself back in the day. I think guys these days—and even in my day— overestimated the value of good looks. Women may *seem* shallow, Buddy, but the truth of the matter is, all a woman really wants is to feel wanted. And if you ask a woman about herself, and really listen, and you say some insightful bullshit that proves you were listening, you can be the ugliest schmuck on the planet and still have a supermodel eating out of the palm of your hands. And Marissa, she was no supermodel, and she knew she was pushing thirty and still single, so after a cocktail or two, it didn't much matter to her that I wasn't the best-looking guy in the room, because I was listening to her."

Margot hated with every fiber of her being that at least a small part of what he'd said was true. Say what you want about psychopaths, but there were few people in the world who were quite as attuned to what other people were thinking as they were.

"Did you just talk?"

"We talked, we danced, we drank, we danced some more. What are you really asking me? You want to know if we fucked?"

Margot schooled her features to not respond, but there was a natural aversion tied deeply to her inner child, the teenager who had stopped being a normal little girl that fall day he was taken away; that part of her wanted to openly gag at the mention of her father having sex.

Which was precisely why he'd said it.

She was starting to see all the insidious ways that this Ed— this true Ed—wanted to mess with her. And it made her wonder why it was, exactly, that this was so important to him. Why, after over twenty years apart, did he suddenly want so badly to worm his way back into her life?

He hadn't known she was a cop because he didn't know who she was now. That was information she had given him. And maybe he had tried to reach out before. Maybe he'd sent a hundred letters. She would never know that because her lawyer had explicit instructions to destroy anything that might have come from Ed himself.

How long was his long game here? And what was it he ultimately wanted? She couldn't get him out, couldn't get him a stay of execution—he wasn't likely to ever be scheduled for one, even with his death sentence—and he could never have her forgiveness.

Forgiveness wasn't hers to give, so she had opted to do his penance instead.

"I don't care if you had sex with her, but if you did, there would have been evidence that connected you to her sooner. So, I don't think you did. See, Ed, the thing is, I know things about you now too. Things you didn't have to tell me, because all the bodies you left behind told a story on their own."

"Oh yeah, what did that story tell you?"

"That you very rarely sexually assaulted your victims before killing them. I think you probably tried a few times and couldn't get it up." Margot raised a pre-emptive hand before he could unleash another outburst about her being disrespectful. "Don't interrupt, you asked me to share. I think the sexual gratification for you was in the act of killing itself. The knife was a stand-in for you. You got off on cutting them up." She stared at him a long time, refusing to flinch or look away from his dead eyes. "I don't think you needed to *fuck* to get what you wanted from them."

What settled between them was a silence so deep it was screaming. Margot briefly thought of a room she'd read an article about, where the sound was so dampened that in the silence a person could hear their blood moving through their veins, and no one could stand to be in the room longer than a few minutes at a time before they slowly started to feel themselves going insane.

That was how cavernous the silence between her and Ed was in the moment she finished speaking.

His jaw was tightly set, eyes frigid.

Margot would not be the first to speak, because she knew she was right. She knew that the science, the research, every shard of evidence that had been pored over after the murders told her more about Ed and who he was than anything he could offer her here. Because all that Ed could offer was lies and half-truths meant to flatter himself or make her uncomfortable.

The irony of that being that the whole truth would have made her the most uncomfortable.

He worked his jaw loose a moment before he spoke, and when he did his voice was a lower pitch, rougher than usual as though the words were clawing their way out, leaving his throat ravaged by the efforts.

"You think you're really smart now, don't you? Think that you listen to some lectures and read a book by some piece of shit FBI agent, and you know me? Hmm?"

"No, Ed. I think what reading the book by that piece of shit FBI agent told me was what I already understood deep down. That I *never* knew you."

"When I killed Marissa, she was telling me something about her best friend. It was some inane story with no point, but she was explaining how her best friend just had the worst luck on blind dates, and she felt bad that things hadn't gone worse between us that night so she could one-up her friend." The corner of his mouth ticked up in a smile as he remembered the last living minutes of a girl's life. "She was sitting in the front seat of my car and I think she wanted me to kiss her, there was just that kind of vibe in the air. When I leaned in she stopped laughing and closed her eyes and that's when I..." His voice drifted and he lifted his handcuffed wrists up to mime jabbing a knife into his throat. "Good night. I had to replace the seat covers after that. Spent hours cleaning. I told your mom Justin had spilled something."

And there it was, the truth of Margot's childhood. She and her brother were somehow always accidental tourists in Ed's world. She wondered if Justin knew that he'd played scapegoat to their father's crimes.

He couldn't, at least not in this case, since no one outside this room knew Ed had killed Marissa.

A guard near the door cleared his throat loudly, and the two men who had helped guide Ed into the room came to stand behind him again, easing him out of the cafeteria seat.

"Wait," Margot protested. He hadn't told them where to find her.

One guard shrugged apologetically as Ed shuffled away with them. He took one look back over his shoulder and gave her the most insidious smile.

"Guess you'll have to come back if you want to know more."

# SEVENTEEN

"I'm sorry I called you a piece of shit," Margot said, staring up at her apartment building from the front seat of Andrew's car.

"What?"

"When Ed called you a *piece of shit FBI agent* I'm sorry I agreed with him." She wasn't looking at Andrew so she couldn't see his reaction. Her building manager was stringing up Christmas lights on the front of the complex and was having a heck of a time doing it without someone to help.

Andrew chuckled. "If Ed Finch had a kind word to say about me it would only be at my funeral to praise me for finally shuffling off this mortal coil. The feeling is mutual, trust me. You don't need to apologize for doing what you had to do to keep him talking. And you did a damn fine job of that, kid. Not sure what got into you back there but there are seasoned negotiators and profilers who couldn't have gotten that much out of him."

Margot hefted a sigh. "Don't tell me that. It makes me think you need me."

"We do need you." That was all he said. He didn't remind her that they'd need to revisit Ed if they wanted to find out where Marissa's body was. They both knew the truth—though it lingered unspoken—that Marissa wasn't the end of the list. They were just getting started, and what Margot had unlocked during her discussion today meant that Ed was bound to just keep chattering away so long as he could get in his fair share of digs while he was at it.

And what did it matter that every one of those digs chipped away a little piece of Margot's carefully constructed shields? Who cared what it was doing to her as long as it was for the greater good?

"I need to do some thinking," she said finally, though what she really meant was *drinking*, because there was no way she was getting to the end of this week without a nip of *something*. "You'll expedite that ballistics requisition for us?" she reminded him.

This time she did look at Andrew and he was watching her like he was worried about something but didn't have the means to express it to her. He opened his mouth like he was going to say something, then closed it again. "Yeah, kid. I'll get them to see what they can find on your guy. But I need you to start thinking of something uncomfortable while we do that."

"More uncomfortable than spending more daddy–daughter time with my *paterfamilias*?" She raised an eyebrow. "Perish the thought."

"I know you guys have probably explored the military angle on your shooter, but has anyone started looking into former SWAT-trained police who might have a bone to pick with the department?"

Margot felt a chill creep over her and shook her head. "I mean, I'm sure *someone* has considered it, but it's not an idea that's been popular for obvious reasons."

Andrew nodded, scratching his gray beard thoughtfully and staring out into the waning daylight as the sun started to set in earnest. "Just... don't ignore options, OK? That's all I'm asking.

No one wants it to be cops, but we don't want to put blinders up."

He offered her a soft smile which she didn't have the where-withal to return. "I'll talk to you later, Andrew."

"I hope so."

Margot approached the front of her apartment where too tall and too beautifully dressed Wes Fox had been wrangled into helping her super hang the lights. She paused to watch his lean frame move effortlessly, the hem of his shirt lifting as he handed up inches of light strings, exposing a bare flash of toned abs.

No one whose age started with *forty* should have any right to look as good as he did right then.

"Wes, if you needed a side hustle, I'm sure I could have found you something more befitting your skill set than this."

He glanced over at his shoulder at her but to his credit didn't abandon his place at the base of the ladder. Margot's landlord, a portly Italian man in his sixties named Lorenzo, glanced down at her from the top of the ladder where his round belly pressed into the top step to provide him a little extra balance.

"Your boyfriend is very nice, Miss Detective. But remember, no extra occupancy without rent amendment."

"He's my partner," Margot sighed.

"I don't know what you call it, Miss Detective, but no extra tenants without an amendment."

Wes did absolutely nothing to hide his smirk.

"I was going to feel guilty for openly objectifying you a minute ago, but now I'm glad I did," Margot said. To Lorenzo she added, "He isn't moving in, don't worry."

Lorenzo stapled the last of the lights to the arch over the doorway. "That's too bad though, he's very handsome and you are not so young now, you know? Get married, have babies. He helps me, maybe no rent increase." He gave a shrug. "Such nice-looking babies."

"Maybe no rent increase, Margot. Think about it." Wes waggled a brow at her, and all of the weight she had been carrying with her for the last days, maybe the last months, lifted in one brief moment of perfect reprieve.

She laughed.

She genuinely laughed.

"I'll consider it. Come on." She made sure Lorenzo was OK to get down on his own then unlocked the front door and headed inside. The evening security guard was on shift and looked prepared to question Wes—who he had surely seen before—until he spotted Margot next to him and simply gave the pair of them a nod.

Up at Margot's apartment, she shucked off her shoes—a habit that Ed had engrained in her that she never got over. He *hated* shoes being on in the house, said it was just one more way to trail dirt from outside in. Her mother had thought it was odd —as had all of her friends—but they all got used to it and Margot had never shaken the habit. Wes took her cue and shucked his own off before making himself comfortable at her small dining room table.

"Not that I'm not thrilled to see you on our day off, but... what are you doing here?" She wasn't going to bother being shy with him about having a drink. She opened the cupboard above her fridge and grabbed a bottle of Glenfiddich. She added ice to two glasses and poured some for each of them. Misery loved company.

Wes took the drink and clinked his glass against hers, as if they had anything to cheer in that moment. Once he took a sip of the whisky he set the glass down on the table and Margot took a good look at him. He was in his normal casual apparel, dark-wash jeans and a shirt that fit just a little too well to have been selected lazily. His dark blond hair was pushed back off his forehead but had a more relaxed vibe about it than his normal workday hair did. She couldn't exactly explain the difference, but it was there.

"I'm worried about you," he said.

Margot glanced down at her untouched drink, wondering if this was about to become an intervention, but reminding herself that while the drinking was a crutch, she didn't let it run her life. He had no reason to be concerned about it.

Did he?

"Why?"

Wes raised an eyebrow making a *seriously* face. It was only then that she realized he was worried about her because she'd had a week from hell.

He was here because he was a good friend, something she had in wretchedly short supply.

"Are you OK? I don't mean in a bullshit way, Phalen, I mean seriously. You should have canceled your meeting today after what happened."

Margot sipped her whisky and the glow of warmth that went through her was akin to stepping into a bright, sunny afternoon after being stuck in a room without windows all day. She let out a sigh of relief, her tensed shoulders easing slightly.

"I don't think it would have made things any easier to reschedule with Ed. It can be hard to get in there even when you're escorted by the FBI. We might not be on a ticking clock but putting it off would just give me more opportunity to bail later. Not like it matters."

"He didn't talk?"

Margot laughed but without any humor. "Oh, he talked plenty. If there's one thing to know about Ed it's that if you wind him up, he's going to *go*, and he didn't want to stop talking today once he got started. It's just that he said a lot of useless garbage to get under my skin and we ended up running out of time before I was able to find out what he'd done with Marissa's body. Though we did get to have a lovely chat about his sex life."

Wes didn't have the ability to hide his expression of immediate confusion and disgust. "You... what?"

"Oh, I suggested he liked to knife-fuck his victims because he was impotent."

Wes stared at her for a long moment before reaching across the table and taking hold of her hands, wrapping them inside his much larger ones and fixing her with a look of intense scrutiny. "Margot, are you actually OK?"

"Currently or in general?"

"Both?"

"No." She shrugged with a *what are you going to do about it* gesture and took another sip of her whisky. "I haven't been OK in a long, long time. This week has just been a little icing on the shit cake, y'know. You want Thai? I could go for some Thai."

Leaning back in his chair so the full, long length of his body was angled out into the tiny dining room, he laced his fingers together and rested his hands over his flat stomach. "I mean this in the kindest way possible, but I sincerely hope you're in therapy."

"Dr. Singh, once a week for six years, baby. Crab Rangoon?" She wrote down a note on a piece of scrap paper in front of her and when she realized Wes was still just observing her like a hawk who had forgotten how to hunt, she set the pen down. "Wes, I'm *fine*. I'm as functional as one can expect, given the circumstances. Maybe one day I'll lose it and you'll need to haul me off to the looney bin, but today is not that day, so tell me what you want." She slid a wrinkly well-worn menu across the table to him. It got used with such frequency she didn't bother to put it away, even though she had it largely memorized.

Wes glanced at it like he was seeing an exhibit in a museum. "Jesus, I haven't used a paper menu for delivery in a decade, I didn't even know they still made these."

"That might be as old as a decade. Not sure. I've been here ten years, it's at least that old."

"I'm going to ask a question I probably won't like the answer to, but... why don't you just order off an app like a normal person?"

"Same reason I don't take Uber." She half-shrugged. "I don't like strangers knowing where I live."

"Then how do you get this delivered?" He waved the menu at her.

"I get Brody at the front desk to order it for me. It gets dropped down there and I go get it—or he brings it up. It's what works for me, and he gets a hefty tip every month, so he's cool with it."

"Do you think that's a little paranoid?" Wes asked.

Margot made a face. "Unless you're auditioning to become my therapist, I think that question might be pushing the boundaries of our friendship somewhat. But to answer it anyway, no. No, I don't think any of the things I do that you might think are *too much* are actually too much, because do you know who taught me to look in the back seat of my car before getting in? Who taught me to keep my curtains closed at night and never take rides from strangers?" Her look was pointed now.

"Ed Finch."

"Ed Finch." She fake-clapped. "So, you tell me if I'm being paranoid. I could let you read some of the fan mail I've been sent—or that Megan has been sent—over the last twenty years. There are plenty of people who would love to know where I live, and I don't feel like making it easy for them to find out."

Wes took the menu back and then grabbed the slip of paper she had in front of her and wrote down a few numbers. "I can't pretend that I'm ever going to be able to say I know what it's like to be you, Margot, but I think I can at least tell you that I won't be a shit about it."

"That's more than I get from most people."

# EIGHTEEN

## 1988

Petaluma, California

It wasn't cold enough outside for Ed to need the heat on in the car, but he'd turned it up anyway. There was the faintest early fall chill in the air, and the warmth of the car had felt nice when he and Marissa had first settled into the front seats.

The scent of cigarette smoke was clinging to them both, and it quickly permeated the car's interior. He cursed the thick cloud of it that had hung around in the bar, knowing he was going to catch hell from Kim later when she assumed he was smoking in the car. Since telling her the truth would be impossible, he would just have to accept the tongue-lashing and let her believe she was the superior partner for however long that lasted.

Ed was a saint as far as he was concerned.

Marissa's cheeks were flushed pink from the warmth and the faint sheen of sweat beaded on her neck and down to her cleavage. Ed's gaze drifted downwards, unable to resist the view, and when he looked up again it was obvious to him that she had caught him. Her expression had a different color to it, less light-hearted and now with an element of heat.

She liked that he was looking.

The knife was tucked in beside him in the place where he normally stored fast-food napkins and a pair of gloves for keeping his hands clean should the car ever need a roadside repair. At least that's what he told Kim they were for.

"I had a really nice time tonight," Marissa said, and then laughed. "I think I'm surprised. You weren't..." She was obviously pausing to find a polite way to phrase what she was about to say. "You weren't quite what I was expecting, but I'm so glad we did this."

She gently pushed a lock of dark hair behind her ear, and for a moment, Ed's rage was incandescent. Everything she was doing, every flutter of eyelashes, the downward cast of her eyes, the way she subtly nibbled at her lower lip to draw his attention in, it was all so practiced, so cultivated, that none of it felt genuine. The little bitch had done this before, God only knew how many times. How many Mr. Right Nows. She was a master manipulator, pulling men into her web, and she thought he was just the newest victim to buy into her coy-girl act.

Ed knew better.

He knew when a girl was just a talented liar, because in their hearts weren't they all liars? Some were just better at it than others, and he had to admit that the lure Marissa was dangling was a tantalizing one.

He had different plans for her, though.

Ed smiled, a slow honeyed smile meant to both flatter and entice. He wanted her to feel safe and comfortable. When her guard went down, he would be ready. His fingertips brushed the handle of his knife and his skin burned, a deep, primal hunger stirring in his belly and below.

Cool metal teased him, the only thing in the car not too hot for comfort.

He wondered how hot her blood would feel as it spilled onto his hands.

"I'm really glad we did this. And I know I'm not much to look at, especially to someone as pretty as you, but I'm glad you hung around. I think we had a really nice time."

Marissa's hand fell on his wrist and a faked expression of concern twisted her features. "John, don't say that. I think you're very handsome." Her hand lingered on his, and the faint scent of the red wine on her breath trailed by his nostrils, twisting his stomach. "I just didn't know what to expect. I sure did like your voice on your message."

Ed thought that her lies tasted of cheap Pinot Noir. He knew he wasn't ugly, but Kim reminded him constantly that he was average at best. Not so much with words, but the way she would cast appreciative looks at other men, the way she would sometimes recoil from his touch. He *felt* her ambivalence.

He should be ecstatic about the attention of a woman like Marissa, but the way she was spoon-feeding it to him just made him furious. He wasn't special, no men were special to a woman like that. He'd be doing the world a favor to keep her from doing this to anyone else.

Schooling his features into a mask of gentle interest, he smiled softly but didn't lean in. He knew she wanted him to kiss her, but she was playing a game where she wouldn't make the first move.

Patience.

She smirked, tossing her hair over her shoulder, and the intense fragrance of smoke and wine were temporarily broken up by the sharp scent of her hairspray, a chemical baby powder smell that reminded Ed of both Kim and Megan—Kim for her similar spray, Megan from her baby powder days.

Justin was just out of diapers, but the fragrance didn't conjure up visions of his son.

Ed's conviction faltered, just for a moment. He didn't like

having Megan in his mind when he did this. It brought him back to the girl on the highway, when his daughter was in the backseat and had slept through the whole thing. It had been the only part of that encounter that gnawed at him afterwards. He didn't like to think about his daughter with a knife in his hands.

"I almost feel bad," Marissa said, laughing lightly and dragging Ed back to the present and his frustration with this young woman's pretenses.

"Oh?" he asked.

"I promised my friend Tamara I would call her after I got home from the date to commiserate. She's been on so many terrible dates lately that I thought I might be able to cheer her up by telling her my own first-date horror story. But now I don't think I can."

This brought a natural smile to Ed's lips, and he hoped she wouldn't understand what had sparked his enjoyment in her statement. "I think you'll need to wait to call her until you've had a different first date. Or perhaps a bad second date."

"Are you planning to be a bad second date?" She leaned forward and closed the vent in front of her, her skin now dewy with sweat.

"I guess we have to finish our first before you can decide if I'll get a chance to screw up the second."

"I don't think you'll screw up the second." Once again, she bit her lip, giving him a long look that was an obvious invitation for him to make a move.

This time he did not demur. His hand closed around the handle of the knife, and he leaned close to her, waiting for her eyes to flutter shut as she prepared herself to be kissed.

Ed's lips brushed against hers.

The blade slipped easily into her neck, barely any resistance as it slid through her skin and only meeting pressure as it nicked her trachea. Ed was no stranger to this resistance; he kept pushing until he heard the familiar hiss of air leaking out.

Marissa squealed, but the sound died as blood burbled up onto her lips, which was when Ed withdrew his kiss, licking her blood from his own mouth and drinking in the terror and confusion plastered over her face. Her eyes watered, tears thickening her lashes. Fingernails scrabbled at his arm, gripping his sleeve as if she was slipping off a cliff and grasping for purchase on anything that could hold her up.

Ed pushed the knife until the blade pierced the opposite side of her neck.

"It's been a very nice date, but I don't think I'll be taking you out again. I'm sorry."

# NINETEEN

Margot and Wes were back to the day shift, which suited her just fine. Living life at night was often surreal, like being part of a vampire world rather than a human one, which could make it feel like you were in a limbo state somewhere between life and death. This was especially true when your nights were haunted by the dead.

They had tracked down an address for Genesis's boyfriend, Eugenio. The case of the dead sex worker did seem like one that would be easy enough to close, but they still didn't know if it was the Nuestra Familia member that one of the working girls had seen pick up Genesis, or if her own boyfriend might have had a hand in it.

Either way, the attack had been too brutal, too personal to be something random. That level of overkill meant that someone was trying to either make a statement with her death, or they had been so overcome with their emotions during the killing that they hadn't been able to stop themselves from lashing out more violently than they might have expected.

It wasn't clear which was the case in Genesis's death, but

whoever had murdered her wasn't just some random john, that much was obvious.

"I feel weird being here when the task force is meeting today," Margot said, staring up at the apartment building they were parked in front of. Her red hair was down, pushed back from her face by a pair of aviator sunglasses balanced on top of her head. She had swapped out her leather jacket for a thicker khaki green utility jacket with a bit more warmth to protect against the steadily dropping temperatures. Wes wore a peacoat that made him look like a Hugo Boss model.

The apartment building was an old 1920s art deco style that had likely survived its fair share of earthquakes and other natural disasters, and after a while someone had entirely stopped caring how it recovered. The exterior was crumbling with paint that hadn't been touched up in about thirty years, and the windows on the main floor had all been smashed in and replaced with graffiti-covered boards.

If she didn't know better, she would have assumed it was abandoned.

It should have been abandoned.

"Task force will still be task-forcing after we talk to this guy," Wes said. He was wearing Persol sunglasses that he once foolishly admitted to her he only bought because he'd seen both Steve McQueen and Anthony Bourdain wear the same ones.

Margot had never let him forget that tidbit.

They did look damn good on him, though, which took a little of the bite out of her jabs.

"I feel like we should be there."

"You just don't want to be excluded. You have sniper FOMO."

"You're sick in the head."

Wes smirked. "Be that as it may, you don't need to worry. Leon is in charge of things, and you know he's not going to bench you just because you're involved, especially not after all you did to get the FBI labs involved. So can we focus on a case that we can actually clear, please?"

Margot chewed on her thumbnail, her teeth working away at a particularly grisly hangnail, but when she caught herself doing it she stopped and buried her hands in her jacket pocket.

"I don't like the look of this place." She squinted out into the gray afternoon light. Just down the street, apartment blocks—like her own—were putting up Christmas décor and generally diving fully into the festive season. This block looked as if it had just emerged from a shitty version of *Brigadoon* where it was still the 1970s and there were no safe places to walk in the city.

"You think we need backup?" Wes must have been picking up on her unease, because instead of his usual jocularity his tone now had a hint of concern to it.

This was a simple interview, interviews did not typically call for backup, but Margot knew full well that where they were going they weren't going to be the most popular.

She shook her head. "I think it'll be OK, we'll just let someone know we're going in and maybe to do a drive-by in about fifteen."

Wes radioed into the station to relay the message and a cruiser called back to say they'd patrol the area shortly and check in on their location. It wasn't going to do much good if things went south, but in her many, many years of homicide investigation she had rarely felt unsafe in the process of doing her job.

She'd had one interrogation go terribly wrong when a man who had only been a person of interest had felt himself cornered. He'd thrown his chair at her and gotten in a few good swings before he was incapacitated. Margot got a broken finger and some solid bruises out of the experience, but it had taught her to always be prepared no matter what the situation was. The Boy Scouts didn't use that motto for nothing, and it had served her well ever since.

Always assume other drivers will make an illegal merge.

Always anticipate the unlikeliest suspect will freak out on you.

Fight or flight could be a hell of a thing.

Since the incidents with the sniper began, all on-duty officers of any kind were being asked to wear bulletproof vests. Margot was sporting hers under her T-shirt, a lightweight but still uncomfortable fit that made her itchy. She also questioned the practicality of a vest when the sniper didn't seem to have any issues with a headshot, but she hadn't raised that concern at the briefing.

It could prove useful here, though, if shit hit the fan unexpectedly.

Margot and Wes got out of the car and headed into the dilapidated apartment complex. Immediately, the smell of urine outside the building wafted up and hit her in the face, making her eyes water and her hand reflexively go to her nose.

"Goddamn," Wes whispered, as if he feared his voice at full volume might make him breathe in too much of the noxious fumes.

"Are we sure anyone actually *lives* here?" Margot asked, giving the building one more sidelong stare. It seemed more likely to be a homeless squat than a place anyone could legally call home.

"It's on his DMV file." Wes opened the exterior door, and while there was a small vestibule between the external and internal, the intercom system had been ripped off the wall and the interior door was ajar.

The place somehow looked rougher on the interior, making Margot's nerves tick up a few notches. At least the smell had dissipated inside. The power was still on—a sign that it was still an operational building. Either that or an enterprising squatter had rigged a system to reconnect things to the grid again.

There were large hand-drawn signs on the elevator doors

that indicated they were out of service and *Take the Stairs, Motherfucker*. Likely not put up by building management, then.

A light overhead flickered.

The lobby was dead silent but for the buzz from the fluorescent bulbs and the steady thump of bass from somewhere overhead.

"This place should be burned to the fucking ground," Margot said. She probably ought to report the building to someone, but she thought about low-income families who were most certainly living here and doing their best to survive, and if she reported it because of the grim conditions, they would ultimately be left homeless. She wasn't going to be the one to yank someone's home away from them just because it wasn't *her* ideal living situation.

There were places a lot worse.

Margot and Wes headed to the marked stairwell, and while Margot would normally count herself in pretty good shape, she was grateful they only had to hike up to the fourth floor. The building had at least ten floors and if they'd been forced to go all the way to the top, she was going to arrest someone just on principle.

When they got to the fourth floor only every other light in the hallway appeared to be working and they passed by a hole in the drywall, created either by someone's fist or head. No efforts had been made to repair it. The air was thick with the scent of pot, and while it was technically legal now, Margot felt confident the drugs had not been procured by aboveboard means.

They were, after all, here to talk to a drug dealer.

The further down the hall they moved the more a creeping sensation trickled down Margot's spine. While this was a completely standard interview of a person of interest, there was nothing about this that felt *standard* to Margot in that moment.

Wes must have had the same feeling, because when they

approached the front door of the apartment listed on Eugenio Guerrero's file, they both stood to opposite sides of the door rather than in front of it.

An eerie quiet hung in the hallway. It wasn't to say there was no noise at all, because the thump of bass was ever present and somewhere on another floor someone was shouting at someone else in a way that might require some further investigation on their part after this was done.

But the hall just seemed devoid of life, as if they were in a vacuum.

Margot pushed her jacket back over her shoulder holster and unclipped the strap that kept the gun safely fastened within. She wasn't *hoping* for trouble, but all the same it never hurt to be prepared.

Wes did the same, then rapped on the door loud enough to be heard from anywhere inside the apartment.

"Whossat?" came a slurring, angry voice from within. "Esteban, if that's you, fuck off, I ain't got time for your bullshit today."

"Mr. Guerrero, this is Detective Margot Phalen of the San Francisco Police Department. I just want to be clear you're not in trouble for anything, but we have a few questions about your girlfriend, Genesis."

If anything, the silence got deeper, or perhaps Margot was deafened by the blood throbbing in her ears. She and Wes exchanged glances.

"Eh. Whatever she did, it ain't my business, OK? I don't want fucking five-oh in my shit today, feel me?"

"Mr. Guerrero, we'd just like a few minutes of your time, please," Wes said. "And we don't *want* that time to be downtown, but it can be if you'd prefer."

Margot wasn't sure she'd have gone directly from hello to *don't make us handcuff you*, but she couldn't take back words that someone else had said. Her hand itched to pull her weapon, but no one had threatened them yet.

Yet.

Footsteps thumped from inside the apartment and the sound of several locks being disengaged followed.

The door opened, but a thick gold chain stayed firmly in place, showing them only a sliver of the apartment's interior, and its glowering occupant. "Police?" the young man said, his lips curling around the two syllables as if he was saying a foul word that tasted bad in his mouth.

Margot remained standing beside the door. She couldn't see the man's hands and didn't know if he was holding a weapon. She held up her badge and he scrutinized it for a long while before grunting.

He closed the door again, and with a rattle the chain was disengaged and he opened the door up for them. His hands were empty, and both Margot and Wes relaxed at the same time, knowing there was not any immediate need to arm themselves.

Eugenio walked away from the door in a cavalier *come in if you want* gesture and flopped himself back down on a nearby couch.

The apartment was hazy with old smoke, though the only scent Margot was picking up at the moment was gravy. Remnants of a microwave dinner and the dregs of mashed potato tossed on the counter next to the sink gave her a clue to the source of the scent.

*Bachelor pad* came to mind while she looked around, as the apartment was a quintessential single man's space. There were no feminine touches to be seen—most obviously in the cleanliness department. Dishes littered the sink, empty fast-food wrappers and cans of cheap beer lined the counter. The linoleum tiles in the kitchen had seen better days and were also in need of a good sweep.

In the living room where the man was sitting on his couch, an old sheet had been pinned up over the window in lieu of curtains. More beer cans dotted every visible surface, and one wall was taken up by an enormous television which was presently muted but displaying a courtroom reality show.

Eugenio cracked a beer. There was a loaded ashtray next to him, but the apartment surprisingly didn't reek of either tobacco or weed. Margot would have been impressed if the overall feel of the place didn't make her skin crawl. All the furniture except for the television was old, likely secondhand, or perhaps belonged to whoever had lived here before him, since the place had the look of maybe once belonging to an aging grandparent.

Margot and Wes lingered in the kitchen, but Wes at least closed the door so no one could surprise them from the hallway. Wes inclined his head toward the living room, and Margot got the unspoken suggestion. She would distract their suspect, Wes would make sure there wasn't anyone else in the apartment.

"Mr. Guerrero," Margot moved closer to the couch, but only went as far as a faded old recliner; not wanting to sit down, she just hovered, her hand still itching to rest on her weapon. "We have reason to believe that you were in a relationship with a young lady named Jennifer Covington, who went by Genesis?"

He snorted, gaze barely moving from the TV screen. "*Relationship*. Is that what she said?"

Margot took a good look at him since he was distracted. He wasn't an unattractive guy, though he had taken the bad-boy persona a little far. Since he wasn't wearing a shirt, it was easy to see his vast array of tattoos, many of which had criminal connotations. Spiderwebs fanned over his elbow—confirming what Margot already knew about a past stint in prison—a teardrop tattoo, and several specific to his own gang. It was nothing she hadn't seen before.

His head was mostly shaved down with fresh, dark stubble filling in, and his sweatpants hung low on his hips, showing off the band of his boxers. He was lean, not overly muscular, but seemed like he'd probably be a scrapper in a fight.

"You did know Genesis, though, yes?"

"Yeah, I know her. Is she telling you I'm involved in something? 'Cause look, she gave me some of that money freely. I'm not a pimp or nothing." He looked back at her, gaze laser-focused. It was important to him that she believe him, and she found that interesting.

She also found it interesting that he continued to refer to Genesis in the present tense even though Margot had not. It could be a ploy, but it was one of the most obvious places that people screwed up when talking about someone whose death they were involved in.

"Eugenio, I'm here from the SFPD homicide division." She leveled him with a careful look, trying to gauge how he was going to react to this.

He went rigid, her words dousing him in a shock of cold water.

"Homicide?"

Margot nodded.

"Hold up, is Genesis OK?" Suddenly he had no interest in the TV or the beer. His focus was locked on Margot and he had gone pale.

"I'm afraid not. We found her body in Jefferson Square Park on Wednesday. I'm sorry to have to be the one to tell you that she was killed."

He flopped back against the couch, his breath leaving him in a *whoosh*. If he was acting, he was the best damned actor she'd ever seen. While he didn't cry, he did grit his teeth until his jaw popped, and when he looked back at her his eyes were red.

Eugenio scratched his jaw as if he just needed something to do with his hands, then looked back in the direction of the TV, but without seeing it.

"Was it..." He drifted, and whatever was waiting at the end of that sentence was lost forever.

*Was it painful?*

*Was it quick?*

*Was it something I could have stopped?*

The answers to those questions were so impossible that she was glad he didn't ask, because she didn't want him to know.

"We have reason to believe that a member of Nuestra Familia might have been the last person to see her alive. Were rival gangs aware of your relationship?"

"You think someone did this to get to me?" He was still looking at the TV, his voice hollow.

Wes had returned and gave Margot a gentle headshake to indicate there was no one else in the apartment. He did hold his fingers up in the shape of a gun, though, inclining his head in the direction of what she assumed were the bedrooms.

No shock there. The real surprise would be if it was the *only* gun in the apartment.

"We're exploring every avenue, but a targeted attack is a strong possibility."

Eugenio adjusted on the couch almost like he was thinking about getting up but his body no longer had the energy for it. He roughly swiped at his face. "I mean, she was my girl. I took her out, she went places with me, we were out a lot. I knew what she did, I'm not a fucking idiot, but that was her job, OK? That wasn't anything. She and I had something real."

Margot couldn't help but think of the cavalier way he'd snorted at the notion of being in a relationship only minutes earlier. Funny how the picture changed once you knew you were alone in it. Now, instead of the tough bachelor who didn't need a woman by his side, he was the devastated lover whose precious jewel had been taken from him.

She wasn't sure which version of him was the real one, and suspected it was a little of both and a lot of neither.

This was a man so accustomed to putting up a front for others that he probably didn't know himself anymore.

"Can you think of anyone in particular who might have—" Margot's question was cut off by a loud pounding sound at the apartment's door.

On instinct, both Wes and Margot's hands went to their weapons, and this time they didn't leave them holstered. That banging was not a gentle *anyone home* entreaty, it was a chilling demand of entry that made every hair on Margot's arms stand at attention.

"Yo, fucker, you come to the door right now or I'm kicking it in, you piece of shit."

*Bang, bang, bang.*

Margot flicked a quick look over at Eugenio, and sure enough the initial concern she had over the number of weapons in the apartment had been justified.

Eugenio had a weapon in his hand, and Margot realized it would have been stuffed between the cushions of the couch the entire time they'd been here.

"Wes. *Wes.* Gun." She stepped into the kitchen, her back against the countertop so she could see both Eugenio and the door, but so she wasn't directly in line with the door in case anyone felt like blasting a hole in it. Wes moved deeper into the living room so they were flanking Eugenio, and both out of the line of fire.

Eugenio, for his part, seemed to have completely forgotten they were there, his entire focus on the door.

Unlike Wes and Margot, whose weapons were aimed carefully at the ground with the precise trigger discipline earned from years of practice, Eugenio's gun was held loosely in his hand, the way a carefree influencer might hold an iced coffee. He used it to punctuate his words as he shouted back through the door, even though whoever he was speaking to couldn't see the gestures.

"I ain't got nothing for you, Juan, go fuck your mother and get the fuck out of my house."

"That's how you're gonna talk to a friend, Geño, eh? I see how it fucking is."

*Bang bang bang.*

It sounded like the new arrival, Juan, was now intermittently kicking the door as well as pounding on it with his fists. Given what Margot had seen in the main parts of the building, she had no confidence whatsoever that any of the neighbors would be calling in police reports about the ruckus. If anything, they were probably just lying low until it passed by. She had a feeling—recalling the dents in the drywall in the hall—that this might not be so uncommon.

Wes took a moment to look at her, and she raised her hand to the side of her face, miming a phone call. Wes didn't even blink—he'd be aces as a charades partner—digging his phone out of his inner jacket pocket and hitting a speed-dial number.

Margot was warring with herself over whether or not to announce police presence. Obviously, Juan should know there were armed officers, but he had to know Eugenio was armed as well, so everything he was doing was already with the knowledge of potential for personal injury. Would her sharing that there were police present make him more or less likely to open fire into the apartment?

And moreover, if she announced herself, he might bolt, and if he barged in she would have a reason to arrest him. She didn't know Juan, had never seen his face, but she did have a good feeling that there were probably some skeletons in his closet that might warrant him taking a trip to the police station.

"Friend of yours?" she asked instead, mostly as a means to remind her *host* that they were still in the room.

He looked startled, staring at her like she was a ghost who had appeared from the ether. "Aw, goddamn."

Wes was speaking on his phone in low tones in the living

room. Margot heard the familiar numbers indicating the address, and the phrase *suspect should be considered armed and very dangerous.*

At least someone would be coming. Not that it did them much good right now.

Wood splintered as the weight of a body thrown against the door cracked the frame and sent the door swinging inward.

A man stumbled in, already raising his weapon, but when he saw three guns pointing back at him he gave immediate pause.

"... the fuck?" He was holding his gun one-handed, finger tight near the trigger. The slightest wrong move was going to cause him to fire and Margot needed to de-escalate things *now*.

"SFPD, lower your weapons." She had her gun aimed at the dominant shoulder of Juan, the new arrival. "*Lower your weapons.*" Heavy emphasis on the plural so Eugenio would know he was included.

The two men briefly seemed deadlocked, ignoring her command even though she knew damn well they could hear her. Were those sirens wailing in the distance or was she just imagining it?

"Don't make me say it again. Guns on the floor *now*."

Eugenio blinked first, having realized she was right behind him and if she was going to fire anywhere it would probably be into his back. It didn't matter that he had incorrectly assumed her intentions, because he raised his hands in a surrender motion then bent down to place his gun on the floor.

"Kick it back to me," she commanded.

He did as he was told, the gun clattering over the linoleum and bumping into Margot's foot. She kicked it lightly away from her so she wouldn't trip over it if she needed to make any sudden movements. She didn't even dare look over at Wes, but based on the silence in the room his phone call was finished.

Juan continued to gape at them, showing no signs of lowering his weapon.

Margot disabled the safety on her weapon and chambered a round. Just that simple step was going to create a mountain of paperwork, but she was *not* leaving this place in a body bag. Not today. Not ever.

"You brought the fucking police in, man? What the fuck?" Juan gave Eugenio an incredulous look as if he'd just been personally betrayed by the man whose door he'd knocked down. "You really gonna do me like that?"

Eugenio, practically reading Margot's mind, indicated the door with a sweeping gesture. "You really gonna do *me* like *that?*" he said.

"This is the last time I'm going to warn you and then I'm going to need to treat you as an active threat. Put that gun on the goddamn ground."

The man considered her. He gave her a long up-and-down look, one that said he was really processing every inch of her, and whatever he saw, he found lacking.

"Aw, suck my dick, bitch." The gun moved from Eugenio to her, just a tiny fraction of an inch, but for Margot the entire scene froze. Her breath caught in her chest and her pulse throbbed in her ears.

There was a shot, but her world had become so clouded she barely heard the sound. Had she fired? Had he?

Her heart pounded and slowly she came back to reality as Juan slumped to the floor. Wes was on him in an instant, kicking the gun out of Juan's hand and keeping his own weapon trained on the man who was now on the floor bleeding. Wes hazarded a quick glance back at her, his expression asking, *you good?*, though he didn't spare the words out loud.

Was she?

Margot looked at her own hands, her weapon still loaded to fire, and at Eugenio, who had dropped to a huddle on the floor next to her, half-tucked under his kitchen table, his arms over his head.

Wes was reading Juan his rights and the injured man was swearing up a storm, holding his bloody shoulder and leveling every insult he could think of at whoever was listening. Margot holstered her weapon and helped cuff Juan as Wes finished Mirandizing him.

She barely noticed as the uniformed officers came through the door, taking Juan and Eugenio out with them.

It wasn't until they were back in Wes's car that her hands started to shake.

# TWENTY
## TWO YEARS AGO

Margot and Dr. Singh were at a stalemate.

He was waiting for her to break first, and she was stubbornly refusing, instead counting down the minutes of her session by staring out the window rather than looking directly at the doctor.

She didn't want to know what his eyes were saying that his words were not. There was plenty they could be discussing, but the weight of it all just felt like too much today. It was petulant, she knew that, but it was her money to waste, at the end of the day.

Dr. Singh lost the battle, clearing his throat. "Margot, I'm not going to force you to talk about anything you don't want to, but I also think it's important we acknowledge *why* today might be especially difficult for you."

She raised her hand to her mouth, almost biting the skin around her thumb, but she stopped herself, dropping her hand back into her lap.

When she finally did look at him, it was as bad as she had feared. He wore a patient, soothing expression, one that told her he was sensitive to what she was going through.

It wasn't pity, but it was nearly as bad.

"It's been a long time since..." She let out a sigh, briefly glancing up at the ceiling and wondering if it might be better for her to simply not speak at all. She had foolishly planned this appointment knowing full well what date it landed on, and yet she had stupidly thought it wouldn't impact her, she'd feel nothing.

Years later she still felt it.

"Your mother went through a lot," Dr. Singh offered. "Even the strongest among us sometimes find they reach a breaking point. Perhaps she felt like she didn't have anyone she could turn to for help."

"She could have come to me," Margot said.

"Margot, you were still so young."

"I was in my twenties," she countered. "I was an *adult*."

Dr. Singh put his notepad on the table beside him and leaned forward so she had no choice but to look at him. He wasn't a large man but his presence was still a commanding one.

"To your mother you were *always* going to be a child. But maybe she understood that because you and your brother were legal adults and independent, that you didn't depend on her anymore, in the literal sense. She waited until you were able to stand on your own before she did what she did. It might not make sense to us, but to her, perhaps, it was different." He leveled her with an intense stare, and when she didn't immediately respond, he continued. "We are not responsible for the actions of others, Margot. You are no more responsible for what your mother did than you are for what your father did. You understand that don't you?"

"Well, not to be a Debbie Downer to your pep talk, Doc, but research has shown a pretty clear correlation between major life events triggering a serial killer to act. So I think it's safe to say I was actually *directly* responsible for inciting my father to his first kill."

"You don't actually believe that's true, do you?" For the first time that day his face showed something other than stoic kindness. It wasn't *shock* exactly, but she had certainly thrown him off some.

Margot lifted one shoulder in a noncommittal shrug. "I know what the research says."

"A lot of people have babies and don't start murdering people."

"I'm not saying that his *capacity* was caused by me. I didn't make Ed Finch a psychopath. I know that. But you can't deny the science."

"Correlation and blame aren't the same thing, Margot. Yes, research has demonstrated that there can be inciting incidents in the life of would-be killers that push them to a breaking point. But that could have been anything. It could have been a breakup, a job loss. You are not the reason Ed killed people."

"And therefore, not the reason my mom killed herself."

The doctor leaned back in his chair and linked his fingers together, resting his joined hands on his slight belly. "You know what I think? I think you're feeling sorry for yourself, but you don't want *me* to feel sorry for you, so you're telling me something that you don't entirely believe to be true."

They were both quiet a long time.

She wasn't sure she'd ever had a therapist be so brutally blunt with her before, and it had stopped her from being able to come up with a quick reply. This time, when she went to bite her thumbnail, she didn't stop herself.

"You're right. I don't think I'm the reason Ed killed all those girls. But I think my mom believed that."

"You can't take on the guilt someone else felt. It doesn't help your mother and it doesn't help you."

"Well Ed isn't going to carry his own guilt, Doc, so I think someone in the family better feel a little fucking bad for what he did."

"No one blames your family for what your father did."

This time she met his gaze full-on just to give him a smug look of incredulity. "We had to change our *names*. We had to leave our lives behind. They might not blame us, but they'd love nothing more than to make circus freaks of us. And then it's all the questions: how could they not know? How could they not have seen? And I wonder that too sometimes. Not just about my mom, but about me. I was old enough to know he wasn't always right, not compared to how my friends' dads were. I ask myself a lot if maybe I should have seen signs. I think that's what my mom asked herself up to the very end."

"Do you think your mom saw signs?"

"Probably. As much as you can in those situations. I know he never got angry, not the way you might think a man gets angry. You could tell there was a rage there, simmering, but he almost never lost it, like yelling or throwing things. I can count on one hand the number of times I was scared of him. The rest of the time he was so quiet, he would just shut us all out if he was upset, until you got to a point where you wondered if *you* were really the problem. I wonder if things might have been different if he just let himself explode a little in smaller ways."

"I think, given all that you know about the psychology of killers, you know that's not how it works. Ed didn't kill because he had rage about his family. Ed was a sexual sadist, he needed to kill in order to feel sexual gratification. That doesn't match with him feeling familial pressure at home."

"I don't think I want to talk about this anymore."

"We can talk about whatever you want, Margot, it's your time to do with as you please."

"I think I'd like to talk about my new partner."

"Work partner?"

"Yes."

"What did you want to talk about?"

"The captain wants to tell him the truth about me."

"And how are you feeling about that?"

Margot looked back out the window and sighed. "I don't know. He drives me nuts, but there's something about him. Something... reliable." She didn't dare say the word she was thinking, not wanting to jinx it. But despite herself, she found there was something *trustworthy* about Wes, and it both terrified and intrigued her. "Maybe it's time someone else knew."

## TWENTY-ONE

Margot stood on one side of the two-way mirror that separated the primary interrogation room at the precinct from a small viewing room on the opposite side. She was clutching a coffee cup, hoping it might help keep her hands from shaking, but the shock of what had happened at the apartment was still holding her firm.

She tried not to let it show on the outside, but in that one moment, a gun trained on her and Juan's finger so close to the trigger that a tremble might have pulled it by accident, she saw everything her father had warned her against, everything she had spent her whole life avoiding.

In that moment the inevitability of death stared her down and told her that it didn't matter how careful she was, or how few routines she built, or how many locks were on her door.

There was always going to be a man with a gun, or a knife, or his hands on the other side of a door, and there was nothing she could do to stop it.

Especially if you were a cop.

Maybe this was just one more way her father had unknowingly put her life in danger.

She sighed and took a sip of the unbelievably disgusting coffee that was lukewarm at best and reheated engine oil at worst. They just needed to take the L and buy a Keurig for the office, because not a single soul in the unit could be trusted to make a half-decent coffee if their lives depended on it.

It was the coffee, then, after all, that helped root her into place and bring her back to herself.

If she could be miserable about a burnt cup of joe, she could interrogate a suspect without being a hot mess. This was who she was, and she was a damn fine detective.

She'd known the risks going into that building, and she and Wes had done everything right. Because of that, both of them had walked away uninjured, and they had someone brand new to discuss Genesis's murder with.

Juan was a member of a third different rival gang, but one with closer ties to Eugenio's rather than a direct head-to-head, shoot-on-sight kind of rivalry. It meant someone could be your buddy one minute and then sinking a knife into your ribs the next, because there was no such thing as friends when it came to gang life.

Margot had her doubts that Juan was involved in Genesis's murder, but it was a lead to follow nevertheless. He obviously had some beef with Eugenio, so there was always a chance he'd gone to Genesis first before heading to the man directly. Anything was possible.

And since Juan had outstanding warrants, he wasn't going anywhere any time soon. Margot would let a narcotics detective have their way with him soon enough, digging for drug-related intel, but Margot got first dibs at him since she'd had to stare down the barrel of his gun.

Wes came into the observation room and gave her a quick once-over. "You feeling up to this?"

"I have very literally never felt more up to something in my life."

Wes smirked and put his hand on the back of her neck just under where her ponytail was tied. He squeezed once, then patted her back with his palm, a rough, brotherly *thump*. "I'm here if you need me."

The two physical gestures were incongruous; one sent a direct pulse of lust right through her body, while the other said, "BUDDY, PAL, FRIEND" in all caps.

She didn't have time to parse through Wes and whether or not she was interested in him or he was interested in her. That was a can of worms that might be compelling to explore, but certainly not when the city was in a state of panic over a sniper, and they still had a full caseload to process.

Not to mention she didn't need to be worrying about potential love-interests while also dealing with the bullshit dredged up by Ed's very existence. She didn't think she could handle much personal life at all while Ed was looming.

She heard her therapist's voice in her head telling her she was making excuses, and maybe she was, but excuses were really tremendous coping tools sometimes, weren't they?

Margot took her coffee with her, and headed into the interrogation room. The space was familiar to her but was designed to feel off-putting to anyone in a particularly guilty state of mind. The wooden chair was uncomfortable and the legs were wonky, meaning no one could quite find their balance sitting in it. The temperature of the room was a few degrees warmer than anywhere else in the station, and Margot had long ago learned the trick of coming into an interrogation like she already knew the person was guilty.

In Juan's case, he would know she was well aware of at least one criminal activity he'd done right in front of her.

Margot wore her simple black V-neck shirt, the bulletproof vest left in her locker and her jacket at her desk. She took a seat across from him, setting a thick folder on the table beside her. She made sure all her movements were calm and purposeful, and at last when she was settled, she sipped her coffee and looked Juan dead in the eyes.

He looked pale. His shoulder had been bandaged up by an EMT that came to the scene at the apartment, and they'd cleaned the wound up—a through-and-through that would leave minimal long-term damage—and made Margot and Wes promise they would get him to a doctor for stitches once they were finished with him. Since the wound wasn't too serious, it could make do with a heavy bandage, some antibiotics, and a painkiller.

But not a painkiller so good it would leave Juan loopy.

So, he was sweating, both from the heat of the room and likely from a bit of discomfort owing to the hole in his shoulder. Under different circumstances Margot might feel sympathetic toward him, but since he'd been about to shoot her, she wasn't in an overly generous mood.

"Yo, isn't this like, a conflict of interest or something? Shouldn't I get a different cop?"

"Why? Do you and I have personal history, Juan?"

"Nah, but like, y'know..." His voice drifted as if he wasn't sure what he could say that wouldn't get him into more trouble.

Margot stared at him coolly, knowing her face betrayed nothing of what she was actually feeling. It was a skill she had long honed, keeping the bubbling rage just a breath below the surface. She *wanted* to scream at him, to throw her coffee in his face, to lash out at him with her fists until he was a bruised and bloody pulp.

But she wouldn't.

She *hated* that that rage was there, though, a hum in her bloodstream that never quite went away.

"You seemed pretty intent on speaking to Mr. Guerrero today, how do you two know each other?"

"We're friends," he replied flatly, sitting back in his chair which caused it to rock uneasily. As he scrambled to find balance again—disturbing his attempt to look cool—he winced from new pain in his shoulder.

"Friends? Yes, I could tell you seemed really buddy-buddy when you knocked down his door and threatened to kill him. So, let's try again one more time. And remember, the longer you dick around in here without telling me what I want to know, the longer it'll be before we get you to a hospital where all the really nice drugs are. I think we can both agree you'd rather be there than here."

"I feel fine." The bracing wince following those words suggested otherwise.

"What did you want from Eugenio?"

"Fine. Goddamn, bitch, you're an icy one, aren't you? I thought redheads were supposed to be fiery but you a goddamn snow queen or some shit. I've seen thugs look less chill after having a gun pointed at them."

Margot declined to answer him.

"Look, Geño owed me some money. He had some... uh... y'-know, products I wanted to sell, and he was supposed to pay me the value of those... products, and he hadn't given me shit, so I wanted what was mine."

"So Eugenio owed you how much for these products that definitely were not drugs?"

"Five large."

Five thousand dollars was no small sum. But was it enough money for Juan to have taken it out on Eugenio's girlfriend over? Especially *before* going to see the man in person? Margot had her doubts.

She opened the folder next to her and slid a series of photos across the table to Juan. He glanced down and almost immediately recoiled. "Damn, Ice Queen, what the fuck is that?"

"Do you know this woman?"

"Bitch, that woman ain't got no face, how do I know if I know her? Jesus."

"How about her?" Margot slid a photo across the table, this time showing Genesis as she had appeared in life, cheerful and pretty, round cheeks and sparkling eyes.

To Juan's credit he took a good, long look at the photo rather than immediately dismissing it. Margot had expected him to just give it a cursory glance and then shrug, but it seemed like he was actually trying to recall the girl's face.

"Yeah, that's Geño's girl, ain't it? I think she works the corner near the park. See her there sometimes. Pretty thing, too good for him, that's for sure."

"Have you ever met her?"

"I mean, I've seen her at things. Parties, out on the street. But if you're asking me if I know her like, *professionally*, then nah. I don't pay for pussy."

He wasn't defensive about it, just matter-of-fact, in a way that made Margot think he was telling the truth.

After a moment he seemed to process that there was a connection between the two photos.

"Aw, fuck, is that her?" He jabbed his finger into one of the crime scene photos. "That's fucked up, she seemed like a nice kid."

"You haven't heard anyone recently talking about killing a sex worker?"

Juan shook his head. "Guys in my crew aren't gonna waste their time killing a ho unless she really fucks something up. Goes to the cops, goes to the other gangs, y'know? Someone really did a number on her. You sure it wasn't Geño?"

"Why would he do that to his own girlfriend?"

Juan shrugged, then seemed to regret it immediately, sucking breath in through his teeth. "I dunno, lady. Maybe he was sick of putting his dick in a used hole? Maybe she was working for him, and she didn't want to pay up. Maybe *he* pissed someone off and she paid the price."

"Pissed someone off. Like you?"

Juan didn't rise to the bait. He just shook his head again. "That shit ain't my style. I didn't touch her. I don't kill women. Kind of a moral code."

Margot leveled him with a wordless stare.

"I wasn't gonna shoot you. But even if I did, you're a cop, not a woman. It's different." After a moment in which she didn't reply he added, "No offense."

Margot reclaimed the photos and put them back in the folder.

"We'll get you seen by a doctor, but then I have a friend from the narcotics squad who is going to come in here and have a nice, long conversation with you about those products you had given Mr. Guerrero, and a few more things we have outstanding warrants for. Plus threatening a police officer. You won't be going home for about ten to fifteen." She got to her feet and took her coffee with her. "Offense decidedly taken."

# TWENTY-TWO

## 1988

Petaluma, California

It never ceased to amaze Ed how much heavier a body was once it was dead.

There was some unspoken science that took place after a person died that made their body weigh roughly twice as much as it did beforehand. This was a lesson he had learned firsthand over years of practice, but it still amazed him that a petite creature like Marissa could weigh so damn much. Her body was so slight, and yet so frustratingly *dense*.

Ed's preference was to kill women in their homes.

Yes, it increased a risk to him, because they would inevitably be found so much sooner—there was a certain *scent* a dead body mustered after a few days—but it was also easier to just leave a body behind rather than having to move it somewhere.

If he had thought this through, he would have waited until Marissa had invited him to her apartment. She had seemed interested enough in him to make a move in the car, but that didn't necessarily translate into a surefire invite back to her home.

The problem was, he couldn't risk setting up date after date with her. For one, she had already mentioned tonight's outing to a friend, meaning someone *knew* Marissa was out with a man. And while he had given a fake name, that still meant that if—when—Marissa didn't check in with that friend tomorrow or the next day, someone would know that there had been a date.

He had been foolish in how he'd executed this, he understood that now, as he dragged her body through the woods, branches slashing at his bare arms. This complicated things, it muddied things, all the repercussions he didn't want to deal with.

When he'd brought the knife with him, he'd anticipated carrying it with him up to her apartment, following her through her door, letting her lead him to the couch or the bed, or perhaps if she was pretending to be a good girl, she would put on some coffee and he would follow her into the kitchen.

This was new for him; he wasn't accustomed to spending *time* with the girls before he killed them. Well, perhaps that wasn't true. He frequently spent hours, days watching them as he decided how to act, but something about Marissa had captivated him. He wanted to know the sound of her voice, but more than anything, he wanted to see what it felt like to turn her calm, even happiness into terror.

He wanted to *trick* her.

This was not something he usually did. Yes, he had talked his way into apartments with charm. He had calmed women he was following on the street. He had shared passing smiles with women he would later gut. But he had never taken one on a date before.

There was just *so much* risk in it. Petaluma wasn't a big town. People could have seen him. Could have recognized him.

If that had happened, he would have needed to abandon the plan and Marissa entirely.

But that hadn't happened, and having her in his car, close to him, *wanting* him, it added such a thrill to the entire thing it had felt completely worth the risk.

That was until the part where he remembered he couldn't just bring a body home with him.

So now he was hauling the literal dead weight of Marissa through boggy undergrowth, her legs continually snagging on low-lying roots and vines, as if the forest itself was trying to claw her back from him.

This might be his sole regret in the evening.

But the night was young, there was still room for more.

Ed stopped, lowering Marissa's body to the ground, and taking a moment's rest. It was convenient, he thought, that the city had developed such a nice park space so close to Petaluma. The two hundred plus acres of the Helen Putnam Regional Park, which had just been opened a few years previously, had put a veritable wilderness in his backyard, one that promised lush lawns to take your kids picnicking, great walking trails to take your dog out for a jog, and most importantly, a huge swath of woodland that wouldn't ever be developed or cultivated.

Eventually someone was going to find her, of course. You could only keep a body a secret for so long. But hopefully by that point there would be so little left of her that any sign of him would be long gone.

The park had more open space than he would have liked, but to take the body out of town to a better location would have required more time than he had to spare. As it was he was going to catch hell from Kim for getting home so late, and he was going to have to come up with some way to placate her. Driving an hour out of town to somewhere more remote simply wasn't an option.

He'd paid attention to the layout of the park on the few

occasions they'd visited as a family, carefully scouting anywhere he might be able to get someone alone if he had the opportunity. He knew ways in that weren't common knowledge or meant for the public.

Ed liked to know where he could hide things.

It was always a good idea to have a plan.

He swatted at a fat black fly buzzing lazily around his head. The deeper he got into the bush the murkier the undergrowth became and the worse the bugs got. Mosquitos were unusual this time of year, but he'd had more than one bite since coming into the woods. This was proving to be a bigger pain in the ass than he had anticipated.

He hefted a sigh and picked up the body again, continuing to drag it, knowing they didn't have much further to go. She was extra heavy thanks to the bag he'd brought along to weigh her down.

First, he needed to get rid of Marissa.

Then, he needed to clean the car.

# TWENTY-THREE

Margot was dumping her shitty coffee into the break room sink when her captain appeared. He was like a silent phantom, slinking through the hallways of the station; he would always pop up when she least expected and least wanted to see him.

Captain Gordon Tate was in his early sixties, certainly beginning to court the idea of retirement, and not shy about telling people when he was sick of their bullshit. He was a handsome man, as men in their sixties go, with a rugged complexion that seemed better suited to someone working on a Montana cattle ranch than behind the desk of a San Francisco police department. His formerly dark hair was now almost entirely silver, and his blue eyes were sharp and attentive.

Under normal circumstances, Margot liked Captain Tate, but she also knew that the last thing any detective wanted on a day like this was to have their captain pop up like the Ghost of Christmas past.

"Detective Phalen. A word?" He inclined his head in the direction of his office and Margot's stomach sank. This definitely wasn't going to be good if it was an in-private conversation.

She passed by Wes as she and Tate moved toward the captain's office. She gave her partner a pleading *save me* look, but knew it was pointless, there was no one who could intervene in whatever was about to happen.

Margot shut the door of the office behind her and sank into a chair facing the captain's desk. The office was dark, filled with old wood paneling that had likely been up since the seventies, and the walls were decorated with little bits of Captain Tate's professional history. There was a letter of commendation from the mayor, framed photos of the captain with various political figures, and a framed service medal.

On his desk was a photo of his family—his wife Nadine and their two grown sons, Henry and Jeremy along with their wives who Margot didn't know—and his mug said *World's Best Grandpa*.

Margot chose to focus on the mug, because it was hard to imagine that anyone drinking from it might be about to ruin her entire day. Then she noticed the folder for the Genesis Covington investigation on his desk and her stomach managed to sink even further than before.

"Great work on the Clark case. That was a quick closure, we needed that."

She gave a tight nod. "He pretty much started spilling his guts the minute we got him into a room. It was open-and-shut."

"The ADA was pleased with your professionalism on covering all the bases. You know that makes their jobs easier."

Margot, who had never much cared for anyone from the district attorney's office, gave a half shrug as her way of acknowledging the compliment. If it meant that someone who was guilty would get justice, then great.

"I didn't bring you in here to talk about that case, though."

"No, sir, I suspected as much."

He gave her a thin smile and tapped his finger on the folder in front of him. "This case you and Wesley are working, it's becoming a bit more complicated than I think you anticipated."

"Complicated, sir? I don't think so." She didn't want to argue with him, exactly, but of all the murder cases that had landed on Margot's plate in her many years as a homicide detective, she didn't think the dead sex worker would even crack the top ten most difficult cases she'd had her name on.

"Perhaps I should reframe my concerns." He tented his fingers together and fixed a serious look on her, one that made Margot wonder what he had been like in interrogations during his prime on the force.

She didn't say anything, focusing all her energy on not squirming like a child who had been sent to the principal's office. Everything she'd done in her current caseload was beyond reproach. Margot knew she was a good cop and she didn't take unnecessary risks, so whatever he was trying to catch her out on, she didn't think it would hold water.

"Margot, two days ago you personally witnessed a fatal sniper assault, and now today you had a suspect threaten you with a loaded weapon. On top of all this I know you've been visiting..." He paused, as if unsure what the best word to use next was. "You've been visiting Ed Finch at the behest of the FBI, doing work for their ongoing investigation there."

Since all of this was factually accurate, she didn't argue, despite the fact she felt like she was helping him dig her a grave. "Yes, sir."

"That's a lot."

"I don't think I understand what you mean?" Her skin itched, a physical manifestation of how nervous she was. She had an idea of where all this was going and she wasn't sure she liked it. In fact she knew if he did what she thought he might be about to, she was going to be fucking miserable.

"I think you need a break."

"A break?" She wasn't sure why she just parroted it back to

him, but she felt like he was suddenly speaking another language.

"Margot, you and I had a discussion when you came to this precinct. We talked about you, and about your past."

"Sir, I don't think that my—"

"Please don't interrupt me." He wasn't cruel about it, but there was a paternal insistence that brooked no arguments. "You said that you would respect my opinion if I ever felt that a case might be getting too close to something personal, too much for you in terms of what you would be comfortable with. You're a stubborn woman, Detective, and we agreed that those decisions could be mine, if I felt that you didn't recognize those limitations in yourself."

She was quiet for a long time, hearing a promise she had made almost a decade earlier getting flung back in her face. Captain Tate was talking about something she had said when she was a fresh-faced, unpracticed homicide detective. He'd wanted to make sure that she didn't over-extend herself, especially with cases that too closely resembled Ed's work.

For a long time she wasn't assigned to any kind of stabbing case where the victims had been women. It wasn't done obviously, she would just be pushed to something different. Over time the leash she was on got longer and longer to the point where she no longer thought she had one.

Now Captain Tate was yanking it back. And for what? A bludgeoned sex worker?

That didn't make sense. Ed had specifically avoided killing sex workers, he thought they were beneath his attention.

Since it seemed that the captain was taking enough of a pause to give her room to speak, "I'm sorry, Captain, but I don't see how that discussion applies here. This case doesn't have any connection to my past. I don't think I need to be put on desk duty because of a murder we're about to solve."

"I'm not benching you because of the prostitute, Detective.

I think given all the stresses you've had in a very short period it's best for you, and for everyone, if you take some time off."

"Respectfully, I disagree."

He sighed, and that was the first sign that things weren't going to go well for her. He was an incredibly patient man, but she was pushing him in a direction of losing some of that patience. Normally that would bother her, but right now she was willing to do whatever it took not to be forced onto the sidelines.

"I don't mean to undermine you, sir, and I can completely appreciate that you're trying to do what you feel is right, but I promise you I'm fine. I don't need to be taken off these cases."

"Well, just as respectfully to you, I'd like to hear that from a professional."

Margot recoiled as if she'd been slapped. "You're requiring a psych eval?" Her lip curled involuntarily. "I didn't do anything wrong."

"I think you're misunderstanding my concerns here. I don't think you did anything wrong. I think you have experienced several traumatic events in a row, and I'd like for you to speak to someone, and they can determine if you're ready to go back on active duty. We would do the same thing in any instance where someone has experienced trauma."

There was no point in arguing with him, she knew that well enough. He had already made up his mind, and no matter what she said to him at this point, the outcome would be the same. "Can it be my therapist?" she asked finally. "Since he's already aware of the complexities of my personal history?"

The captain nodded. "Yes, I think that would be a suitable compromise. Until then, I'm not asking you to stay home or do nothing. I know you have a few cases that are going cold on the backburner, certainly some paperwork to catch up on. I don't even mind if you sit in on the task force meetings, but I just need you to stay put and not go running around town until I know you're handling everything in a healthy way, OK?"

She tried to smile at him, but even without seeing her own face she knew it was more of a twisted grimace than anything genuinely warming. "Of course, sir. Is that all?"

He looked as if he might want to say something else, but after looking at her for a long moment he simply shook his head. "No, that will be all for now. Please close the door when you leave."

Margot left his office feeling like all the air had been released from her body in one fell swoop. There was nothing she could do or say, and no way to change his mind until she was able to meet with Dr. Singh, so until then she would just need to be a desk jockey, doing paperwork and fiddling with cases already at a standstill.

She was being punished not for what she had done, but for what had been done *to* her, and that didn't feel fair.

Though fairness was hardly a standardized concept in the real world.

Still, she wanted to flop down on the floor and scream until she was given what she wanted. It seemed the only logical reaction. Rather than heading back to her office she made a beeline through the station and to the front entrance until she was outside.

The sun was down now and cool air had snuck in along with the evening fog. The world outside the station was misty and cold, but it felt good to breathe in the damp air, her skin dewing over almost instantly. She took a deep breath and leaned against the arm of the staircase.

It didn't take long for her to calm down. Margot recognized that between the rage she felt toward Juan, the frustration she felt over the cases she was working, and the brutal blow handed down by her boss, there wasn't a lot she could *do* about any of it. She'd spent a long time in her life trying to assess the difference between events she could control and those that she couldn't, and this was just a case of knowing it was the latter. Everything was out of her hands at this point, so it didn't make much sense to lose her cool—and potentially her job—by overreacting.

Though it probably would have felt good to just let some of what she was feeling out.

She was about to turn back into the building when she noticed a woman standing by a car parked near the end of the block. The woman was in her mid-to-late-forties, and wore a bulky coat hugged close around her. She clutched her purse to her chest, and every time it looked as if she might take a step toward the building, she took a step back instead, remaining close to the car.

There was a nervous energy about her that was easy to spot even from a distance. *Cagey* was the word for it. Margot had seen it countless times in criminals who were debating their next steps. She'd watched footage of robberies where men made that same uncertain two-step shuffle before pulling out a gun and asking a poor clerk to hand over all the money in the register.

This woman didn't look like she was on the cusp of robbing anyone, though. She looked like she was having an internal war with herself, and Margot wasn't sure which side was winning.

She waited, uncertain if the woman had seen her or not, and after the fourth time the woman took a step toward the entrance and then turned around, shaking her head and reaching for her keys, Margot left the steps and moved a little closer.

"Hey. Hi there. Do you need help?" Margot wondered if perhaps the woman was coming to file a domestic violence report or request an order or protection from someone. She had the nervous energy of someone who was trying to do something difficult but couldn't find the backbone. In Margot's experience women in abusive relationships were often so beaten down—

both physically and psychologically—they didn't believe they were worthy of being helped.

The woman froze when she realized someone had been watching her.

She was plain, the kind of face Margot's eyes might easily pass over in a crowd. There were dense black bags under her eyes, and she had deep-set wrinkles between her eyebrows and beside her mouth. Her clothes looked well-worn, as if perhaps it had been quite some time since she'd gotten new ones.

"Oh. I..." She looked around and Margot could see the way the hands that clasped her purse were trembling.

"My name is Margot Phalen, I'm a detective here. I can help you." She held out a hand like she was approaching a skittish dog, moving slowly so as not to spook her.

For one brief moment the woman gave her a look of such naked longing that it almost broke Margot's heart. Whatever she was going through it had done one hell of a number on her. Margot hoped they could get her away from whoever had made her feel like that.

"I'm sorry. I made a mistake." Before Margot could stop her the woman pivoted quickly and ducked back into her car. She started the engine and was gone so fast that Margot had barely processed she was leaving.

Something about the woman and her presence left an uneasy, gnawing feeling in Margot's gut that she couldn't quite name. But if someone didn't want to ask for help, Margot couldn't force it on her.

Margot hoped she wouldn't see her again, because in her line of work that would mean something had gone terribly, terribly wrong.

# TWENTY-FOUR

Rules were rules, and Margot had no intention of breaking them, but when Evelyn Yao, the chief medical examiner, called the next morning to let her know that their park victim was done being autopsied, Margot wasn't about to decline the invitation.

Besides, was a trip to the city morgue really considered going into the field? Margot didn't think so.

She swung by Wes's desk, pulling her jacket on as she did. "Evelyn called."

Based on the look Wes gave her, she suspected that the captain had already given him a heads-up on her new desk duties, but when he didn't argue with her about leaving, she at least knew her partner had her back.

The drive from their precinct to the morgue would normally have taken about twenty minutes at that time of day, but it took them just over ten. The streets of San Francisco were emptier than she could ever recall seeing them.

Usually the sidewalks were crammed with residents and tourists, not to mention cyclists weaving their way through traffic. Now, though, the sidewalks were barren, and anyone who needed to be out on them seemed to hug the side of the building and hustle at top speed from one location to the next. She saw more than one person carrying an open umbrella despite it being an unusually sunny morning in the Bay Area.

This situation with the sniper was making everyone paranoid, and Margot could hardly blame them. You could only be so careful against an invisible threat. A deranged gunman on the street you might at least see coming, you *might* have an opportunity to do something to protect yourself.

A sniper was a wholly different menace, because by the time he decided you were going to be his next victim, you were already dead.

It made everyone feel like they were already in his crosshairs, and Margot couldn't blame them. Whenever she left her own house the hairs on the back of her neck stood on end. Everywhere she went it felt like there were eyes on her, and at any moment she might simply cease to be.

If there was any positive way to look at being a sniper victim, it was that at least you wouldn't see it coming. If you were the first one he took down, then you wouldn't even have a chance to be afraid.

In Margot's line of work, that counted as a small mercy.

They parked in front of the morgue, but Wes didn't immediately get out of the car. Margot realized she was foolish to expect that they'd be able to get through this day without some kind of discussion about what had happened the day before, both in the apartment and at the station.

Rather than dodge the uncomfortable confrontation, she leaned back in the passenger seat and just waited for him to say his piece. It had taken her some time to understand Wes and how he operated. He came across to most as blasé and sometimes a bit prickly—in a Tony Stark *I'm being mean but I'm being funny* kind of way—but she had come to see a more genuine side to him during their time together.

Sometimes he could drive her mental, but she also knew when he wanted to be earnest about something it was best to let him get it out of his system. He'd once locked her in the car to have his say without realizing it might send her into a panic attack, and she didn't feel like repeating that again.

"You know I'm on your side with this whole thing, right?"

Margot crossed her arms and let out a puff of air. "I was kind of hoping we just wouldn't talk about that."

"What, you figured you would just politely decline going out on any new calls and I wouldn't have any questions about it?"

"It would have been nice for him to at least give me a *chance* to tell you before he ratted me out."

"It's only temporary."

"Yeah, I just need a glowing report card from my shrink and then I get to play with the other kids again."

Wes ran his fingers through his dark blond hair and instead of looking at her he stared out onto the street. It didn't escape her notice that his gaze kept drifting upwards, keeping an eye out for their unseen enemy.

"I hate to be the one to say it, but maybe it's not such a bad thing that you're being forced to take a short breather."

Margot sucked in air through her teeth but resisted the urge to snarl out the response that was on the tip of her tongue. *Let him talk, just let him say it.*

"Oh?"

"Hey, look, don't misunderstand me, because I know that's what every instinct in your body wants to do right now. I'm not saying I *want* you behind a desk. You're the best partner I've ever had, and I want you next to me for the rest of my damn career, OK?"

She didn't *want* to love hearing him say that, but it touched on a base need for encouragement that had gone unsatisfied for a very long time.

"Yeah, I guess you're OK, too," she said quietly, but when she saw the corner of his lip tick up in a smile, she knew he understood her.

"I'm just saying that you've had quite possibly the single worst week one person could have, and I don't think you've given yourself enough time to process that. Hell, Tate wants *me* to talk to someone too based solely on having to shoot a guy before he shot you. And you know what, I'm glad because that was not a great fucking moment, y'know?"

Margot took a moment to really *look* at Wes, even though he was doing his damnedest to avoid eye contact with her. The fact he was willing to be so open with her about his feelings was something she couldn't just let go without acknowledgment, otherwise he might think his candor meant nothing to her, and it was quite the opposite.

She reached out and put her hand over his on the steering wheel, gently squeezing until he let go of the leather and let her hold him.

"Wes, I'm sorry. I was kind of up my own ass after what happened yesterday, it didn't even occur to me to ask how you were feeling. That can't have been easy for you."

He looked at her for the first time then, as if trying to decide if she was being sarcastic or making fun of him, but seeing only an open, patient smile he seemed to relax.

"Look, I'm sorry. I didn't want to make this all about myself, because that had to be fucking scary for you, especially after the whole thing with the shooter."

"I can't say it's an experience I'm eager to relive."

"But you can see, I think, why I can understand why the captain would want you to just take a step back. To make sure everything is OK."

She once again wanted to argue that she thought it was actually pretty damned unfair that *she* was being forced to step aside, while Wes—who had actually shot someone—was only being asked to *eventually* talk to someone. But she also understood that, no matter how long she worked in the department, no matter how good she was at her job, she was always going to have two things working against her. First, she was a woman in a man's world, and there was no escaping that put her at a disadvantage. And second, her boss knew her deepest, darkest secret, and she had a hard time believing that he didn't sometimes hold it against her.

The thing about Wes's little confessional was, Margot didn't *mind* hearing it from him. From the captain it had felt like punishment. From Wes, it helped her understand why maybe it *wasn't* a bad thing for her to take a moment to re-center herself.

This week had been hard, and with another Ed visit on the horizon, and still no sign of their sniper, there were plenty of reasons she might be feeling tense or volatile. Things that wouldn't make her much good to anyone as a detective.

"OK. I get it, I get it. I'll do my time like a good girl. I'll talk to Dr. Singh and be honest with him about how I'm feeling. But you have to *promise* you aren't going to let me get pushed out of the loop on our cases. And so help me God, if you team up with O'Halloran for something I'm going to slit every single one of your tires."

He smirked and shook his head. "See? How could anyone think you aren't a mentally stable person?"

Margot dropped his hand, having almost forgotten she was holding it, and socked him in the arm. "Just for that I'm going to tell Evelyn you had a sex dream about her."

"You wouldn't dare." He followed her out of the car and up the steps of the morgue. They traced a familiar route down to the basement—really just a hair below street level rather than a proper basement—and into the cool chamber of the morgue proper.

Evelyn Yao was awaiting their arrival with her usual bubbly enthusiasm. She had recently dyed over the purple streaks in her hair, giving her pixie cut a more subdued all-over black tone that surprised the hell out of Margot the first time that she saw it.

While they'd seen each other several times now since the dye job, Margot still missed Evelyn's former bright patches.

Still, even with hair that might be more age-appropriate, Evelyn herself was nothing of the sort.

"Morning, you two cutie pies. How are we doing this fine November day? Wes, you reconsider my offer to get married, or are you still secretly pining for this one?" She winked. From anyone else it might have felt bizarre to field pickup lines while standing beside a dead body, but it was just par for the course here, and Margot found it helped buoy the atmosphere.

Evelyn never made jokes about the bodies themselves; when it came to her job, she was dead serious and incredibly gifted. But she seemed to understand there was an inherent need to lighten the vibes in her workspace before they got into the nitty-gritty of it all. Margot wasn't sure how anyone else felt about it, but she for one was grateful. Their work was hard enough as it was. Little pockets of humor made it survivable.

"I've already told her I'm madly in love with her, Evelyn, but she won't have me. I need you to talk some sense into her." Wes dramatically wrapped his arm around Margot and pulled her against his side.

The contact made something inside her twang with desire, a hungry pull that *yearned* for more contact, and it made Margot wonder how long it had been since she'd let someone touch her. Months? More than a year, certainly. And in those situations, the connection might be sexual but it was never *intimate*.

Wes touching her, even as a joke, made her come alive in ways that she might need to add to her list of things to talk to her therapist about.

*Dear Dr. Singh, I would very much like to roll around naked under my partner, do you think that will ruin the only healthy adult relationship I have?*

Margot sighed and shoved Wes off her. "You show me that you can be more useful than my building handyman and my vibrator, and maybe we'll talk."

Evelyn snorted with obvious delight. "Smart woman."

With the opening ceremonies out of the way she ushered them over to the metal table waiting behind her.

While it had only been a few days since Margot had first seen the girl in the park, the state of her head still managed to be shocking. It took a lot to trigger a queasy stomach in a homicide detective, and Margot *had* seen worse, but it was still a grisly sight to behold.

Perhaps even more so now that the body had been cleaned up.

The corpse was fully nude on the table, her chest cavity sewn back up after having been assessed, and with her clothes off Margot was able to see plenty that hadn't originally been visible the first time around.

Genesis's body was covered in bruises of varying stages of healing. It was immediately apparent that not all of them had come from her recent violent beating. In fact, Margot was willing to bet good money that very *few* of them had come from the beating that led to her death, because bruising just didn't work the same once the heart stopped pumping blood.

Under the victim's left breast was a swirly tattoo with the name *Eugenio* distinctive in the cursive, surrounded by lurid red roses and pointed thorns that looked like they were piercing her skin. Margot wasn't sure she'd ever seen a more appropriate version of a name tattoo, if her deductive skills were right and those old healing bruises had been a gift from the woman's boyfriend.

She let out an unintentional sigh. She tried to keep herself distanced from who these women were as people, and only focus on how they had ended up in her path, but sometimes that was harder to do. And while the world at large might look at a dead sex worker as just an inevitability of the trade, Margot couldn't help but see a million tiny life mistakes and tragedies that had gotten this poor girl to where she was today.

Nothing, especially not a job, made what had happened to her justifiable.

"As you can see, we have plenty of antemortem bruising on our victim. Much of what you're seeing here is at least a few days, if not a few weeks old." Evelyn indicated a few older bruises that had faded out to a blotchy yellow. "I think, given the victim's known job, we can assume maybe *some* of this came from her work, and we all have one or two unaccountable bruises on us, but in my professional opinion I think what we're looking at here was probably domestic violence. Unless we uncover that she was also a semi-pro kickboxer." Evelyn offered a wan smile, but it didn't reach her eyes. "X-rays showed a fair number of broken bones that were healed up. Fingers, arms, and a fracture in her skull as well. I think if there was more of her face left, we likely would have seen even more."

"Son of a bitch," Wes grumbled.

"Cause of death?" Margot asked. "Blunt force trauma?"

Evelyn paused for a long moment, steeling herself. Not a good sign. "Asphyxia. She was still alive after the beating was done. She drowned in her own blood."

Margot heard the words and processed them, but still couldn't quite comprehend. The death had seemed bad enough when she'd thought it was a savage beating, but knowing that Genesis had continued to suffer, to experience her pain and likely know that help wasn't coming... it made Margot sick to her stomach in a way that the girl's appearance never could.

"Jesus," she whispered.

"I'm sorry to say it gets worse."

The detectives waited, neither sure how it could go downhill further, but knowing she wouldn't disappoint.

"Jennifer Covington was three or four months pregnant at the time of her death."

There it was.

Margot thought back to the previous day, to the way Eugenio had acted so shocked to hear about Genesis's death. The way he'd immediately started talking about her like the lost love of his life. While she hadn't bought into all his bullshit at the time, she *had* believed he was genuinely surprised to learn Genesis was dead.

Now she wasn't so sure.

Based on the bruises, the broken bones, the baby... the signs were starting to point away from a gangland homicide and right back to good old-fashioned domestic murder.

"I'm sorry, kids," Evelyn said softly. "Not all sunshine and rainbows, as much as I'd like to bear only good tidings, it's an unfortunate drawback of the job."

Margot tried her best to smile but found it exceedingly difficult to force her mouth to do what her brain was asking. After her efforts went unrewarded, she just gave up. "It's OK, Evelyn. We all knew what we were signing up for."

Except that was and wasn't true.

Margot knew, she *knew* the horrors that one human could enact on another, because that violence was her birthright. But when she decided to become a police officer, she thought what she was doing might help keep people *safe* from that kind of evil.

Instead, all she'd managed to do was learn that there was no rock bottom in terms of human cruelty. Whenever she thought she had seen the worst the world had to offer, she got a pregnant woman drowning to death in her own blood.

What Margot had learned was that there was no such thing as fairness.

There were no scales that she was helping to balance.

And yet she kept on trying, because the only other option was to give up, and that seemed worse.

But on days like today she struggled to see the benefit, and wondered why it was they kept fighting against evil, when it was an unrelenting tide that would just eat away at them like a river chews down a gorge.

She did it because she didn't know anything different.

And some days that had to be enough.

## TWENTY-FIVE

Neither Margot nor Wes had much to say on the drive back to the station.

The sun was high in the sky, and it would have normally been a day where the streets were packed, but once again it was a ghost town. Margot wondered how much pressure the department was getting from the mayor's office simply due to the lost income from tourists.

A bottom line tended to inspire men of power into action better than almost anything else.

They were finding parking near the precinct when Margot spotted a familiar figure. At first her wandering gaze skated right over the woman, eyes scouting for an open space rather than a person.

It was the coat that triggered her memory first. The shabby brown overcoat, pulled tight, like it was protecting her from some unseen force. The woman looked just as lost as she had the previous night, pacing about a block from the entrance, her face tight with obvious concern.

"Stop the car," Margot instructed.

"But I'm not—"

"Wes, just stop the car."

He did as he was asked, eliciting a sharp honk from the car behind him, which ceased abruptly when Margot flashed her badge at the car and gave the driver a stern look.

The man held his hands up in a brief gesture of surrender, and Margot closed the passenger door. Wes watched her go for a moment before he continued his search for a parking spot, not wanting to hold up traffic any longer.

If the hubbub had pierced the woman's bubble at all, it didn't show. She was still staring up at the precinct as if the building itself had her in a trance.

Margot waited until she was just about directly behind the woman to speak.

"Excuse me, ma'am?"

The woman jumped and spun around. Now, in the light of day, Margot could see her better. She was probably in her fifties, with deep-set crow's feet by her eyes. She'd looked younger before, it was almost as if she had aged a decade since the last time Margot had seen her. Her dark blond hair was flecked through with gray and tied at the base of her neck in a well-practiced bun.

After what Margot had just seen at the morgue, she felt like she was hyper-fixated on this woman, looking for physical signs of abuse, some logical reason for why she kept appearing outside their office.

"I saw you here last night," Margot reminded her.

The woman looked around her, expression etched with obvious worry. Margot got the idea that given the opportunity the woman was going to bolt again, except this time Margot was standing between her and her car.

"I... I just..." Again she looked around, seeing where she might be able to run to.

Margot thought about touching her arm, trying to give her some kind of comfort, but she worried that the woman might shatter like glass the moment anyone got close. Instead, Margot mimicked the driver she had just seen, raising her hands up so both palms faced the woman and taking a half-step back.

All she wanted to do was help, because it was evident this woman was in a great deal of distress, but one thing Margot had learned both in her life and in her career was that you couldn't help someone who didn't *want* to be helped. She assumed that some part of the woman did crave assistance, otherwise she wouldn't be here, but something was clearly frightening her and Margot didn't want to make that worse.

"I'm a detective. If you need help with something, I can help you."

"No," the woman said flatly. "No, I... I'm sorry, I shouldn't have come here."

She moved around Margot, head down, going in the direction of a familiar car. Margot memorized the plate, unsure if it would be useful, but wanting some way to be able to find this woman later.

"I can help you," Margot repeated. "You don't have to be afraid."

The woman stopped in her tracks at the side of her car and looked back. Her expression seared into Margot's memory it was so haunting.

"I'm sorry, Detective. No one can help me."

As she drove off, her eerie words trailing behind her, Wes came down the sidewalk and stood next to Margot.

"What the hell was that all about?" He watched the car leave, then looked at Margot, concern and confusion etching his features.

They headed back into the building, not wanting to stay out on the sidewalk, and Margot explained the encounter from the night before. "There's just something about her. She obviously *wants* help, but something has her so scared. I got her plate number; I'm going to see if I can find her. Maybe there's a history of domestic abuse there, something that could warrant a drive-by."

Wes's expression made it obvious he thought Margot was overstepping, but what else was she supposed to do? She was, for all intents and purposes, under house arrest.

When he said nothing, Margot was grateful. She needed something to occupy herself with, and while the Muir Woods case loomed large as her biggest outstanding case, she wanted something that might be a win, no matter how small.

"I'm going to talk to Eugenio," Wes announced. "You want to watch that before you go on your little crusade?"

Eugenio had been held overnight thanks to some outstanding warrants. He and Juan were in side-by-side holding cells, which they had been hoping might elicit some intel, but the pair had largely ignored each other all night.

Now, with this new wave of information about Eugenio, they certainly had some more to discuss with her boyfriend.

Margot would have liked to have been in the room with Wes, but obviously given her current predicament she couldn't. Going to see Evelyn had probably been pushing it, but thankfully the captain hadn't been standing at the entrance when they returned like an over-eager parent whose children were late for curfew. She had dodged one bullet but didn't feel like tempting fate further for one day, especially not when the captain could easily walk past an interrogation room and see her inside.

She knew he liked to sometimes step in on the observation side just to see how his detectives were handling themselves, so the last thing she needed was for him to see her so boldly disobeying his directions, no matter how much she disagreed with them.

Leaving their jackets in their office, Margot headed in the direction of the interrogation rooms while Wes went to collect Eugenio from holding, but she was stopped by Leon.

"Hey, kid." His hand went to her arm, giving it a brief squeeze, and the concerned look on his face told her that the police station gossip mill had been working overtime since the previous night.

"Don't give me that look," she said, feigning a teasing tone, pretending she didn't care. "I'll be back before you know it."

"Oh, I have no doubt. But are you doing OK? I mean really?" Though he dropped his hand, his concern still cloaked her like a blanket.

"I mean, are any of us OK, Leon?" She smiled. "I promise I'm good, all things considered."

"It's the *all things considered* that has me worried."

She nodded. "Yeah, well. If anyone can handle being knee-deep in the suck, it's yours truly."

"I suppose that's true, isn't it? You're a tough lady, Margot, but don't forget that it's OK not to be tough all the time?"

"Thanks, Leon."

"But that's not why I stopped you. I have an ulterior motive."

That made Margot laugh for real, a short chuckle right from the belly. "Of course you do, you sneaky old man. Playing the doting friend card just long enough to make me feel beholden to you. I see how it goes. All right, what do you need?"

"I got a call from Rebecca Watson's old housekeeper." Rebecca had been the first of their Muir Woods victims. "She said she might remember something that could help us out, but she was a little hesitant to share when I called her. I thought she might respond better speaking with you. You know, women supporting women sort of thing."

"I don't think you actually know what that means, but the intent is very sweet, Leon. Yeah, give me her number I'll call her once I'm done watching this interrogation. I'd like to call Wally Albright again, too, see if he's feeling up to another chat. But I figure he might not want to meet in person again, given what happened last time."

"You think there's something to that angle? That this guy has been at it longer than we thought?"

Margot shrugged. "I'm not sure. If we're going with the possibility that the two victims *are* connected, then his window is really confusing. They died less than a month apart, but that was four months ago. Violent offenders, especially serial killers, tend to start escalating their kills rather than extending their cooling-off period. I think I'd just like to see if there's anything that has a similar MO, with a series of frenzied kills close together then a long period of inactivity."

"There's a more obvious way to account for that," Leon said. "Prison."

Leon nodded. "Or something happened in his personal life that sharpened focus around him. A wedding. A baby." He gave her a meaningful look.

"Or it's not a serial killer at all," Margot offered. "Let me talk to the housekeeper and we'll see if that helps us in any way."

"All right, I'll leave her number on your desk."

Margot wanted to ask him how the sniper case was advancing, but she had wasted enough time talking to Leon, and needed to get to the interrogation room to see if Wes could crack their case open.

# TWENTY-SIX

The interrogation room seemed different from the opposite side of the mirror.

Margot generally enjoyed the act of interrogation. She liked trying to bend and manipulate a suspect into telling her something they might not have intended to say, and she liked to unlock the secrets of a case based solely on her ability to speak to someone with intention.

Being on the outside looking in, she felt like a voyeur, seeing something she wasn't meant to. Often, she forgot that people *could* sit in here and listen in as she questioned suspects. It never bothered her because she didn't think about it.

Sitting on an uncomfortable metal chair, watching Wes do his job, she had an uneasy feeling that she was doing something wrong, even though he knew she was here.

For some reason, she thought about Ed.

She thought of the way he would linger outside the apartment and house windows of his victims, the way part of the enjoyment for him was observing them in their natural setting without knowing he was there. A shark just outside the kiddie pool, waiting for his opportunity to strike.

Margot shook it off, burying thoughts of Ed deep in her subconscious where her therapist would argue they did more damage, but her day-to-day life disagreed.

On the table in front of her, her phone buzzed.

*David.*

Her brother was calling?

While instinct told her to pick it up in case it was an emergency, she was also in the middle of her workday. Things had been hard for Justin recently. His girlfriend had left him shortly after their baby was born, not wanting to deal with his constant mood swings and stumbles back into drinking. He was trying to get his life back together to rebuild his family, but lately that had just resulted in a lot of tearful phone calls and requests for money. If something had happened to the baby, Cruz, she would have heard about it from Justin's ex, Tamara.

She didn't have the patience for Justin right now, so she declined the call.

A few moments later a voicemail notification appeared. She waited to see if there might be a follow-up text, but none came.

It couldn't be that important, then.

She turned her focus back to Wes. Unlike Margot, who liked to sit on the same level as her suspects and look them in the eye when she spoke, Wes prowled the room like a caged animal, turning the entire space into a stage show. It was more theatrical than she would have preferred, but this time it was his room and not hers, he could do this how he wanted.

Eugenio looked casual and easy in his chair, even though Margot knew full well he was probably straining his core muscles trying to keep the chair from wobbling around; it couldn't have been comfortable. Still, he exuded an air of indifference that was in marked opposition to his heartbroken display from the previous day.

Margot couldn't help but wonder where this guy landed in

the DSM—the textbook that collected all known psychological conditions for diagnosis—because he was giving her shades of sociopathy and narcissism, but she was no expert.

Certainly, he was adept at projecting what people wanted to see.

"We went to the morgue to review the autopsy of Jennifer Covington this morning. I'm wondering if you might have some idea of what we saw when we were there?" Wes crossed the room and then back again, pausing only to fix Eugenio with an intense stare as he finished asking his question.

"How should I know, do I look like a morgue doctor to you?" Eugenio picked at a broken nail on his hand, and Margot wondered how it had gotten broken. Evelyn told them there had been multiple skin samples under Genesis's fingernails, but owing to her job and to her existing relationship with Eugenio, it was hard to know if those were from work, her personal life, or from her actual killer.

Evelyn had submitted the samples to test against known samples in CODIS, the national criminal DNA database, but Margot knew, even if they got a match, it wasn't a smoking gun to the prosecutors.

They needed a confession.

"How long had you and Genesis been together?" Wes asked.

"It was an on-and-off thing, you know how it is."

"I can't say that I *do* know how it is, since I wasn't dating you. So why don't you answer my question and tell me how it actually was?"

Eugenio, for the first time, seemed to realize that this wasn't just another easygoing conversation like the one he'd had in his apartment with Margot. This wasn't a simple questioning anymore, this was him being *grilled*. She watched the way his demeanor changed, his shoulders hunching up around his ears and his devil-may-care smirk fading into a tense grimace. He was suddenly a different person.

"We were together about a year. With breaks."

"Why did you break up?"

"I dunno, man. Stupid shit. I didn't like her job, but she couldn't just change what she did. It's not like you can take your résumé into Walmart and say *I've been a hooker for ten years, can I have a job*. It doesn't work like that in the real world, she was kinda fucked. And like, don't get me wrong, she didn't let it bum her out too much. She didn't like doing it, but she had some regular guys who were pretty nice to her, treated her good. And she had those other chicks she hung out with, her weird little street family, she called them. But we would fight about it sometimes. One time a john overstepped, I thought, and he gave her this purse. It wasn't like, Gucci or nothing, but it wasn't cheap, and I said she should just hawk it, get the money, but oh my *God* you'd think this fucker took her to Louis Vuitton and let her pick out whatever the fuck she wanted. She was so proud of that fucking purse." He pronounced Louis Vuitton as *Lewis Vitten*, and Margot wasn't sure if it was an intentional choice or if he really didn't know how the brand was pronounced.

She was sure they were on the right track with Eugenio, but all the same she made a note about the bag, wondering if Genesis might have mentioned to the other girls which john had bought it for her. If she'd been as proud of it as Eugenio was indicating, she certainly would have shown it to her friends.

"Why else did you break up?"

"Aw hell, I dunno. I cheated on her once and she was pissed, which is kind of rich when you consider she spent all day with someone else's dick in her mouth, y'know?" He shrugged. "She got over it, we got back together."

"Did you make a habit of hitting her when you weren't happy with her?"

Eugenio's brows shot up, and again, Margot was impressed

by his acting skills. She probably would have believed he was surprised in different circumstances. "Hey now, I don't hit women. That's not a thing I do. My momma raised me better than that."

Margot might have pointed out, "But your momma did raise you to sell drugs and join dangerous street gangs?" As if taking the words right from Margot's mind, Wes asked that very question.

She couldn't help but smile. Eugenio frowned. "Naw, man. She taught me that you do what it takes to take care of yourself and your family, and no one else matters beyond that."

"Did you consider Genesis family?" Wes asked.

"She was my girl."

"That's not quite the same thing, is it?" Wes braced his arms on the back of his own chair, leaning over to stare at Eugenio. "And what about the baby?"

The silence that filled the room was deafening. Margot waited, holding her own breath, to see if he would deny knowing about the pregnancy, or immediately jump to a new lie to cover his tracks, but instead Eugenio stared down at the scarred tabletop in front of him, his rigid posture sagging.

"Yeah, I knew about the baby."

"And you decided, what, you didn't feel like having a baby with a hooker? You didn't want to be tied to her forever, to make her and the kid a family you needed to look out for, so you killed her?"

"Holy shit, dude. No. I didn't kill Genesis, and I sure as fuck wouldn't kill my own damn baby."

Margot watched his face, focusing on his eyes, looking for anything that might suggest this was just one more act, one more bullshit front, but the truth was the rage in his eyes and the broken way he held his body, she just didn't *see* the lie. And while she already knew he was a particularly gifted actor, and a lot of what he'd said even the last few minutes was contradictory, she just didn't feel his guilt in her stomach the way she thought she would.

She'd left the morgue absolutely certain this was their guy, but now she had to wonder if she had just been looking for an easy solution. And when her gaze flicked from Eugenio to Wes, she could see his own uncertainty there. It was subtle, and if she didn't know him so well, she would have missed it entirely, but it was there, mirroring her own.

"We saw the bruises. She was covered in them."

"Well, no fucking shit, didn't you say she was beaten to death?"

Margot tried to recall if she *had* said that, but considering everything there was a good probability he could have heard it elsewhere, too, even from Juan overnight. It wasn't a confession and wouldn't hold water as one, unfortunately. They needed something a lot more concrete.

"I'm talking about the old bruises. You might not be a morgue doctor, but we have a pretty good one of those, and she can tell us how old bruises are. Jennifer had bruises that were days and weeks old. She had healed fractures. You want to tell us about those?"

Eugenio fell silent again, considering. The fact that he wasn't immediately denying his participation in those injuries was all Margot needed to hear to know he was responsible for them, but she was curious how he would try to defend himself.

"OK, look. Sometimes things got heated. I told you that we argued."

"You also told me your mom taught you better than to hurt women," Wes reminded him.

The deep red flush over Eugenio's cheeks spoke louder than any words. "I tried to be good to her. I did the best I could to be a good man, y'know. But sometimes I just got so fucking mad at her. And when I get mad, I can get mean, and I'm not saying that's OK, I'm not like, proud or nothing, but it is what it is."

"Were you mad and mean the night she died?"

Eugenio shook his head. "Look, I know you want to pin this on me. I get it. I'm the bad boyfriend. I'm the guy with the rap sheet. But I didn't kill Genesis. I wouldn't do that, and I have someone who can vouch for me. 'Cause I *was* a bad boyfriend, and the night she died I was fucking someone else."

# TWENTY-SEVEN

"Well, fuck. That wasn't how I saw that going." Wes flopped into his desk chair, his long legs stretched out in front of him.

Margot sat on the edge of her desk. "At least we have a couple new leads to chase. We can ask the girl he was with when he left. There's still a chance there's a window where he might have been able to kill Genesis."

"I guess, but I'm not sure it feels right. I was so positive he was going to be our guy, but now I'm not convinced anymore."

"Me either, but we're not taking his word for anything," Margot insisted. "He's too good at faking. Gives me the heebie-jeebies. I was *positive* when we talked to him yesterday that he was really torn up over her murder, and now we find out just how much he was keeping from us. I need independent corroboration before I believe a single thing that he says."

Wes nodded. "What else you got?"

"I think we... you... need to talk to the girls again. Eugenio mentioned something about a john giving Genesis a purse, and that stuck out to me. Shows that maybe someone was getting a little too attached to her, too personal? I think that's a lead worth following just to keep all our options open."

"OK. Gotta say I don't feel right going out and talking to these people without you."

"You need my warm and fuzzy personality to win over a group of sex workers?"

"Naw, I can do that just fine on my own. I'm *very* charming." He winked at her.

"And modest. Don't forget modest."

"Hey, I didn't lead with how handsome I am, so I think I'm doing pretty well."

"You're gross."

"You love me."

"You're lucky." Margot settled into her own desk chair and took the lid off a banker's box that was sitting in front of her, a sticky note from Leon on the top of the lid.

Until she was allowed to leave the office again, she'd need to bide her time with the Muir Woods case. It felt insane to her that any other case could exist or need attention when someone was taking civilians out one at a time, but murder didn't wait for a generous gap in her schedule.

An unfortunate truism of investigating homicides was how much time was of the essence, and how fickle memory could be. If she didn't follow up on these leads, stories and details could change or be lost.

And the Muir Woods case was just one more excuse in a long list that gave her permission not to think about going back to see Ed again in a couple of days. She wanted to call Andrew and ask if they'd had any luck getting something useful from the ballistics on the sniper's bullets, but she was also avoiding Andrew because she didn't want to be reminded about Ed.

She was also avoiding calling Dr. Singh. She knew she needed his approval to get back to work, but something stopped her from picking up the phone. Hell, he took bookings by text and email, she didn't even need to talk to him. Still, her stomach lurched with waves of anxious nausea when she thought about picking a date. Their discussion was going to be an intense one. Whether she wanted to admit it or not she'd been through a lot of emotional and mental turmoil all packed into one very bad week. She was worried Dr. Singh might be on the captain's side about being on desk duty.

Worse still, she was starting to wonder herself if the captain had made the right call.

"You go, I've got plenty to keep me busy here." She waved a folder at him.

It had been months since she'd done a real deep dive into the Muir Woods case files, and it was a much-needed reintroduction to the case to pore over the old photos and files.

Two women, found within days of each other, both brutally stabbed and left to the elements of the protected redwood forests. One had been well hidden, her body decomposed and feasted on by wildlife; the other left within plain sight of a hiking trail and discovered within hours.

At first glance the women had little in common beyond their gender and their horrific murders. But with the gift of hindsight on her side, and the graphic crime scene photos at her fingertips, it became more clear to her than ever that the two deaths *must* be connected. There were just too many similarities in the scenes and in the way the women had been killed.

Every bone in Margot's body told her this was a serial killer case and not just two disconnected women whose bodies had been found in the same park.

She suspected that Leon felt the same, he was just trying not to let an assumption color his perspective. Margot was all for being open-minded, but she worried if they *didn't* treat this like a serial killer, they were more likely to miss connections elsewhere.

Making some notes about the victim profile, she thought it might be worth a casual mention to Andrew next time they were together. The last thing she wanted was to start using the

FBI as a crutch in her own investigations, but the sad truth was that police departments—no matter how good the detectives were—were woefully unprepared to deal with serial killers.

The FBI were the pros, there, and they had the ability to help craft a potential profile for their killer, not to mention deep reserves of information on other cases out of the state that could potentially be connected.

Margot knew those same FBI resources were how Ed got tied to six murders in New York state, committed during family vacations to visit her grandparents. Those killings—at the time—had been a godsend for Ed's lawyers because the cases were discovered and tried later than the California cases and gave them a reason to move Ed to New York, where there was no death penalty.

He had *chosen* to come back to a death penalty state to be closer to her.

Margot's grip tightened on the file in her hands, wrinkling the stiff cardboard folder. She didn't *want* to think about Ed right now, but it seemed like everything was bringing him to mind. She tossed the file down on the desktop and ran her hands through her hair, releasing a sigh that would have felt better as a scream. This was why she liked the distraction of being out in the field, it kept her busy, let her thoughts focus on the job in hand.

Here she had too much time to be in her own head and that was no good for anyone, especially not her.

She picked up her phone and placed a quick call to Dr. Singh's office, leaving a voicemail with his message service that she would like to book an appointment for something police-related, knowing that this might get her seen sooner rather than later.

Margot was then reminded of the phone call she had received from her brother earlier and tapped on the voicemail icon awaiting her attention.

"Hey Margot." From the hesitation in his voice, she could tell that, twenty years on, he still struggled not to use her original name. Considering she still *thought* of him as Justin, she imagined he likely did the same for her. She wondered—though she had never asked him—if he was more comfortable thinking of himself as David.

It was odd, she thought, that she clung to his old name, but embraced her new one so easily for herself.

"Sorry, I know you're probably working, this isn't a big thing, but..." He drifted off thoughtfully. She listened for any slurring in his words that would be a dead giveaway that he was calling her while drunk—it was often the only time he called her —but his voice was steady, and he sounded sober. Her next thought was whether or not he was calling her for money, which seemed likely.

And she'd give in, too. She told herself time and time again that she shouldn't coddle him, shouldn't let him take advantage of her, but the truth was he was the only family she had left in the world, and if he needed her help, she would give it to him. She just had to hope that one day he'd wake up and realize he needed to help himself.

"... I know this might sound out of left field, but Christmas is around the corner, and I was thinking it might be nice to come see you. Do a little family Christmas thing? I wouldn't even make you put me up, I know how much you hate having people in your space."

Margot sagged. She'd hosted Justin a few times since moving back to San Francisco and hadn't realized how obvious she'd been about disliking his presence. It wasn't that she didn't want to see him, but he was a slob, and Margot's whole life existed with strict routine at its base. Justin upset her routines.

She tried to be nice and welcoming whenever he visited, but she found it exhausting, and apparently he had noticed.

"Anyway, give me a call back and I'll book a ticket. My own

money. I got a job and everything. I'll tell you about it later. Love you."

Margot saved the message, in case she ever needed a reminder later that he *could* sound like he had his life together. She wasn't crazy about the idea of him visiting for Christmas—she liked to ignore the holiday completely—but maybe it was time to start building some new family traditions.

Maybe they *could* have something that resembled a nice, normal holiday.

Now wasn't the right time to call him back and sort out plans. She'd need to think this through and have a conversation with him about the logistics, but she also didn't want to be Sister Scrooge, turning him away when he finally wanted to act like her brother and not her dependent.

Setting her phone aside she dug further into the Muir Woods files, pulling out the one specific to Rebecca Watson. Rebecca had two personal photos in her file, one before she'd become acquainted with her Los Angeles plastic surgeon, and the second was the way she had looked in a social media post just before her death. The two women looked so dissimilar Margot wouldn't have even taken them for sisters, let alone the same woman.

The old Rebecca had a somewhat forgettable face, the type you might pass over while scanning a crowd and never come back to. She hadn't been ugly by any means, there was just nothing arresting about her that commanded attention.

She'd had a weak chin, her nose had been slightly too wide, and her smile showed uneven, slightly yellow teeth. In other words, she'd been human, totally unique even if she wasn't a stunner.

What Rebecca had become after her surgeries and dental work was almost as bad. She looked like every other reality show star, with a fake tan, perfect veneers, a pert nose and hollowed out cheeks. Her eyelashes were extensions, and so was her bleached blond hair. Her boobs were fake. So much of the original woman had been removed that in order to identify her body they had needed to trace the serial number on her implants.

Typing the woman's address into Google Maps, Margot pulled up a street view of her house. Rebecca hadn't lived in San Francisco, she had been from Sausalito, across the Golden Gate Bridge. The area Rebecca had lived in was stunning, with the kind of homes people dreamed of.

Sausalito was most famous for its floating homes, permanently settled houseboats that people spent hundreds of thousands of dollars customizing. Margot had long yearned for one of the houseboats, even if it meant abandoning much of the security that she had in the apartment. She loved the anonymity of the water mooring and knew many of the floating neighborhoods were better protected than her apartment. Sadly, even the ones that required a massive amount of work were well outside her budget.

But Sausalito also extended up the side of the hills around the Bay, its beautifully situated properties looking like bejeweled Italian coastal villages rather than something bordering a large California city.

One of these cliffside homes had been where Rebecca lived. The ownership paperwork indicated it belonged to a wealthy investment banker named Richard Downey, but Richard was evidently rarely around—spending most of his time working in Europe—and leased the property to Rebecca for a song.

It allowed Rebecca to live her Beverly Hills dreams on a smaller scale and portray herself as living in the lap of luxury, even if the luxury wasn't all hers. They had grilled Richard during the initial investigation, but his alibi was airtight, he'd been in London for a full month before Rebecca died, and activity on his passport indicated he hadn't been in the US for at least three months surrounding the time of her murder.

They had taken an angle wondering if he had hired someone to have her killed—he was wealthy enough—but a forensic accountant had scoured his records, and they were squeaky clean.

It hadn't taken long for Richard to fall off their list entirely.

The housekeeper whose number Leon had left for Margot must have been one that Richard employed, because, based on Rebecca's finances, she wasn't covering anyone's salary.

Margot dialed the number from her desk phone, and it rang three times before a cautious voice answered with a, "Hello?"

"Hi there, I'm hoping to speak with Constance Esparza."

"Yes, that's me."

"My name is Margot Phalen. I'm a detective with the San Francisco Police Department."

"Oh. Oh, yes, hello. I was expecting a call."

"I appreciate you taking the time, I'm not interrupting your work, am I?"

At this Constance chuckled softly. "I'm taking care of an empty house, I can talk."

"Are you still working for Richard Downey?"

"Yes, ma'am."

"And that's at the same residence where Rebecca Watson was living?"

"Yes."

"OK, wonderful, thank you. My colleague said that in your message you mentioned something you thought might be useful to us in the investigation?"

"Well, I'm not sure if it'll be helpful or not, but I remembered something and thought it would be best to tell you about it either way."

"Sure." Margot had heard that same spiel a thousand times from a thousand different people. Ninety-nine percent of the time it turned out that their information was useless, but she always listened in case it was the one percent chance that it might actually help them solve a case.

Those rare instances made it worthwhile to follow every lead, no matter how tenuous it seemed. She liked to remind new detectives who didn't feel like doing the boring legwork that not one but *two* people called in to report thinking that Ted Bundy might be a match for a person of interest sketch, and unfollowed leads were the reason that he hadn't been immediately arrested.

That was generally a more sobering reminder than offering up concrete examples from their own office—of which there were plenty. That was the trouble with homicide, you never ran out of cases, and never stopped being bombarded by leads from those cases. Things fell by the wayside.

Constance's call probably would have been one of those things, thanks to Leon being focused on the sniper case, so perhaps it was almost a hidden blessing that Margot had been shackled to her desk and unable to go and interview witnesses with Wes.

Still, she was miserable knowing he was out there without her.

"So, I'm not sure if this got mentioned in your original investigation, but Rebecca liked to host parties at the house a lot. Richard didn't *love* that, the house is filled with expensive things, not to mention the wine cellars that he has spent a ton of money stocking with old vintage wines." It did not escape Margot's attention that she had said *cellars*, plural.

Richard had declined allowing the police to search the house following Rebecca's death, one of the reasons he had initially seemed so suspicious. Because of his alibi—and likely some connections higher up the chain politically—they hadn't been able to secure a warrant, and so the house had remained something of a mystery.

Before Margot finished the call, she'd have to ask Constance if anything seemed amiss at the residence after

Rebecca disappeared, but Margot didn't think the mansion was their crime scene, despite Richard's attempts to keep it hidden.

Still, she was sorry not to see the multiple wine cellars in person.

Rich people were wild.

"She continued to host parties after being asked not to?" Margot asked.

"Yes, but she would always pretend they weren't house parties. I'd come in the morning to clean and she would be very friendly and tell me that she just had *a few guests* over. But the thing is, no one took anything, no one broke anything. I think she was just afraid Richard wouldn't like it."

Margot wasn't sure what the parties had to do with Rebecca's death. They'd already cleared Richard of suspicion, so it wasn't a motive for him.

"Do you know if she was doing anything illicit at these parties?" Margot prodded, hoping to help Constance get to the point.

"Illicit?"

"Illegal. Drugs? Maybe Rebecca was involved in sex trafficking?" This wasn't out of the question. High-end parties were often a place where surprisingly well-to-do folks would trap young women into being trafficked. Everyone saw one or two movies and assumed that a trafficked woman was thrown into the back of a truck and taken to another country, but the truth was often much more insidious.

"No, I don't think so. I didn't see anything like that."

Margot was starting to wonder if Constance had seen *anything* or if it was just the presence of the parties she felt like reporting on, which felt like the most useless potential lead they had received yet.

Before Margot could push to see if there was any reason to stay on the call, Constance spoke again, this time her voice lowered despite the fact that she'd already told Margot she was alone in Richard's house.

"About a month before she died, Rebecca had one of her parties. When I came the next day, she wasn't acting like herself. Rebecca was a very fancy woman, she liked to have her hair and makeup done early so that by the time I came in the morning she was already done up. She told me once that she would get up most mornings around four so she could get in a workout—the house has a very nice gym—and get her 'face on' as she liked to say. Even on mornings after parties I never saw her hungover or not put together. So that morning I got there, and she was on the couch, still in her pajamas. It was the first time I think I'd ever seen her without her hair done, it was just in a messy bun. I was shocked. She was a beautiful woman, you know, I'm sure you've seen photos, but she was so particular about how people saw her. And she had this big bruise on her neck."

"On her neck?"

"Yes. I remember it because I was a bit scandalized at the time. I don't mind telling you I thought she was a little too old to be going around with a hickey. But now that I think about it, and about what happened to her, I wonder if it wasn't a hickey at all."

Margot mulled this over. It wasn't necessarily anything, but it wasn't *nothing*. If someone had been violent with Rebecca that close to her death, it was certainly worth digging into.

"Constance, Mr. Downey lives in a gated community, right?"

"Yes, ma'am."

"People need to check in with a security guard?"

"Yes."

"OK, thank you very much." She was about to hang up when she recalled one more thing she had wanted to ask the housekeeper. "Before I let you go, do you go to the house every day?"

"Yes. Except holidays. Mr. Downey is very generous with vacation time."

Margot thought it was pretty generous to pay the woman to clean a house no one was using, but she didn't dare question Constance's opinion of her boss. "You were there after Rebecca went missing, then?"

"Of course."

"And you didn't think it was unusual that she hadn't been home for several days?"

"No. She would go on last-minute trips all the time. And since my schedule was so regular, it wouldn't change whether she was there or not. She was an adult; she didn't feel the need to tell me her plans."

There was something in the housekeeper's tone that told Margot she would *prefer* if her charges did keep her in the loop with their plans, but she was too well-trained to say anything about it.

"Nothing in the house looked out of the ordinary? Nothing was missing, or out of place? No signs of a struggle?"

Constance thought about it for a minute. "There were a few dishes left in the sink, which was strange only because Miss Rebecca was very good about loading the dishwasher. She didn't like to see clutter in the sink, she told me. And she hadn't taken anything with her. No suitcase, no toothbrush. By the time it occurred to me to start wondering where she had gone, I heard from Mr. Downey about the murder."

"OK. Thank you very much, Constance. This is my direct line at the precinct, so if you think of anything else, please don't hesitate to call."

"I will."

As Margot hung up, she stared at the picture of Rebecca Watson on her desk.

"What happened to you?"

# TWENTY-EIGHT

## 1988

Petaluma, California

Ed considered himself a smart man. He was a careful man.

But he was also a married man.

It was after midnight when he stepped through the side door of his house. Cleaning the interior of the car had taken him over an hour, first parked down a dark side street where no one would see, and then at two different car washes so he could be thorough without drawing attention to himself. He was exhausted, but grateful to see the lights were all off.

Kim and the kids must have gone to bed hours earlier.

Only when he passed through the living room and a lamp snapped on with an accusatory *click*, did he realize his mistake.

Kim sat on the couch in her nightgown and robe, wearing an expression he'd never seen on her face before. She was furious, that much was obvious, but there was also something *sad* in the way her mouth sagged and her eyes glistened.

When she spoke, though, it was only the anger he could hear.

"Where were you?" Her tone was hushed but it still cut him.

"I told you I'd be working late. There were some last-minute print changes, it was all hands on deck." Ed was grateful he'd had the foresight to take his clothes off before dragging Marissa's body out into the lake. His lie would have been much harder to sell if he'd been sopping wet.

Kim's lips formed a thin line and Ed's mind was racing. This lie had been solid, he'd used it a number of times and it worked because it was something that often *did* happen. While Ed worked in classifieds, there was sometimes a need for all able-bodied employees to rally in order to shuffle things around and get a fresh edition ready to print.

"Don't lie to me," Kim said.

"Kim, don't be like that. I had to work, I'm tired. Whatever this is it can wait until morning."

"I called the paper."

Ed, who had been about to bypass her and head for the bedroom, ending the argument by ignoring it, froze in place, trying to decide how he would make his next move. Did he cling to the same lie or pivot?

"Megan left her homework in the back of the car. She had a project she needed to work on. I was going to see if you had time to just bring it home. But the funny thing is, when I called, they said everyone had gone home for the day. It was just the printers left."

Silence hung in the air between them, so thick he thought it might suffocate him.

"So, I'll ask you again, where were you?"

He considered, just for a moment, how easy it would be to kill her.

The thought had crossed his mind before: whenever she was being uptight, or in an especially shrewish mood, he thought about how much easier his life would be if he could just slide a knife between her ribs and end that ceaseless whining once and for all.

But it wouldn't make life easier.

It would mean he'd be the only one to look after the kids. It would mean scrutiny and too much attention, police, and a link between her death and dozens of others.

Killing Kim might end some of Ed's miseries, but it would just be the start of brand-new ones.

He couldn't divorce her either, because he was certain that the minute they were no longer married her attention on all of his activities would become an obsession even more than it was now. She'd look for anything she could find to bury him in court, and it would be just one more nightmare ordeal.

No, the only thing to do was to coax, to coddle, to calm.

He needed to bring her back to a point of suburban bliss. In the past, she was at her most calm when pregnant, but that ship had sailed after Justin's difficult birth. She didn't want more kids.

He thought about perhaps getting her pregnant again by *accident* but that was unlikely to serve as the balm it had before.

"I don't know what you want me to say, Kim," Ed said, his tone calm and even as he tried to soothe her, to iron down her frayed edges. She had caught him, and now he just needed to give her a lesser evil to find him guilty of.

"I want you to stop *lying* to me for starters, Ed," she spat back. She was keeping her voice low so she wouldn't wake the kids, but he could tell she wasn't ready to give up her anger just yet.

"I went out for a few drinks, OK?"

"Alone?"

"If you thought I was alone you wouldn't be sitting up right now, would you?"

"I want to hear you say it."

"No. I was with someone else."

A small sob bubbled out of her throat, and it was a relief to him. He hadn't been sure, up to that point, what Kim actually knew and didn't know. There had been a chance that her suspicions had run deeper than just cheating, and that would have made it a lot harder for him to let her live.

If she only believed he was guilty of infidelity, that was something he could handle. It would mean no more late nights, and he'd have to be a lot more careful about how he hunted and when he killed, but it was a problem he could solve.

"Ed how could you?"

And now he would placate. He would beg. He dropped to his knees in front of her and let her pepper his arms with slaps. She didn't *want* to hurt him, he could tell from the softness of the blows, she just needed to get out the anger inside her and with him right in front of her she was able to do that.

He wrapped his arms around her legs and buried his face in her lap, letting his shoulders shake and tremble as if he were crying.

"Baby, I'm sorry. I'm sorry. It was only once, and it didn't mean anything. And as soon as it was over, I knew how wrong it was. I only want you, you're the only woman for me, and I don't want to lose you. I'm so sorry."

Kim was rigid at first, her own body racked with sobs, but soon she seemed to sag, bending over him and running her fingers through his hair.

"I hate you," she whispered, but the rage and passion were gone and it was just words with no fight in them.

"I know. I know. I deserve that and I'm sorry."

Her hand tightened in his hair before she yanked, pulling his head up to look at her. Ed was surprised by the violence of the gesture, and in no small part aroused by it, though it wouldn't be right to show her that response.

Kim stared at him, her gaze boring into his.

"If you *ever* hurt me like this again, I will take the kids and you will never see us again, do you understand?"

Ed nodded solemnly.

"Never again."

# TWENTY-NINE

Margot had just gotten off the phone with the security station that monitored the gate of Rebecca's neighborhood when Leon came tapping at her office door.

"Hey Margot, you busy?"

"Just following up on that lead you sent me. The housekeeper."

"Anything there?"

Margot shrugged. "Hard to say, might be some kind of a pre-existing exposure to violence, but I'm just checking in with the gate to see if I can narrow down anyone who regularly visited Rebecca's house in the month before her death."

"You want to take a break? We're just going to have a sit-down with the task force, I thought you might want to join since you missed the first meeting yesterday."

Margot stood up and grabbed her bag. She didn't need to be asked twice. The security team had said it would be hours before they could get back to her, and while she had other work on her desk, none of it felt as immediately important as the sniper case, and focusing on an active investigation would be a great distraction from the looming figure of Ed that always seemed to sneak into her thoughts whenever she stopped working.

She just wanted to feel useful, and it would be good to have a break from sitting at her desk, even if the alternative was sitting in the huddle room.

There were already a dozen cops in the room when she arrived, and she headed toward a seat next to Detective O'Halloran, an older homicide detective who usually worked opposite hours to her and Wes. He was gray. That was really the best way to describe O'Halloran; shades of gray. His hair was almost white—even though he was younger than Leon—and his skin had an overall pallor that might best be labeled *fresh corpse* if it was a makeup foundation. Even his eyes were steely gray.

His clothing was the only difference. There, he favored brown for reasons that were beyond Margot's comprehension. Brown loafers, brown corduroy trousers, and a faintly yellowing short-sleeved dress shirt with a brown striped tie.

O'Halloran looked as if someone had found a cop who had died in 1976 and brought him back to life, then forced him to return to work.

He was nice enough, though, Margot didn't mind being around him.

He gave her a nod as she took her seat.

Leon was joined by a detective Margot didn't recognize, but she knew the task force was a combined effort between three different precincts, so there were several faces in the room she wasn't familiar with.

"Good afternoon, everyone," Leon began, causing the low murmur in the room to die out completely. "We're just going to jump right into it. The hotline we opened Tuesday has received over twelve hundred tips in the first twenty-four hours. While we have managed to pare that down considerably by eliminating some obvious *my dog is the killer* nonsense, we do have over four hundred viable tips that we have tried to categorize in terms of potential. We're going to be divvying that up between all three precincts, plus calling in some extra help since the tip line is still active today. You'll each be getting a folder with transcripts of the messages we need you to follow up on. If you think any of these warrant an in-person follow-up, please let myself or Detective Romanski know, and we'll make sure those are prioritized. We know this has been a rough week for everyone, and I don't think we need to remind you that the pressure is really on from the top brass, so let's buckle down and find this fucker, got it?"

A chorus of noncommittal agreements went through the room and Leon handed each of the detectives a thick folder. Margot took hers and gave Leon a quick look. "So glad you took me off doing grunt work to do more grunt work," she teased.

He smiled softly. "But this is top-tier grunt work, Phalen. You'll have a great time. Now get to it." He patted her shoulder, and she was thusly dismissed.

Back at her desk she set aside the banker's box with the Muir Woods files and tidied her space enough that she wouldn't get her multiple ongoing cases muddled together. She checked her phone to see if there was anything from Wes, but instead there was a text from Dr. Singh's office saying that he could get her in the following week on Wednesday. While it wasn't as soon as she would have liked, it was better than waiting several weeks, so she tapped out a reply agreeing to the date.

Margot opened the folder Leon had given her and started to read through the call transcripts. A lot of them were doubtful—people who believed the shooter could be a neighbor or an ex-boyfriend—but they were coherent enough to be possibilities. She'd give each of them a call.

There was a message in the middle of the pile that caught her attention, tugging at her.

Caller, female, does not identify name.

Time: 11:54 p.m.

Transcript of message:

Hello? Oh. Yes, I, um… [indistinct noises] I guess I'm calling about that shooter? [pause] I shouldn't be doing this. I don't know why I'm doing this. But I think my husband John—[call disconnects]

It wasn't a lot, and the people reviewing the calls would have thrown out others with less reason. In fact it was likely only the inclusion of a first name that made them move the transcript into a *keep* pile.

Margot read the entry again, something about it nagging at her. Since the call wasn't any more specific than the others on her list she started from the top, committed to getting through her pile of thirty calls before she left for the day.

By her fourth call, Margot was regretting her decision to become a police officer.

"Hello, is this Frank Marzano?" she asked, trying to keep her tone light and friendly—not overly bubbly—but enough that people wouldn't hang up out of fear.

"I don't want any," an old man grumbled.

"Sir, I'm calling to follow up on a tip you left on the sniper hotline yesterday."

"Whosis?"

"I'm calling from the San Francisco Police Department." Margot was already ready to write this guy's tip-off as plain useless, but he seemed to perk up slightly.

"Oh yeah, yeah. I called you yesterday."

"Yes, sir, you indicated that your next-door neighbor might somehow be involved in these shootings and I was just wondering what made you think that? Your call wasn't clear about the specifics."

"My neighbor, name's Joe, anyway he's a bit of a gun guy, if y'know what I mean?"

"I think so, yes."

"Well, anyway, you listen to Joe talk, and Joe *loves* to talk, and eventually it always ends up the same. He goes on about how the government doesn't care about us—and mind, he don't care what government. Liberals, conservatives. I think a monkey could be president and old Joe still wouldn't trust the government."

Margot resisted the urge to agree that a monkey president might not be their best option, but she let Frank continue.

"After he finishes complaining he always says, 'Just between us, Frank, I think one day I'm gonna find myself a tower and start shooting people until someone listens to me.' So when I saw the news about those shootings I thought to myself, *Damn, Joe, did you really do it?*"

"Have you seen him since the two shootings?"

"Oh, yeah sure, he's outside in his yard right now, staining his fence."

"So his general demeanor hasn't changed?"

"Same old Joe."

"And has he said anything to you to indicate that he might have been the one to do it?"

"He waved the paper at me the other day. Said, 'Someone's got the right idea.' That seemed a little suspect, y'ask me."

Margot was inclined to agree. She got Frank's address, as well as Joe's next door. Frank wasn't clear on Joe's last name, but he thought it might be Dobson or something similar, which—along with the address—should be enough for Margot to get a name.

She set aside the stack of transcripts and did a title search on the address Frank had listed for Joe. The address had been registered to one Joseph Robinson for over thirty years. Margot next checked Robinson's name for any criminal history and was unsurprised to find he had one.

There were a handful of calls from other neighbors complaining about Joe's activities and tirades. Apparently in addition to being staunchly anti-government he was also racist and homophobic and made no secret of it. One neighbor had filed a complaint against him for continuing to tear down her pride flag and leaving behind hateful pamphlets when he took it. Another had called in several times saying that Joe had used verbal threats against her young son for being black.

He had a string of DUIs, a suspended license, and it looked like the police were at his house almost once a month to talk to him about something. It was evident that Joe wasn't a well man, but what interested Margot was that he was former military. He'd served in Afghanistan with the army. There was no indication of whether he'd been a sniper—she'd need to contact the military to learn the specifics—but his current behavior made more sense to her. PTSD could exacerbate existing mental health conditions. If Joe had already had an underlying issue that the military screening had missed, then the stress of being in a war zone could have easily made that a lot worse.

She printed off his file and attached it to the call transcript from Frank before heading off to find Leon.

The other calls in her folder would have to wait.

# THIRTY

Wes was in their office when Margot returned, and there was a steaming cup of Philz coffee on her desk, its enchanting deep-roast aroma wafting into the space.

"Did you ever know that you're my hero," she sang softly to him.

"Yeah, yeah, wind beneath your wings, I get it." He waved dismissively at her, not looking up from his computer. Wes at a desk—like, actually working at a desk—was always a comical sight to her. He was simply too tall to fit the standard desks in the office, so he had to hunch over, his knees crooked up to his elbows like he had been seated at the kids' table for dinner. He tended to put off doing paperwork until it all had to be done in one crunch just because he hated sitting at his desk to do it.

Margot flopped onto the musty couch, taking her coffee with her. Wes finished what he was working on, then rolled his chair away from the desk and propped his feet up on the couch beside her.

"What did you keep busy with while I was gone?" he prodded.

She took a sip of her coffee and shook her head. "Nope,

we're not going to play the *how was desk duty* game, I want to know what you found."

"It wasn't easy to track the girls down before nightfall, but I found one of them who was willing to talk to me. She said she remembered Genesis getting the purse and everyone was a bit jealous. Apparently, it was Coach, she was able to specify for me."

"Coach isn't exactly cheap. It's kind of baby designer. Achievable, but out of a sex worker's price range," Margot clarified.

"Well, Genesis loved it, took it everywhere with her. I asked if they could remember who gave it to her and she said that Genesis only knew his first name—Owen—and that he was something of a regular for her, came around once a week or so."

"Have they seen him since Genesis died?"

"They have *not*."

It hadn't quite been a week since Genesis died, but it was interesting that the guy hadn't shown up at all.

"Any chance the girl remembered what he drove?"

"Would you believe our luck if I told you she did?"

Margot raised a brow at him. She wasn't in a mood to play games.

"A maroon Dodge Caravan."

"You have got to be shitting me," Margot replied. "The ultimate dad van? How is someone driving a *Caravan* affording Coach bags for sex workers?"

"I don't know, but I *do* wonder how many people are still driving the lamest car of the nineties in the year of our lord 2017?"

"They still make Caravans, you know."

"I choose *not* to know that. Besides, she seemed to know her cars—I guess maybe you need to in her line of work—and she was insistent it was a late nineties or early two thousands version. She said it was old and looked *rusty a-f* to quote her exactly."

"Interesting." Margot sipped her coffee, eternally grateful to not be chewing on old grounds as she did, and stared thoughtfully at the ceiling. "Owen might not be his real name, but it would be worth looking into DMV records to see if maybe it *is* real, or possibly his last name. There can't be more than a couple hundred late model Caravans still kicking around. We might need to touch base with surrounding communities in case he's driving in from Oakland or Berkley, but it gives us something to look at anyway."

Wes was quiet. "I still have feelings about her boyfriend."

"Are the feelings that he's a piece of shit, because if so, then same."

Eugenio was still in holding, and thanks to his existing criminal record he wouldn't be out any time soon, giving them plenty of opportunity to corner him for another chat if need be.

"It would be so convenient if he was the one. The existing abuse. The baby. It all points to him being the killer."

"I know. And nine out of ten times I'd agree this was open-and-shut, except the problem is his alibi checks out. A girl named Desirae confirmed he was with her that night, and her roommate verified it. Guess they were pretty loud. I think we need to find and question this Owen guy. If it's not him, we go back to Eugenio and press him harder, see if he folds. There's always a chance the alibi falls apart under pressure." She patted Wes's leg before getting up and returning to her desk. The folder of calls still waiting to be returned stared up at her, and she let out a sigh. "Meanwhile I'll be here, glued to my desk for at least four more days, forgetting what sunshine looks like."

"You're not a serf, Margot, you can go outside."

"I don't want to push my luck with the captain, I feel like if I leave my desk for longer than fifteen minutes he's going to come around and find me missing. Visiting Evelyn this morning is about as risky as I feel like getting."

Wes picked up the folder on her desk. "Hotline leads?" he asked.

"I think calling them leads is a bit generous, but I've had one worthy of a follow-up at least. Better than nothing."

"We need to figure out who this guy is. It's eerie out there. I normally like to bitch about tourists as much as the next guy, but I've never seen it look so barren outside. It's depressing."

Margot took the folder back. "Well, maybe what we need is in here."

"You get anything back from your FBI buddy?" Wes asked.

"Funny you should ask, I was thinking about calling him to see if he might have some insight on Muir Woods when I was going through those folders, so I might be able to kill two birds with one stone. At least I'll look less naggy if I call about something else and just *happen* to ask if the ballistics are back."

"Yes, subtlety is one of your strongest assets." His eyes twinkled.

She smacked him in the chest. "I thought I missed you while you were gone but now I'm seeing that I was wrong, and you are terrible."

He took her place on the couch, flipping through his notebook to review what he'd written during his interview with Genesis's friend, JJ. He closed it with a snap. "You want to look at those DMV records, or are you busy with the hotline calls?"

"Why, you have somewhere better to be?"

"At the moment, no, actually. How about I pull the DMV records and get started there, you finish what you're working on, and then we regroup. I'd like to see if we can get you a stay of execution to go speak to this Owen guy if we can find him."

"Good luck with that. I know the captain likes you, but I don't think twenty-four hours is enough to change his tune."

"Well, I can always bring the guy to you, then."

"Let's find him first before we start planning out the best ways to question him, shall we?"

"Too pragmatic. That's boring. I'm already thinking ahead to the arrest. It's called manifestation, you should try it."

"Why don't you manifest us lunch while you're at it?"

"Dino's?"

"Yeah, that would be great."

Wes disappeared, leaving Margot to her pile of calls, and the one waiting on the top was the one she had pulled earlier. A creeping sensation crawled up her spine. *Someone just walked over your grave*, her Grandma Pat has always said.

It wasn't Margot's grave she was worried about.

*My husband John.*

It wasn't as obvious a lead as her call with Frank, but it was enough to pique her interest. She sat down and dialed.

# THIRTY-ONE

When the mystery wife didn't answer, Margot decided against leaving a message. If the number she'd called from was a home line, and the husband was a suspect, she didn't want to put the witness in danger with a voicemail from the police.

Margot couldn't shake the nagging feeling at the back of her mind that there was something to this caller. She kept circling back to the woman who had appeared twice at the police station but refused to come and make a statement. While she had initially thought there was a domestic abuse situation behind that visit, she was beginning to wonder if there was more to it.

The first thing she did was a reverse search on the phone number, which came back registered to a John Savoy. Home phone, then, for sure. Before she did a background check into John, she checked the records for the license plate she'd memorized earlier, hoping her brain was up to the task, because she had forgotten to write it down.

The license was for an early 00s brown Chrysler sedan which lined up with the car she had seen the woman climbing into. The car was registered to Erica Savoy.

Margot's pulse tripped when she saw the name Savoy on her computer screen.

She pulled up Erica Savoy's license and while the women in the photo—age 52—looked a little warmer and happier than the woman Margot had seen, it was undoubtedly still the same person.

"What the fuck?" Margot whispered to herself.

The sound of the station around her had grown to a dull throb, where all she could hear was her pulse in her ears. She did a quick search of John Savoy and found something that surprised her even more.

John was a thirty-five-year police vet. He'd retired about two years earlier with his pension and a thank you very much from the union. That was it for his record, there was nothing to indicate a history of issues on the force, no calls to his address, nothing to suggest a single hair had been placed out of line in his entire life. He didn't even have any parking tickets, which seemed almost impossible for someone living in San Francisco. Even Margot had parking tickets.

She glanced back at the transcript from who she now assumed to be Erica.

*My husband John.*

Margot printed off John and Erica's information and headed to Leon's desk. He saw her coming and his brow went up.

"Another one?"

She sat in a chair next to him, handing him the file. "I'm not sure about this one. It's more just a feeling than anything else. I'm pretty sure the caller was here last night, and again this morning."

"Like at the station?"

Margot nodded. "She never got as far as coming in, but she was lingering outside like she was just *dying* to talk to someone, but both times I approached her she bailed out quick."

"And you're sure it's the same woman?"

"I couldn't swear beyond a doubt, but the evidence all lines up. Same last name, picture on her license is the same woman. And her husband was a cop."

Leon flipped through the sheets, settling on John's file, his mouth falling into a frown. "His record is flawless."

"I know."

"I'm not sure I'm seeing the same red flags here as I did with the other guy you brought me." He raised his hand to her before she could interrupt. "But I'm not dismissing it, Margot. We'll investigate it and see if there's something here. I trust *your* gut, and if you're telling me this is worth looking into, I'll look into it. But more likely than anything else it's just an uneasy woman whose bored husband is making her paranoid."

"Maybe."

"I promise you, Margot, ninety-nine percent of these calls are people getting bent out of shape because their cousin once mentioned he'd like to shoot someone, and they took that to be a real threat twenty years in the making. I had callers reporting their mailman because they still think *going postal* is a thing. It's astonishing how easily people can become convinced that people they've known their whole lives are killers. Times like this you really get to see how paranoia works. On the plus side, I think we might have our best month ever for seizure of unregistered firearms, so that's certainly a small win out of this whole mess." He set the papers down on his desk next to a stack that had grown since her last visit.

She wanted to volunteer to drive to the Savoys' on her own, but she couldn't.

Her inability to take control of this lead was driving her nuts.

"OK, thanks, Leon. Let me know if anything comes of that, OK?"

"Of course, kid. But don't hold your breath."

Margot left his desk feeling like she had been dismissed.

Leon was usually a warm and open mentor-figure to her, he respected her, so it felt strange to have what she considered to be a worthwhile lead be dropped in a pile with the rest. Yes, it was possible all those other names were more worthy of investigation than her hunch, but it hurt that he hadn't at least humored her about it.

Was she grasping at straws? His disinterest made her question whether or not she was reading too much into Erica's appearances at the station and the phone call. Maybe she really *was* just a nervous wife whose newly retired husband had gotten under her skin now that he was home and bored. She knew plenty of retired cops who took to working on cold cases once they were off active duty because it kept their minds sharp and more importantly kept them from annoying their spouses.

Since Margot didn't know *why* Erica thought John could be involved in the shootings, she didn't have much else to go on. She googled his name, but he was only mentioned in a scant handful of newspaper articles and nothing relevant to the case.

She had to admit that, despite what her gut was telling her, all the actual evidence at her disposal suggested that John had no concerning indicators he might be their guy. For the time being she had to set the Savoys aside and move on to other things.

Wes had returned with their food, and she picked at her Greek salad while sorting through the remainder of her hotline calls. There would be a whole new batch to parse through come tomorrow, an unenviable task that she knew would continue to land on her plate as long as she was on desk duty.

She continued to work the calls while Wes tried to make headway with DMV records on local Caravans—over a hundred and eighty dark red or maroon models that fit their timeframe. He had his work cut out for him.

By the time the evening shift change came on, Margot's

folder was empty, and she'd had her fill of crackpots, and Wes was only about an eighth of the way through his list.

As he walked her out to her car he said, "Is it wrong to admit I hope it *is* the van guy just so all of these calls are worth it?"

Margot smiled. It was dark out and the air was damp with fog. "At the very least, once we find him, I think we'll know one way or the other who Genesis's killer is. I know the gang angle felt flashy, but I think this is going to turn out to be something a lot less convoluted."

"In a way that's good. I think we've had our fill of convoluted this year." Wes stared at her a beat longer than was just friendly, his skin dewy from the fog. For a moment it felt like gravity was pulling them toward one another, like nature itself was acting against logic and common sense. She knew he felt it too, the way he focused on her too sharply, eyes searching hers. Finally he patted her shoulder a few times, shaking off whatever spell had come over him. "Let's do it all again tomorrow."

Margot let out a short laugh, and the weight of some unseen force lifting off her chest was the first sign she hadn't been breathing that entire time. She watched him walk away, not sure if she was relieved or sad to let the moment pass. She wished that people were as easy to solve as murders were.

# THIRTY-TWO

Things in life have a funny way of timing out.

At least that's what Margot thought when Andrew called her—as if he knew she had been thinking of calling him to cancel—and asked if they could bump up her next meeting with Ed.

Ed, it seemed, had told his lawyer that he was in a talking mood, but implied he wasn't sure how long that mood would hold. And while the FBI weren't in a habit of bending to the whims of incarcerated serial killers, they knew they were on the cusp of solving the Marissa Loewen case, and her living siblings were evidently putting a lot of pressure on the FBI now that rumor had started to circulate that the case was once again being investigated.

Margot got it, really she did. Wes was continuing to narrow down their list of van owners, and she had spent several days looking into possible leads in the sniper case without much advancement. So when Andrew asked if she wanted to take one of her days off and head to San Quentin in the hopes of actually *closing* a case, she grudgingly accepted.

The fact that the visit would fall the day before her psych

evaluation with Dr. Singh was both terrible and somewhat hilarious. Of all the set-ups to have her at her absolute worst psychologically, she was practically dooming herself to failure.

And yet, if she could show her therapist that even *after* sitting with Ed, she was still holding it all together, then surely he would give her the thumbs up to get back to active duty after her days off were over.

She had hoped she might be able to use the time to rest and refocus herself, but apparently the universe hadn't received that memo.

By now, Margot had the routine of going to the prison down to a fine science. The clothing restrictions meant she now had a designated *prison* ensemble, which was fine for her. She never wanted to wear those clothes anywhere else after wearing them to visit Ed. And by wearing the same thing every time she went, it gave Ed nothing to use as leverage to learn more about her. She wore no jewelry, nothing personalized. The clothes were plain and nondescript, which was sort of Margot's personal style anyway, but she usually leaned more toward cool-toned neutral V-neck tops and a pair of jeans she loved so much she had four of them.

She looked slightly more like a schoolteacher in the outfit Ed saw her in, and that was fine. She liked to keep him at arm's length from who she was as a person, because she knew he was capable of weaponizing every fact he could get his grubby little hands on.

What should have bothered her more than the knowledge that she had a prison outfit, was the fact that on her drive to the prison she didn't feel any of the same apprehension she had en route to previous visits. The first time she'd seen him she had to pull over to the side of the road to have a panic attack, and when she'd left, she threw up.

Now, she felt almost disconnected from herself. This was not her visiting her imprisoned father. She was here to do a job for the FBI. She was here to help solve Marissa's case and bring her home so her family could finally have the closure they had been so desperate for for decades.

She stepped into the visitors' center and Andrew was waiting for her.

"Thanks for making this happen, Margot. I know it's not a lot of time since we saw him last, but we wanted to strike while the iron was hot, so to speak."

"Mmm," was all she said, leaving her car keys and jacket with the security desk. She had to sign in with her legal name, which made her nervous every single time, as if Ed might somehow be able to check the records. But Andrew had assured her that her anonymity was being protected, even if he never explained how.

She loved Andrew the way someone only can when they bond through mutual trauma, but as she had grown into adulthood, and especially now, she was realizing he was just human. It put a bit of a damper on her childhood idolization of him as a man who could do no wrong, because now she knew he *could* do wrong, and was frequently in the habit of doing it to her whenever it suited his own needs.

Margot fundamentally believed that Andrew cared about her. He showed it by helping keep who she was a secret well into her adulthood, by shielding her from the prying eyes of the public, and by asking very little of her in return. She knew he cared because he hadn't vanished from her life the moment Ed's case was closed.

But now, and especially over recent months, there was an insidious doubt creeping into her mind, wondering just how much Andrew *actually* cared, and if what had once been a paternalistic, protective relationship was now a parasitic one.

She didn't want to dwell on that too long, because it had the damaging potential to ruin her entire opinion of him, but sometimes the thought snuck in and it was hard to shake off.

If he *really* cared, he wouldn't be asking her to do this. And he'd told her time and time again that he wouldn't force her, that she could back out whenever she wanted, but he would say those things and follow them up by telling her about the families of victims or walking her past a wall of smiling black-and-white photos showing Ed's possible additional victims.

He gave her an out the way a kidnapper could open a door but leave your shackles on.

He knew she couldn't back down. And maybe he thought that was because she was a good person, but sometimes his belief that she would do the right thing felt oppressive.

Of course, Dr. Singh had pointed out in their sessions that Margot's opinion of Andrew tended to change drastically depending on how recently she had visited with Ed. He had suggested—or rather, outright told her—that she might be passing the bitterness and rage she felt toward her father onto one of her father figures.

Margot hated Dr. Singh's insights.

Mostly because they were right.

But it didn't change how she felt in that moment.

Andrew left his own things with security, and they waited for their escort. The prison halls were becoming familiar to her, the scents—antiseptic but covering something revolting—the sounds of shouting around every turn, the way everything just felt *damp*. It was a space she was learning, and she *hated* that.

The escort brought them into the same familiar dining hall, where Ed's lawyer was parked at his usual table and the guards were gathered at the entrances, weapons ready.

For a brief second Margot wished Ed would step out of line today and give one of those men a reason to shoot him.

She wondered how frequently the guards hoped for the same thing.

Andrew sat at the same table as the lawyer, where they exchanged icy greetings. Margot had no real connection to Ed's lawyer beyond her fury at him for finding her when she didn't want to be found. But she had a slight twinge of sympathy for him. There's no way he wanted to spend this much time sitting around a prison listening to his client incriminate himself in fresh murders. That had to be a miserable job, really.

Margot quietly took a seat at the usual table and waited. She was too tired, too worn down to feel anything other than resignation. Ed had to tell them where Marissa was today, otherwise even he knew he risked drawing it all out too long. Ed loved a good cinematic climax, but he knew his audience would be bored if he wasn't careful. Telling Andrew he was in a talking mood let him control the narrative, but Margot was determined they'd leave here with what they wanted.

She wasn't sure she'd come back again if he tried to be coy with them, and she had no problem letting him know that.

Ed was guided in, and Margot couldn't help but smile to herself. Not because she was pleased to see him, but because it occurred to her in that moment that Ed *also* had a dedicated prison ensemble. He wore the same navy sweats and blue tee every time they were together. Today he was wearing a shabby cardigan she'd never seen before.

"They let you have normie clothes?" she asked him, jutting her chin at his sweater.

"I made this," he replied casually.

"They let you have *knitting needles*?" She was more incredulous about this than about the notion that he'd learned to knit.

"Under supervision. And they aren't very good." His expression was vaguely amused. "You think I'd kill someone with knitting needles?"

Margot's gaze moved to the two guards who had just finished seating Ed at the table. They didn't react to his statement, but she knew they heard him just fine.

"Not really your style, but you never know, desperate times call for desperate measures."

"Yes, well. You can rest assured they are very vigilant about keeping track of the needles as I use them."

"Someone in here taught you?"

"We have a video library that we can use to learn basic skills if we choose. They let us have certain craft supplies if we're on our best behavior. Someone was kind enough to send me the wool when I mentioned I was learning."

Someone.

Another groupie hoping for what? A shot at love with a serial killer on death row? A chance to hitch her wagon to the Finch horror show? Margot couldn't understand these women and what made them tick, but there was a never-ending supply of them. Whenever Ed got bored of one—or they wised up and moved on—there was always another one waiting to fawn over him.

Margot knew that was how he sourced most of his money in here, since inmates still needed funds for the commissary and phone credits. She sure as fuck wasn't sending him anything, but she had it on good authority his prison account was flush.

It made her sick.

"If you like it, I'll make you one," he said, as if this was the most normal suggestion in the world. "Not as if I'm doing much else with my time."

"I would rather strangle myself to death with the loose threads than wear something you made for me," she replied before she thought about whether it was a good idea.

Ed didn't say anything back, he just watched her appraisingly, which might have been even worse than if he lost his temper. She didn't want to be assessed by him, and she hated the way he wore such a knowing look on his face whenever she had a moment of weakness around him.

The small smirk on his lips might as well have said, *I see you.*

"All right then. Having one of those days, are we?"

"I'm not sitting here having a parental chit-chat with you about how my fucking *day* is going, Ed. I'm at a prison, how do you think it's going?"

"Well all of my days are at a prison and some of them aren't so bad." He gave a self-deprecating shrug. "We all have days, Meg."

She ground her teeth together, her fingernails digging into the palms of her hands. For some reason it was even harder to talk to him when he was pretending to be nice.

He was doing the psychopath thing today. The one where they speak and act the way they think normal people should. He was putting on a show, but she didn't understand why, because the audience in the room had seen him scream in her face before. They all knew he wasn't this nice.

Was it just a way of keeping them on their toes, so they were never sure which version of Ed they were going to get on any given day? Or was he doing this because he wanted something? The latter option seemed the most likely.

"I hope you know you don't have more bargaining chips to play here, Ed. You asked to see me, and I've come, but that's it. There are no commuted sentences, there's no bonus activities or extra time in the yard. You don't get to ask for more now that you've gotten us this far."

"I'm hurt that you think so little of me that you'd assume I'm planning to *bargain*. That's a bit crude, don't you think?" He smirked slightly, making her blood boil.

"I think you've played games with us this entire time and you're willing to push to see just how far you can go. But I'm telling you right now, this is it." She gestured to herself. "You get your one-on-one time and I listen to you, but at the end of it all you need to live up to your side of things and tell us where Marissa is."

He looked away for a moment and then turned back and held her gaze. "You know, the night I buried her was the first time I ever thought your mother suspected something." His expression was almost wistful.

"What?" Margot couldn't have been more surprised if he had reached out and slapped her. Her mother had been oblivious. They all had.

"Oh yes, I don't think you ever knew about that. I came home and she had caught me, but she didn't understand what she'd caught me in. I had to convince her it was infidelity. I had to make her believe I had strayed so she wouldn't ask too many questions. I think deep down she must have known that wasn't really what happened, but she told herself a lie that was easy to believe. No one wants to think their husband is a killer, it's so much more palatable if he's just fucking around, isn't it? You can complain to your friends about a cheating husband, but she learned the hard way no one wants to be friends with you if your husband kills people."

The anniversary of Kim's suicide had just passed, and Margot had done her best to ignore it. She'd called her brother just to make sure he wasn't drowning himself in gin, and he'd sounded OK. It seemed like there were enough years between them and their mother's death to allow them to acknowledge the occasion without too much self-destruction.

Ed's words were not without intention, but he misjudged the pain they would cause her. Margot ignored him, not rising to the bait.

"Is that when you started being home more?"

"For a little while, yes. She had the leash nice and tight; it was hard to go hunting."

Margot swallowed down her revulsion and kept her face neutral.

"I still shopped around, you know, there are ways, but the thing about killing is you can't do it all in your own backyard. People start to ask questions. I really pushed my luck with Marissa, she was my riskiest kill, and maybe that's why people

didn't think I did it. Well, that and they never found her body."
He smirked, proud of himself.

"Where is she?"

"We'll get there. But you're here now, let's have a little chat
first, shall we? Make the visit worth your time. Tell me what
you're working on now."

Margot would have rather gouged out her own eyeballs with
a rusty spoon than let Ed know she was being forced onto desk
duty, so she skirted it with a variation of the truth. "Wrapping
up that dead sex worker case. The sniper investigation."

"Oh, well now. That *is* interesting, isn't it?" He wasn't refer-
ring to the sex worker and they both knew it. "What an unusual
case. Snipers are quite rare, you know, as killers go."

"Yes, I'm aware of the statistics."

"I'm just saying most people who go nuts with a gun usually
do it in close quarters. Mass shootings are a dime a dozen,
there's a new one every day. For pure body count they're the
way to go. Haul your AR-15 into a busy shopping mall and fire
until someone takes you down."

Margot grimaced. The reality of mass shootings was a bit
too *real* to have Ed glaze over it so brazenly.

If he noticed her discomfort, it didn't slow him down.

"But if you want to incite *fear* then people have to know
you're out there, waiting in the shadows. It makes things harder
sometimes—trust me—but when you know that people are
huddled inside their homes with the doors locked because
they're afraid of *you*. Oof, baby. No thrill in the world like that."

"So you think he's doing it to create fear."

"Well, sure, doesn't that make sense to you? I assume he
hasn't sent any demands, any kind of manifesto that lets you
know what his crackpot whims are?"

"I'm not at liberty to share the details of an active investigation."

Ed snorted at this, and Margot deserved it, because she was

already guilty of discussing active investigations with him. Nothing huge, nothing she wouldn't mention to a colleague. She knew what she was doing, offering Ed breadcrumbs to keep him talking. And if she was being honest, it made her feel powerful to have something he wanted. But something about this was different. For some reason she didn't *want* to talk about the sniper case with him, not because it was a state secret—the perpetrator *hadn't* sent them anything and telling Ed that wouldn't damage the case at all—but because he seemed too delighted to be talking about it, and she didn't want to feed into that by offering him unnecessary details. Maybe she could give him just a little something. What harm could it do?

But Ed didn't wait for her to change her mind. "All right, you play it your way, kid, I'm not here to do your work for you." Then he laughed as if this statement were particularly funny. "Actually, I guess that's not true, is it. Because I'm here to do *his* work for him." His head swiveled to look at Andrew, who seemed surprised to suddenly be the center of Ed's focus. "Tell me, Andy Boy, just how many open cases do you need me to solve for you, hmm?"

"I don't know, Ed. How many of them are yours?"

A slight smile passed over Ed's lips before he clucked his tongue scoldingly. "Now, now, that would take the fun out of this, wouldn't it? No, I think we'll keep doing this piecemeal, it's a lot more exciting, isn't it? Christmas morning every time you visit."

It was Margot's turn to make a scoffing noise, and the second it was out of her throat she loathed how much it sounded like the same noise he'd made.

"Watch your tone, Megan," he said smoothly, keeping the venom in his voice to a minimum.

"How can I have a tone without saying anything, *Ed*?" she countered. God, she sounded like a teenager picking a fight with her parent, not a woman of nearly forty trying to solve a murder. She hated what Ed brought out in her, she hated who she *was* in his presence.

As much as she wanted to solve Marissa's case and get out of the prison, she knew this wasn't going to end here. Ed had a hold on them, and God only knew how many other victims were out there waiting to be found. Was it two or two hundred?

He'd already admitted to the murders of seventy-eight women, counting Marissa Loewen. Margot suspected the actual total had to be considerably higher, solely based on the number of potentials who littered the boards back at the FBI offices.

"Of course, Christmas mornings don't really look the same for us anymore, now do they?" Ed said, pivoting away from the argument.

Margot was surprised. In her previous visits with Ed he had been quick to anger, rising to every perceived slight or disrespect with rage. Now he seemed to recover more quickly. She could see that he was upset, but rather than picking a fight with her or enforcing his need to be the parent—a leg he no longer had to stand on—he was trying his best to avoid the argument.

She didn't understand why, or why in doing so it made her want to fight with him even more. There were a good two decades' worth of her own anger stewing inside her, and all of it was demanding that she poke the bear.

She took a deep breath, still staring him down, and she let it drop.

"Can we please talk about Marissa?"

"I want to talk about the sniper first. Then I will tell you about Marissa."

Margot bit her tongue, because if his only demand was a bit of information, then she didn't see the harm. She wasn't even lead on the sniper case—meaning if he went digging through newspaper articles about it later, he wasn't going to uncover her name—and her insider knowledge was limited to what she had gleaned from sitting in on task force meetings.

The gist of that was: not much.

Margot was more than willing to share the nothing details of a case with Ed if it meant he'd finally stop dicking around and tell them where they could find Marissa's body. Andrew had a team ready and waiting back at headquarters for any word from him, and they could mobilize a field team for body recovery in mere hours.

Marissa would finally come home.

"There's not a lot to tell you, honestly," she admitted. "We suspect it's someone with some training, just based on the weapon and the approach. He seems to be pretty accurate, so we don't think it's some amateur who bought a long-range rifle." She avoided mentioning the fact they were looking into ex-military members. That felt *too* specific to share.

"Could be a prepper," Ed offered.

"A prepper?"

"You know, those doomsday freaks who build bunkers in their backyards and have a lifetime supply of rations sitting there. They spend their days beating off and hoping the world will end. Those guys fucking love guns. Their biggest hard-on in life would be protecting their inbred families from Mad Max and his goon squad after the government collapses."

"Mad Max was the good guy in those movies," Margot said.

"Was he really though? Were there good guys in those movies?"

Margot frowned, now not entirely certain she'd ever actually *seen* a Mad Max movie the whole way through, aside from the new one.

"I don't think it's a doomsday prepper," she went on. "In that instance the violence would only make sense if they were defending themselves from some kind of threat: real or imagined. Like Waco."

"Then I guess you know what you're looking for. Someone who knows their way around a gun. Someone who knows the city and the habits of crowds. I don't know about you, kid, but to *me* that says cop."

Margot felt a chill from his words. She'd avoided mentioning military, but Ed had managed to find the one alternative that said *the call is coming from inside the house.* The suggestion that someone close to her could be responsible. He knew what he was doing.

Her mouth formed a thin line and she worked to keep any kind of expression off her face. She couldn't let him see that he'd hit home, and worse, because she had been considering the same thing herself. She let herself look at Andrew quickly, wondering if his face might give anything away, considering he was the one who had been helping her investigate the ballistics, and he'd also been the first one to suggest she consider a police angle.

He was as stoic as ever, giving every impression of having no opinion, no interest at all.

Helpful.

Margot couldn't help but wonder if Ed was simply goading her. He had to know that the suggestion would get under her skin, because she wouldn't want it to be true. And it was hard to shake the feeling that there was something *accurate* about his reasoning.

She squirmed uncomfortably in her seat, willing this conversation to come to an end. "That is certainly an angle we can explore."

"If you're saying that, then I know it's an angle you've already explored. You don't need to placate me."

"Jesus, then what are we doing here?" she snapped. "This whole farce is just about placating you. And before you jump down my throat and tell me to be polite, tell me to respect you, you can just save it. This is *exhausting.* And this is the last time we're doing things your way, Ed. I'm not coming for multiple visits again just so you can hem and haw about whether or not you want to share something with us. The next time you dangle a victim in front of us, you better be willing to *talk*, because I'm not going to sit here and spoon feed you tidbits of my life and my work and anything else you haven't earned the right to know."

Ed looked surprised by her outburst, as did Andrew, frankly. There was a long, uncomfortable silence.

Ed gave a small smile and opened his hands placatingly. "I was simply offering some insight."

"Shove your insights up your ass."

His jaw tightened, eyes gleaming like a dangerous predator who has just spotted something and can't decide if it's prey or a threat. Margot met his gaze without blinking.

"Helen Putnam Park. There's a small lake. A pond, really, but it was deep enough. I weighed her down with some gym equipment from the car."

Margot knew the park well. She and her family had gone there often to picnic or play in the wide-open fields. She didn't remember the lake, but Ed would know if he'd put a body there.

Andrew was looking impatient now, gaze darting from her to the door. Since they couldn't bring phones in with them, she knew he was antsy to get out and set the ball rolling.

The guards came to collect Ed when Margot gave them a nod, and he got up without protest, though she noticed a frown of disappointment.

"Don't think I didn't hear it," he called over his shoulder, as he shuffled away.

"What are you talking about?" she grumbled.

"You said *next time*."

# THIRTY-THREE

The whole drive back to San Francisco, Margot tried *not* to think.

She was doing a bang-up job of it right up to the point where she saw the first sign advertising Muir Woods exits, and she was forcefully drawn back to reality.

There was only so much disassociating one person could do when literal lives were on the line, and as much as she'd like to bury her head in the sand—or hide out in her apartment with a bottle of vodka and an unholy amount of Thai food—there was still work to be done.

It was her off day from the precinct, meaning the work that needed her focus today was the Marissa Loewen case and parsing through what they'd learned from Ed and what the next steps would be to recover the body. She made her way to the FBI headquarters, where she found a beaming Greg rather than Andrew, who'd driven separately, waiting for her in the lobby.

Greg's sinewy awkwardness was a surprising balm to Margot's nerves. There was no pretense with this guy, he was just... Greg.

As they rode up in the elevator together, Greg shuffled

nervously for a moment before breaking into the silence. Margot was surprised it took him that long.

"I just wanted to say, the information you were able to get out of Finch during your visits has been unbelievably helpful to my research."

Margot nodded. "I'm glad it was good for something."

"He's such an interesting case study." Greg stared right ahead, rocking back and forth on his heels like a child who was excited about something.

Margot appreciated that he said *case study* and not *person*.

"You think he's more interesting than any other killers? I think he's pretty derivative."

"Oh, no, definitely not." Greg was about to launch into a well-practiced lecture, she could tell, but she gave him a quick, knowing smile, and he seemed to read it instantly. "Oh, you were being sarcastic."

The elevator doors announced their arrival with a *ding* and Greg followed Margot as she headed for the main boardroom where they had previously met. She caught sight of Andrew outside the room talking to an agent she recognized from previous visits, but not one of the three she'd been dealing with recently. Agents Alana Yarrow and Carter Holmes were just heading into the boardroom together, and Carter held the door open for them.

"Welcome back, Margot," Alana said with a nod of greeting. Today she looked more austere, her suit a deep navy and her platinum blond bob pinned back in a tiny ponytail.

The three agents took their places, and Margot settled in to one of the seats on Greg's side of the table, not wanting to have all the attention on her when things got under way.

Greg, it seemed, was still interested in continuing their conversation. "I know it's not your first priority, but I'd be really interested in learning more about his victimology from his perspective. Obviously, we can see certain similarities across his known victims which has helped us narrow down the most likely candidates in existing missing persons' cases, to see which girls might fit his profile, but getting some insights directly from *him* would be just... game changing."

"Greg," Alana said with a sigh. "We talked about this."

Margot gave Greg her most patient smile. Honestly, she kind of appreciated his enthusiasm, and the way he didn't try to handle her with kid gloves. In fairness, she thought that was most likely due to him forgetting the basics of decorum, but she wasn't mad about it.

"It's OK. I don't know how often I'll see him going forward." *Hopefully never.* "But if I can find a way to ask that he won't think is me being intrusive, I can try. He *loves* to talk about himself."

Greg's enthusiasm was boundless, he vibrated like a puppy. Margot knew the others didn't care for him much, and she understood how guys like Greg could be a bit *much*, but all the same, there was something about him she liked. He had no artifice, but more importantly he didn't view her as someone that needed to be protected and patronized.

And while she knew he wanted to use her connection to Ed for his own benefit, Margot was pretty sure he simply didn't understand how much of herself she gave up every time she sat across from Ed. Andrew *did* know, and that was the source of her growing resentment toward him. Greg just craved knowledge.

Andrew came into the room and settled into the head seat without greeting any of them. He plugged his laptop into one of the aux cables in front of him while Carter dutifully got up to dim the lights. Margot thought it was an unnecessary step, considering they were in a glass box in the middle of a brightly lit work floor, but then Carter also tapped a switch that instantly fogged over the windows, casting the room in darkness, reminding Margot they had FBI money.

She sat back as Andrew opened a PowerPoint presentation and she wanted to applaud whichever lackey agent had been responsible for putting it together in the time it had taken for them to drive back from the prison.

Sometimes people *said* they were proficient in PowerPoint, other people were actually pros, and this person knew their stuff. The menus were animated.

Margot watched as Andrew carefully walked through what they knew. "Based on our information, coming directly from Ed Finch, with thanks to Margot." He paused to nod in her direction, and she pretended not to see it, her hands clenched in fists in her lap. "We know that Marissa was killed the same night she went missing. The believed location of death is this parking lot." The slide changed, showing an overhead still of an overgrown lot. "This is a current angle of that lot, the building that was formerly there has since been abandoned. We're obviously going to check the lot for any signs of evidence, but at this point we don't imagine we're going to find anything relevant. If Finch left the murder weapon there—again unlikely given our knowledge of his previous MO—there's no way it wouldn't have been found at this point."

The slide advanced again, this time showing a satellite view of dark green trees, some small access roads, and a lake that reminded Margot of the shape of a motorboat from above.

"This is Helen Putnam Regional Park, and this is the lake where Finch claims he disposed of Marissa's body. Now Finch didn't have access to a boat, so we have to assume the body isn't that deep out there—not that it's a very deep lake to begin with. I'm surprised nothing was unearthed during any previous drought seasons. That said, she's had a fair amount of time to decompose, so we're not expecting to find her all in one piece. We have a dive team prepped and heading out there in the hour, and a forensic anthropologist and her students meeting us as well to review what we find."

"Is draining the pond a possibility?" Alana asked. "Might make it easier to ensure we get all the pieces."

"That's certainly on the list of possibilities, but as it's a state-owned park we're going to need a higher authority approval on that, and they're going to need a good reason. So let's find her, and hopefully we don't need drastic measures to get the job done."

Andrew closed his laptop, unplugging it, and casting their chamber into complete darkness until Carter was able to get the lights back on again. For that brief moment, Margot's heart was in her throat. She wasn't afraid of the dark, but she *was* unsettled by not being able to protect herself from things she couldn't see. And while she knew logically she was perfectly safe, logic and fear had little to do with one another.

Her pulse was still pounding when the film over the windows was lifted, the bright light of day filling the room once more.

"Margot, do you want to join us?" Andrew asked. "This is your victory more than anyone else's. Good work." She appreciated him giving her the credit, and even the nods of approval she got from the others, but this didn't feel like a case she had solved.

Much like the Theresa Milotti case a few months earlier, this just felt like a little sacrifice of her soul that had been necessary in order for someone else to find peace. Margot didn't regret the efforts she'd made to solve Marissa's case, but she also didn't feel like celebrating them.

"Thanks," she mumbled, pushing her chair back from the table. She considered declining the offer—she had no interest in another visit to Petaluma so soon after her last—but she *did* want to see this case through to the end. Maybe it would heal something in her to watch them actually pull Marissa out of the water.

Somehow she doubted it.

## THIRTY-FOUR

Margot had never noticed how many dog kennels had popped up around Petaluma since she had left. It was astonishing just how many specialty breeders there were in the area.

As she followed the FBI convoy north to her old hometown —wanting her own car with her, so she could leave without needing an escort—she kept seeing signs. Breeders specializing in golden retrievers, in French bulldogs, in something called a Pomskie which Margot was imagining as a terrifying hybrid between a Pomeranian and a husky and therefore the loudest dog alive. Aussies and doodles and Great Danes. Just sign after sign advertising expensive purebred dogs and designer mix-breeds that were probably thousands of dollars each.

The only pet Margot had ever had growing up was a hamster named Phillip, and once it disappeared—something she purposefully avoided putting too much thought into—she never bothered asking for another one. Justin had begged and pleaded for a dog, especially after their neighbors got a beautiful German shepherd puppy, but her parents had dodged the request year after year, claiming there was no room for a dog in the house and the kids weren't responsible enough for one.

Even when Margot started to babysit and Justin had a news-paper route, they still shot down the idea.

Finally, Justin stopped asking and just volunteered to walk dogs for seniors who weren't able to exercise their pups as often as they would like. It had given her brother the hit of doggy dopamine he wanted, and their parents had presumably been grateful they stopped asking.

Justin had a dog now, though Margot would argue he was less responsible as an adult than he had been as a kid. Margot had never met his dog, a shepherd mix of some kind, but Justin mentioned her sometimes when he called. Bailey.

It was such a painfully nineties name for a dog, like he was trying to live out the fantasy life he had wanted back then, before everything went to shit.

They dealt with things their own way. Perhaps neither of them was doing it particularly well.

The local Petaluma police had opened the maintenance access roads inside the park, allowing the convoy of FBI vehicles to easily get right up to the pond without having to traverse the big lawn between the public parking lot and the water.

Margot took in her surroundings as they drove in. The park was usually bustling with people out enjoying the weather—even in November—but it looked like the local cops had done an impressively efficient job of chasing away poten-tial onlookers. The parking lot was empty aside from police vehicles, and uniformed officers were walking the trails to stop anyone who might have come by bike or on foot and send them out.

A service road gave them access to a paved walking path, and they parked and walked over to the waterside. Margot thought calling it a *lake* might be a bit too generous. It was a pond, but a decently sized one, with a little sandy patch down a set of wooden steps where people could wade in if they so desired, and there was a small dock where people could go fishing. Margot assumed the pond must be stocked regularly if that was the case, but she didn't know for sure.

The pond couldn't be that deep—ten, maybe fifteen feet? Maybe that *did* qualify it as a lake. She wasn't certain how those designations were determined.

All she knew was it was deep enough to keep a body hidden in its depths for nearly thirty years. That in and of itself was astonishing now that she was standing on the shore. With all the people coming and going from the park on a daily basis, people wading into the marshy waters on the banks, people casting fishing lines in regularly... how had *no one* found Marissa here, even by accident?

If Ed had told her that he'd left the body in the trees surrounding the pond she might have believed that more readily, but she was astonished by the fact that, if he was being honest about his dumping ground, sheer dumb luck meant that he must have put her in the deepest and best hidden part of this little manmade patch of water.

There was a dive team of four people in black wetsuits—their genders indistinguishable thanks to the bulky breathing apparatus and thick neoprene—and they had bypassed using a boat entirely and were just wading into the pond. A motorized dinghy was attached to the back of one of the FBI trucks, but it seemed like everyone had unilaterally agreed it was more effort than it was worth to try getting it on the water. Two of the divers had bypassed flippers as well, donning only water shoes before they headed into the murky pond water.

Margot's morning visit to the prison felt as if it had happened months ago rather than hours. It was astonishing how quickly this whole circus had come together, how one phone call from Andrew had unleashed a tidal wave of productivity onto the park.

She stood back from the shore, glad that they were well distanced from the public, so she didn't need to be mindful of reporters. She didn't *look* like Megan Finch anymore, but she still avoided speaking to the press as a matter of maintaining a small shard of her anonymity. On any case she worked, she let her partner, or the captain, do all the talking.

The only exception she made was for Sebastian Klein, her friend over at the *Sentinel*.

Now that she knew Ed was out there watching, and knew she was a cop, she didn't want her new name and face appearing together in print anywhere. Maybe it was a silly thing to worry about. Her father was never getting out of prison, maybe it didn't matter if he knew what her name was now. But the problem with giving up her name was that she didn't know where things stopped after that. First her name, then little tidbits of information about her life after he had been caught, tiny pieces of a person he was never supposed to know.

She and her brother hadn't changed their names to protect themselves from Ed, they had changed them to protect themselves from his legacy.

She realized now, with a shiver, that what kept her awake at night lately wasn't the idea that Ed might pick up a newspaper one day and see her name dangling at the end of a quote.

What worried her was that she might be the one to share it with him.

It seemed more and more since their conversations she was asking herself *what harm could it do*, and that was a very frightening line to toe.

Two of the divers worked in opposite directions, walking the shoreline, and getting deeper and deeper with each pass, while the other two went right for the middle. Margot assumed, given the depth of the lake, they would finish their work in minutes, but it was almost a full hour of the slow-moving work before one of the divers emerged, pulling out their oxygen mouthpiece and said, "I think we've got something."

Margot's pulse quickened, as a crowd of agents wearing

matching FBI windbreakers converged on the small shoreline and a raft was sent out to the diver. It took twenty more minutes and several loud complaints about thick silt before two divers working in tandem were able to bring something up to the surface.

Margot watched them work and the agonizing precision of it, the slow-going progress to ensure they didn't miss anything, made her feel like the scene was being played back in slow motion.

At first it appeared to be little more than reeds and pond detritus, but as they worked to lift the object onto the raft—the other two divers helping to steady it—Margot could make out a skeletal human arm. More bones followed until the raft risked being too weighed down to stay afloat and it was pulled to shore.

Margot watched, barely feeling anything as each bit of Marissa's remains came out. She had thought she might feel horror. Relief. *Something*. But after years of working in homicide she had been conditioned not to react to the dead.

She was a professional at feeling nothing.

The sun had begun to set by this point, dusk surrounding them, but spotlights had been set up angled at the pond's surface and the divers were equipped with underwater lights. Bugs swarmed the lights, battering themselves against the bulbs and creating an eerie flicker to the illumination.

Margot was standing in an area that had been set up on the shore under a portable tent with several folding tables and tarps laid out. The FBI's forensic anthropologist, who had introduced herself as Dr. McHugh, was giving hushed directions to a group of three grad students. Despite there being several spotlights on the tent, all four of them were wearing headlamps.

Margot had no idea what half of the tools they had were for, but she knew that the square wooden frames with metal screens set into them were to help sort through debris to find smaller bones like teeth and finger bones. In the morning, after the bulk of the main skeleton had been collected, buckets of silt would be pulled from the pond floor in the area of the body's discovery to see what else they could find.

A crime scene photographer snapped photos as the raft came ashore, then made way for the agents to bring the tarp that had lined the base of the raft into the anthropologist's tent. Alongside the forensic anthropologist was an FBI medical examiner, and the grisly power duo would work together to help identify all the pieces of the body to ensure that this *was* Marissa they were looking at.

Margot had seen her dental records in her file, along with some old X-rays showing a broken tibia from when Marissa was a soccer player in high school. Provided the necessary bones were available for comparison, they should be able to make an initial confirmation that night.

Margot's feet were beginning to protest against all the pacing she'd been doing on the uneven patch of shore, but with an answer so close at hand she wasn't about to give up and call it a night now. She was still waiting for something, for that *feeling* that would tell her this had all been worth it.

So far all she felt was a grim sense of loss.

Andrew made his way over to her as the forensics team worked on sifting through the thick muck and plant life that had come to the surface with the bones. They painstakingly cleaned every bone they identified and laid it out on one of the waiting tables, while the silt was kept on the tarp to sort through later for smaller items.

After another hour of work, it was pitch black outside and Andrew was still with her, like they were standing vigil together. Team members would drift over to ask questions or get his approval as the agent in charge, but for the most part it was just him and Margot standing in the darkness outside the circle of light around the tent, watching them put Marissa back together like she was a puzzle.

Finally, the medical examiner came over, pulling down his mask and wiping sweat from his cheeks.

"Sir, we still have a ways to go, but given what we've got here we have roughly eighty percent of the skeleton intact now, and it's enough for us to make a confident assessment. The subject is a female, roughly twenty-five to thirty years of age, Caucasian. The tibia shows a healed fracture identical to the one on Miss Loewen's X-ray, and while we don't have all the teeth, there are substantial similarities, especially on the occlusion, and she had a fairly distinctive gap in her central incisors which is present with our remains."

The ME waited a moment, as if giving them a chance to reply, but when they didn't, he made the findings crystal clear.

"Obviously we'll want to confirm one hundred percent with DNA, but we believe that this body is Marissa Loewen."

## THIRTY-FIVE

After seeing the contents of the bag used to weigh Marissa down, Margot waited until she got back to her car to start crying.

She wasn't sure what part of the whole ordeal triggered the response, whether it was the confirmation of the body being Marissa, if it was the stress of seeing Ed and then seeing one of his victims in the same day, but she sat in the driver's seat of her car, both hands on the wheel and her keys sitting in her lap, and she sobbed.

Back on the shore she had wanted to feel *something*, instead she was feeling everything.

With the darkness deepening outside, she felt safe to give in to it. It didn't matter that there were dozens of FBI agents passing by her car in a steady stream. She just needed to let it out, because if it wasn't crying, it would be screaming, and she thought that might garner a lot more negative attention.

She cried for a good five minutes, full-body airless gulps, trying and failing to breathe, which only set her sobbing more. When she felt wrung out completely, she let go of the steering wheel and roughly swiped away the tears on her cheeks and down her chest.

One gulp of air, then another, and by the third she almost felt like she was human again, though it was hard to feel tethered to humanity when she had just walked away from a pile of desiccated bones, slick with algae, that had once been a person.

And that the thing weighing her down to the bottom of the lake hadn't been *gym equipment* as Ed suggested—how had she believed that when Ed had never set foot in a gym a day in his life?—it had been an old garbage bag filled with Margot's toys, ones that he had meant to take to the Goodwill but found another use for.

Seeing them open the bag had been it for her.

She'd recognized the old lawn bowling set immediately.

She didn't believe for a second that Ed had forgotten what he had used. He would have remembered the burial like it had happened yesterday. Sexual sadists *loved* to relive their crimes. No, he hadn't made a mistake. He had set her up to discover it for herself. To what end? Would he ask her later how it had felt?

Margot squeezed the steering wheel and for one flicker of a moment, she imagined it was her father's throat.

It felt good.

Margot had almost regained her composure when there was a knock at the passenger window. Andrew didn't wait for an invitation before climbing in, but what surprised Margot more about that was that she had forgotten to lock the doors when she got in.

She couldn't make mistakes like that.

That was how women ended up like Marissa.

Her breath caught in her throat, but she passed it off as an effect of the crying, releasing the air from her lungs in a shaky, audible sigh.

Andrew put a hand on her shoulder and squeezed, his face

etched with an intense, compassionate expression. When she looked at him now, she struggled to see the man he had once been. The salt-and-pepper beard, the glasses. He looked like the father of the man who had jumped into the car with her the day her father had abandoned her to make a break for it.

Climbed into the passenger seat, just like he had now.

"What do you want, Andrew?" She pulled away from his touch, glad that with his door closed they were cast back into darkness so he couldn't see her red cheeks or the tear stains down the front of her shirt.

"I just wanted to make sure you were OK. This was a heavy day."

A million thoughts swam through her mind. A thousand barbed comments begged her to say them. But ultimately, she did the best thing she could, given the situation, and she said nothing.

"Margot..." He said her name like it was a complaint. "I know things between us have changed. I know that stems back to me asking you to visit Ed again. If you think I don't see that, then you have forgotten I have a doctorate in psychology." He let out a little chuckle, she assumed to let her know he was poking fun at himself. She didn't laugh. "I don't know what I can do to make that right. I try to include you so you don't think we're just using you."

"But you *are* just using me." She glared at him, but realized quickly the gesture was lost in the darkness, so she looked back out the window again, watching the activity of the scene. A veritable beehive of crime solving. "You saw a way to get what you want, and I get it. I *get* it. Tonight, a family gets to sleep knowing the truth about what happened to their daughter. To you that's worth it."

"And it isn't to you?"

Margot gripped the steering wheel again, fighting back a new wave of tears. "No. I thought it would be. I thought I could give penance that he couldn't. But you will go home tonight thinking about Marissa's family and what this means to them. I'll go home tonight knowing that when Ed's head hits his pillow he'll be smiling. Because he got *exactly* what he wanted. And he's going to keep getting what he wants, because he knows you've got a hook in me. This worked. We found her, and if there are more of them out there, you'll want to find them all. Ed knows my conscience won't let me walk away. And so do you."

Andrew didn't have a pithy comeback for that. They sat in a mutually uncomfortable silence for a long moment. He opened the car door and she thought he might leave without saying anything, but at the last moment he looked back and said, "We got those ballistics reports. I'll come by the station this week and return the evidence along with the report."

"Fine."

For a moment he hovered outside the car, lingering like he might say *something* to comfort her, but in the end he shook his head and closed the door behind him.

She was about to start the car and make the trip back to San Francisco when her phone sounded a text alert. The vibrating buzz set her nerves jangling all over again, and she cursed the stupid thing as she opened it.

Wes.

> I know it's getting late, but I thought you should know. We got a hit on the Caravan driver. I'm going with Garvey to have a chat. I'll let you know if there's anything worth coming into the station for.

Margot didn't hesitate.

The only thing waiting back at her apartment was a cabinet full of liquor and closets full of skeletons.

She headed for the station.

# THIRTY-SIX

Margot listened to police radio the whole way back to San Francisco because she needed the kind of distraction that shitty pop couldn't provide. She followed along as dispatchers sent squad cars out to different parts of the city, familiar codes translating themselves in her mind.

A calm dispatcher requested units for an 11-65. Signal light out. One person replied they were Code 7. Mealtime.

Another dispatcher requested immediate assistance for a 246. Shooting at an inhabited dwelling. As the officers replied they were given more details and the soap opera drama of a San Francisco night unfolded, bringing her back to a calm state where she could function normally again.

She was about ten minutes from the station when an even-toned voice doing a great job of hiding the edge of panic came over the radio.

"All units, all units. We have a code 966 at the intersection of Broadway and Powell. Repeat, code 966."

Margot almost veered into the oncoming lane, steadying herself in time to avoid the car whose horn shrieked and whose driver was clearly screaming at her.

Code 966 was sniper.

She was only about five minutes from the location of the shooting, and despite not being on active duty she *was* probably closer to the scene than anyone else on the task force. She could beg forgiveness later.

Throwing her dash light on, she wove through the traffic, channeling her inner Steve McQueen. Breathlessly avoiding other cars on the narrow streets of San Francisco, she made it to the scene of the shooting and came to a halt near to where a cruiser was parked. Its lights were flashing and its door was open, and on the street next to the vehicle, a uniformed officer lay crumpled on the asphalt. It was impossible to see the person's face from where she was parked, but she didn't expect to know who they were. Margot's initial gut reaction was to get out and check the officer for a pulse, but the 966 call told her that there was no safety to be found outside.

Broadway and Powell was usually a busy intersection, right where the Broadway tunnel ended. But whether it was the late hour, or the recent shootings, the wide street was nearly empty of traffic. Margot saw a car emerge from the tunnel and immediately pull a dangerous U-turn back the opposite direction.

People were running up the sidewalk past her car screaming. Car horns blared and sirens filled the air, but as far as Margot could tell at first glance she was the only living officer on the scene.

Someone was huddled in the front seat of the car in front of the police cruiser, and while she couldn't make out much about them, based on the way they held their head, she was pretty certain they were alive.

The officer on the ground was the only body she could see.

"Fuck. Fuck fuck fuck." She slammed her hand on the steering wheel, desperate to do something, but not to put herself in the line of fire. She'd seen up close the damage this guy was capable of, and as much as she might get mired down in her depressive moments, she still wanted to live.

She grabbed the radio from her car and chimed in on the main line. "Dispatch, this is Detective Margot Phalen. I'm on location. Officer down, I repeat officer down. No other victims visible. Tell officers to avoid Broadway specifically, it appears our 966 has a perfect angle. Put someone on the other end of the tunnel to divert traffic."

"10-4, Detective."

There was no additional chatter on the line aside from officers indicating they were en route to the scene. Margot wanted to warn them against using the open frequency to announce their position, but it seemed like they had all made the inference from her first message and were simply reporting the number of minutes until arrival.

Her phone started to buzz almost immediately and she glanced at the screen.

Leon.

At least it wasn't the captain.

Margot was about to answer when another cruiser pulled up. These officers were apparently either too distracted by the sight of a fallen comrade to think straight or simply hadn't been paying attention when the code for *sniper* was used, but they got out of their car, guns drawn, looking side-to-side for an assailant but never *up*.

Not that they could have seen it coming.

Margot opened her door a crack, and was screaming, "Get back in your car!" when the first one went down.

The haunting thing about it was the complete lack of sound. Just a dull *thwack* where the bullet hit the officer in the chest, and the surprised grunt he made before falling.

The second officer barely had time to turn their head to see what had happened to their partner when a fine pink mist appeared as a halo around their skull, and they, too, collapsed onto the street.

Margot ignored Leon's call, letting it go to voicemail. She grabbed the radio again. "Dispatch, dispatch, all officers responding to the 966 *stay in your vehicle.* Two more officers down, I repeat two more officers down. Keep the damn ambulance out of here."

Protocol for unsafe scenes was to keep non-police services at bay until the scene could be cleared. And right now, this scene was far from clear. Denying medical care to those who might be on the cusp of death could have heartbreaking consequences, but Margot wasn't about to let some poor, unarmed EMT run headlong to their death.

And nothing could help those officers who were already dead.

Her phone started ringing again and this time she answered it immediately. Leon didn't even wait for her to talk. "Phalen, get the hell out of there now. If you are in a position to turn your vehicle around and get to safety you do it, do you understand me? Right now, you are a *civilian*, you are off duty. Are you even wearing a fucking vest?"

"No." She didn't know why she answered, the question was so obviously rhetorical.

"Then I don't want to hear a single peep of argument. You get out. We have officers coming."

"The shots are coming from the west. Don't go near Broadway, Leon. You stay the fuck off Broadway, do you hear me?"

Leon was saying something to someone else in the car, but even though she couldn't hear every word, she knew he was telling whoever was driving to avoid Broadway.

"Can you leave?" he asked, his voice quiet.

"No." And she didn't think she could. When she had yelled out her car window she had drawn attention to herself. If she peeled off now, she would most likely put herself in the line of fire.

"Then you hunker down and *stay put*."

For once in her life, Margot wasn't going to argue.

She wasn't sure how long she stayed tucked in the front seat, ducked low so that she could see but her head was covered. She didn't think the sniper could see her car based on the angle where the others had been shot, but she didn't know *what* he could see, so she wasn't about to try moving herself or the car.

She hated this, hated not being able to *do* anything. From her vantage point she could see the three bodies on the ground, and the person huddled in the sedan, doing the same thing as she was.

Sirens screamed, and red and blue lights bounced off the side of the buildings around her as the side street was suddenly filled with cruisers and unmarked cars.

A car pulled up close alongside hers and inside she spotted Leon's familiar face in the passenger seat. She rolled down her window, staying low. He was hunched down too.

"You OK, kid? See anything else?"

Margot shook her head. "No, he's been pretty quiet since he took out those two officers."

Leon grimaced, mirroring how Margot felt. "Any movement from them?"

"No," she said, wishing she had any other answer to offer.

A big, armored truck pulled onto the street, the bright white lettering on the side announcing SFPD SWAT. These guys were the only option they had right now. Helmets and armor and expertise meant they would at least be able to get to the person in the sedan and check on the fallen officers.

Margot watched the highly trained SWAT unit, equipped with military-level gear, move in formation down the block. They stopped at the cruiser near the mouth of the street where the first officers on scene after her had been shot down.

While she wasn't expecting anything, a strangled sob of relief bubbled out of her when one of the SWAT officers turned and shouted, "We got a live one here."

A second crew moved in from somewhere Margot couldn't see, converging on the spot with the fallen officer. The one who had been shot in the chest must have been wearing a bullet-proof vest, as they'd been instructed to.

Son of a bitch was the luckiest man on the street today if he made it.

The second SWAT crew formed a huddle around the fallen man while the primary group headed out onto Broadway in the direction of the first shooting. Margot waited, holding her breath, expecting a hail of gunfire to litter the street, but there was only silence.

Everyone waited. The SWAT crew on Broadway moved in toward the cruiser first and after confirming the downed officer was beyond saving, they headed toward the sedan. After a few more moments they moved away and back toward the side street Margot was on. She craned to look at the car, which was now empty, meaning that the person was somewhere amid the huddled group of armored bodies.

Still, they waited, dozens of officers and task force members stuck in their cars just itching for the moment they could move into action.

Silence owned the street.

The sound of heavy footfalls echoed as two groups of SWAT members shuffled back toward their van. One had the sedan driver, one the injured cop. As soon as they were back at the armored truck the two survivors were loaded in and the truck backed out of the lane.

One of the SWAT team broke away from the group, and came and tapped on the driver's window of Leon's car.

"We've got the survivors out. Looks like it's clear, but I'm going to recommend no one go out on that street for the foreseeable future. This street is good to go." He pointed to the side road they were on. "Survivors are being taken to the waiting ambulances a few blocks over."

Leon gave the man a nod. "Thank you." As the SWAT team disappeared from view, presumably heading back to another truck Margot couldn't see, Leon looked at her. "We're going to meet back at the station, if you're feeling up to it. I can have a word with the captain on your behalf if you'd like."

Since Margot had quite literally broadcast her presence on the scene over the radio, there was no way they could play it off like she hadn't been there.

"That's OK, there's no point in us both getting in trouble."

She waited for the street to clear. A few cruisers set up near the end of the road, but further back from the abandoned cruiser. At some point someone would need to come in and help remove the two bodies, but there was no safe way to do it yet, and putting anyone at risk—even the well-armed SWAT crew— for men who were already dead just wasn't worth the danger.

Margot stared at the bodies as she waited for her turn to leave.

Ed's words reverberated in her memory as if he were whispering them in her ear again now.

*That doesn't necessarily scream* military *to me. To me that says* cop.

Margot started her car and headed back to the station, the thought on her heels, chasing her every step of the way.

She didn't *want* to think it was a cop, especially not when he'd now taken down two men in uniform, but maybe there was something to the theory. Had he been listening in to the radio, as she had? Waiting for the perfect moment, where he knew a cruiser would be in his line of sight before striking? Had the police been his intended target? That seemed likely in this case, more so than the others before it.

As Margot made the trip back to the station, she knew that there were going to be a lot of hard truths the task force would need to face after this shooting, and the hardest of all might be acknowledging that someone with a badge might be behind this rampage.

# THIRTY-SEVEN

The first person Margot saw when she came through the police station doors was Wes.

She wasn't sure what it was about his presence, about the solid figure of him, or the way his brows knit in concern as soon as he saw her, but she almost broke right on the spot.

Had she not spent a good chunk of her evening crying beside a pond in Petaluma, she would have lost it then and there. As it was, she still let Wes wrap his arms around her in a wordless hug. And while she didn't cry, she felt something leave her body as she curled into the warmth of him, letting the smell of his cologne and his general Wes-ness create a shield between her and the rest of the world.

She knew she couldn't stay there, and it was just a temporary balm, but she needed this more than she could have put into words. Margot didn't know if Wes instinctively understood what she needed in that moment, or if it was the only move he knew how to offer in a time of hardship, but whatever the reason, she was grateful for him and his strong arms.

When he released her from the hug, he kept his arm around her, guiding her with the flow of traffic toward the meeting room. Even though it was after eleven at night and it should have only been the overnight crew working, the station was packed, and it was standing room only when they got into the task force's meeting space. Wes dropped his arm as they entered the room, and Margot felt emptier without it.

Leon was already waiting at the front along with the captain. Margot was aware of the captain's gaze sliding over her as she entered the room, but his expression remained unchanged. It was hard to know if he was going to read her the riot act for her involvement or just let it go. He *should* have been furious, but Margot knew that any cop in her shoes would have done the exact same thing—including him.

Maybe he understood that as well.

There were battles to be picked in their situation and she had a feeling this might be one she was allowed to walk away from.

And if not, then she would deal with the repercussions.

For the time being there were two dead police officers to be mourned and a killer who wasn't going anywhere unless he was stopped. There was no doubt he was targeting the police intentionally now. As Leon reviewed the details of the shooting, he brought up pictures of the two deceased officers. One was in his forties—Margot assumed this was the one who had died making the traffic stop—his name was Thomas Yoakum. The responding officer who had been shot in the head had only been twenty-three. His name was Chris Reade. Leon was monotone when he explained that Reade had just gotten married four months earlier.

Reade's partner, who had survived and was presently in the hospital, was an older vet of the force named Duncan Plymouth, and Leon let them know his condition was serious but good.

"Let that be a reminder to everyone here that we *do not*

leave this station without a vest on. All active-duty officers, regardless of detail, need to be wearing their vests."

Margot knew the general view of the team was that the vests had done little to protect Reade and Yoakum, both of whom had been killed instantly by headshots, but no one said anything out loud. The tone of the whole room was a somber one, and, despite how many people were crammed into the small space, a chilly silence hung in the air.

The captain stepped up to speak. "I just got off the phone with Special Agent Andrew Rhodes of the FBI."

Margot's ears pricked up. She felt like she'd just walked into a room where people had been talking about her behind her back.

"The task force had teamed with FBI connections to test the ballistics on some of the bullets we retrieved from the first crime scene, and Rhodes was able to give me the report on those findings tonight."

Well, he had told her he had them; apparently he must have realized the sooner the better to pass over what he'd learned rather than waiting to meet with her later in the week. She wondered if Andrew had also told the captain what Margot had been up to that afternoon.

It wouldn't surprise her.

Maybe it would even work in her favor, but she doubted it.

"We reviewed the data they collected, and we know that the weapon used is a Remington M24 firing a 51mm NATO cartridge. The bad news for us is that the M24, while commonly used in police and military circles is also a non-restricted weapon, meaning anyone can buy it if they have their appropriate license. The FBI is currently doing a statewide check to see how many registered owners of M24s there are, focusing in the Bay Area. We've provided them with a list of names of persons of interest we've gotten from the hotline, but this isn't going to be instant, it might take us a day or so to get any kind of traction on that. I know we all want quick answers and swift action, I know we've been leaning hard on you to get us results, but now in addition to a need for action I must ask you all to be patient."

A buzz filled the room. It was obvious no one present wanted to lie low and do nothing, especially not if it meant the FBI was doing all the legwork, but Margot was just glad to have the computing power of the bigger force on their side. The FBI could cross-check databases that the cops would be waiting for weeks and getting bogged down with request paperwork to gain access to. This was a good thing.

The FBI could follow the leads she had given Leon.

That didn't mean it didn't kill her to be told to do nothing.

The captain raised his hand, commanding their attention again. "Calm down, calm down. I'm not suggesting we do nothing. We still have *hundreds* of tips we need to dig through, and we'll be divvying that work up at the end of this meeting. For the time being we are going on a non-active radio protocol. We will not be broadcasting our assignment locations over a public scanner. All officers will either get a direct contact based on known coordinates, or they'll call in direct to dispatch when they are free to respond to a call. This isn't ideal, it's a pain in the ass, but it's a level of added protection we need right now to keep our officers safe. I expect the same from everyone in this room. No one shares their location on an open radio frequency for the time being. We don't want to create any unnecessary targets."

Not that there were *necessary* targets.

A uniformed officer moved through the group and handed out folders to everyone present. Margot flipped hers open, looking at a familiar stack of transcribed messages. She slipped out of the task force meeting room and Wes was right behind her, his own folder in hand.

When they got back to their office she settled at her desk,

surprised to see a cup of coffee sitting at the desk across from hers. Then she remembered she wasn't supposed to be here right now, and their little office was likely to get pretty tight sharing with the two other detectives who swapped shifts with them.

As if reading her mind, Wes said, "Garvey and O'Halloran are out on a call, we should be on our own for a bit."

He was watching her carefully; she could feel his eyes on her even as she focused on the folder in front of her. Without looking up, she said, "I'm OK, Wes. I promise."

"You know it would be OK if you weren't, right?"

That gave her a little chuckle. She turned to face him. "Trust me, when the opportunity finally arises for me to have a good, proper meltdown, I'll do it. I'll take to my chambers and behave like an old Englishwoman whose daughters refuse to get married. But I don't have the luxury of not being OK right now. Maybe someday the world will stop burning down around me, but today sure as fuck ain't the day."

A knock sounded at the office door, and of course the nature of perfect timing meant that Leon and the captain were standing in the frame, most likely having overheard much of her outburst. That was just the way things went.

"Phalen," the captain said, clearing his throat. "A word?"

She sighed and followed both men to the captain's office, not bothering to take a look back at Wes for moral support. She had been hopeful she could get through the night just doing her job, but it seemed that wasn't going to be the case.

Inside the captain's office Margot didn't bother to look around, she just stared at his World's Best Grandpa mug and hoped this would be over soon. Leon sat next to her, but she couldn't even look at him. She wondered if this was how people felt when they'd been led to the guillotine. Just waiting for the blade to fall, not looking out into the crowd for hope of rescue.

"I don't think you need me to tell you that it was an outrageously stupid idea for you to drive onto an active sniper call without adequate gear or preparation or backup." The captain rearranged some already perfectly tidy folders on his desk.

Margot wasn't sure if this was a statement that needed her acknowledgement, so she nodded her head uncertainly. "Yes, sir. I happened to be close to the area when the call came across. I acted more on instinct than planning. I'm sorry."

He cleared his throat again, forcing her to look right at him. When she did, she was surprised by how unexpectedly... kind his expression was. "Margot, I'm not here to censure you. Yes, you completely ignored my requests to stay out of the field, and perhaps that's my fault for not placing you on a true suspension, but you're a good police officer—a great one, even—and I don't feel that your record deserves to be besmirched by a suspension. When I asked you to step back from active duty, I did it out of a place of genuine concern, and that concern still stands. But all the same, I think both Leon and I agree that your actions today and quick response at the scene probably saved a lot of lives."

"I wish it had saved more," she said, thinking of Reade, whose new wife was now a widow.

"We always wish we could save more, Detective." He opened a folder, giving it a brief review. "Special Agent Rhodes had a lot to say about you during our conversation this evening," he continued.

"Oh?"

"Says we should be grateful you never applied for the academy. That you would have made a damn fine agent. And I never like to agree with the FBI, but I suspect he might be right about that. He told me that your work with Ed Finch has been instrumental to the FBI in helping close not one but two cold cases this year, including the Marissa Loewen case. That's been a blight on the California cold case list for decades."

She wasn't sure what response felt right, so she just said, "Thank you, sir."

"You and I briefly talked about my concerns about you interacting with Ed, and how I don't necessarily think it's good for you. But after speaking with Special Agent Rhodes, my opinion might be swayed slightly."

Margot wanted to tell him his first opinion was absolutely correct, and that frequent visits to her father were doing more damage to her psyche than she thought possible. She wanted him to tell her to stop immediately. To say that if she didn't stop, her job would be on the line.

Instead, he said, "I'm going to reconsider my opinion on keeping you deskbound. For now. I need you out on the street working this sniper case, and it's clear to me that the work you're doing in your spare time hasn't impacted your ability to do your job. So effective immediately I'm going to reinstate you, but I *would* still like a report from your therapist letting me know his independent assessment of how you're handling all this, OK? This is highly irregular, given everything you've experienced, but I think what you did tonight—however foolish— shows me who you really are in a situation of stress. And that's someone we need on our side."

"Thank you, sir," she said again, this time meaning it.

He handed her the folder he'd been holding. "I want you to take a small group over and speak to this caller that you flagged. We've been unable to reach anyone in the household by phone, and his history with the police department, while excellent, is not without its concerns. He applied several times for SWAT and was denied each time. I think you're right, there's a red flag there, so proceed with abundant caution."

The sheer *force* of the vindication Margot felt in that moment outweighed her relief at being taken off desk duty. She had felt in her gut that something wasn't right with the Savoys, and hearing her opinion parroted back to her from the captain made her feel euphoric.

She took the folder and shook the captain's hand, then gave

Leon a grateful nod of acknowledgment. There wasn't much she could say in the captain's office, but she knew her restoration to active service had a lot more to do with Leon and Andrew than it did with her own merits.

Later, when she had a real opportunity to mull over what she'd heard tonight, she might start to wonder about Andrew's game plan. He had outright lied to the captain about her mental state, and while he might have thought he was doing her a favor, Margot had serious doubts about his motives.

That was for another time, though, when lives weren't in the balance.

Wes glanced up from his folder, a phone in the crook of his neck, and gave her a curious look as she came back to her desk.

"All good?" he asked.

"Defying all logic and expectation, actually, yes. I'm back, baby." She did a miniature victory dance at her desk, which made her partner chuckle. "We need to go check on one of those calls I flagged the other day. Seems like the guy might have reason to feel a bit slighted by the SFPD and he hasn't been answering calls. Neither has the wife, which makes me a bit nervous."

"Oh shit, before we look at that and I forget to tell you, Garvey and I talked to the Caravan driver. He lawyered up *instantly*, but we've got him back in holding for at least forty-eight. Maybe after we talk to Savoy you want to take a crack at him? Something tells me he's the kind of guy who would respond well to the, shall we say, feminine touch?"

She wrinkled her nose. "Gross." She grabbed her jacket, which she'd barely had off. "At least he's on ice for the time being. What vibe did you get?"

"He's married. Kids. And he was definitely cagey, but it's hard to know if that's more about the cops showing up to ask him about a dead hooker when his wife was busy making dinner, or because he actually killed the girl. He's hiding *some-*

*thing* though, and he gives me the fucking creepy-crawlies. I want your take on it; Garvey just assumed he was on edge because of the wife. I think it's something else."

"Wonder how Mr. Suburbs will feel spending a night in holding with some drug dealers."

Wes smirked. "At the very worst he's going to have a hell of a story to share with his golf buddies once he stops shitting himself."

Wes put on his coat, and they headed out into the pen. Margot normally would have grabbed Leon to tag along with them, but he was occupied by task force duties, and the captain seemed glued to his right arm. What they needed for this stop wasn't another detective, *per se*, they needed an armed escort.

Margot moved toward the main lobby of the station—the precinct was divided by divisions, with homicide, vice, and major crimes on one side, and uniformed officers on the opposite side. She found the on-duty lieutenant sitting in his office, mournfully prodding at a rice cake.

He glanced up at them as they entered. "Wife thinks high cholesterol is going to kill me," he said with a heavy sigh.

"Is it at least a flavored one?" Wes asked.

"Buttered popcorn."

"The caramel corn ones aren't half-bad," Margot offered.

"Noted. What can I do for you, Detectives?"

"We're going to question a person of interest on the sniper case. Hoping we could get a couple of your cars to follow us— lights off—and offer some backup if needed. Obviously, we need some vigilant officers on this. No rookies."

The lieutenant nodded gravely and looked at his computer screen, assessing which cars were available, and doing some mental gymnastics to determine who was best for the job. He reached for his radio, and said, "Cars 24, 81, and 53 please contact HQ." He glanced over at the detectives as he set the radio down. "We're working through the new directives. It's not easy to re-train habits overnight. We get 'em to call dispatch for general commands, but HQ is a call to my desk for special instruction. Anything with addresses, y'know?"

"10-4," crackled through the radio in three different voices.

"What's the address?" the lieutenant asked, and Margot handed him the Post-it she'd brought with the Savoy address on it. As the three different units called in, the lieutenant passed on the address, Margot's phone number—also on the slip—and their instructions. "Lights and sirens off. Stay out of direct sight. Await instruction from your lead."

The team assembled, and instructions given, Margot and Wes headed to his car, and as they set off Margot did something she rarely ever did.

She said a prayer.

## THIRTY-EIGHT

The lights of the Savoy house were off, but that didn't mean no one was home.

The screen of Margot's phone said it was 12:17 a.m., a time when most sensible couples in their fifties or sixties would likely be in bed. Margot wouldn't have been surprised to see the flickering blue light of a TV on somewhere in the house, but she also wasn't surprised to see nothing.

Next to her, Wes shifted his weight in the driver's seat. He was a tightly coiled spring, and she was feeding off his tension.

Around the roof of the low bungalow there were Christmas lights, which were the only illumination around the home at all.

The little house had no yard to speak of, just a concrete lot with terracotta planters bursting with flowers and cacti placed around to give the space color. A pink bougainvillea was just entering its winter bloom on a trellis next to the front door.

Overall, the house—located on a quiet but rough-looking block in Oakland—seemed typical of its type, something bought before Bay Area prices chased the working class further and further out, in an area that would likely be a plum target for gentrification in a few years.

The Savoy house was neither overly nice, nor too run-down, it looked like what it was; a small family home.

The car Margot had seen Erica driving was parked out front, along with a white pickup truck that had a few dents and scrapes on the doors.

Did you really live in the Bay if your car hadn't been annihilated by your fellow drivers at some point? Margot didn't think so. Her own car—a vintage model—seemed to garner a little more respect from others, but that didn't mean it hadn't incurred some damage in its time. She was grateful for indoor parking at her complex, a rare treat in the city, but one that had been non-negotiable when she looked for a place to rent.

They'd been parked just down the block from the house for fifteen minutes, carefully observing for any signs of activity. They'd barely spoken the whole time, but despite his obvious anxiety, she was glad Wes was with her. The white truck was registered to John. Margot tried to plot out a timeline of the night. She had left Petaluma around nine and arrived in the city around nine fifty. It had been just before ten when she reached the shooting scene. The ordeal in the street had felt interminable, but she'd been back to the police station by eleven. Given that the shooter had more time to move than they did, since they'd needed to be sure the coast was clear, if it *had* been John, then he would have had plenty of time to move from wherever his sharpshooter nest had been to get home.

If Erica had already been tucked into bed—much like her own mother had been while Ed had been out "hunting"—then he could very easily have just slid himself in beside her and no one would have been the wiser.

The Bay Bridge was a toll bridge, and Margot could make out the familiar shape of the San Francisco FasTrak toll badge, an automated electronic toll reader. For anyone who made regular trips to San Francisco from Oakland or vice-versa it was an essential.

It also meant that if John *was* their man, they'd have plenty of data to trace his movements if and when it came time to prosecute.

For now, they just wanted to talk.

Margot checked her vest, the slight pinch of it under her arms feeling strangely comforting rather than a distraction. She was also keenly aware that there were no high-rise buildings around them, so nowhere obvious for a shooter to be watching from. In a city that was almost all hills and high points, it was nice to find the one place where she didn't have to worry there might be a target on the top of her scalp.

She wasn't foolish enough to believe they were *safe* if this turned out to be their guy, but there was a tiny sense of relief in knowing her lack of a tactical helmet wasn't going to be the death of her.

Leon had called a minute earlier and told them he had rerouted a SWAT crew to her area but was keeping them a few blocks away to avoid raising any alarms if Savoy was their man.

The highly trained team felt like guardian angels or imaginary friends. She knew they were there, she just couldn't see them.

"You ready for this?" she asked Wes.

He hadn't cracked a joke in twenty minutes, which was really the only answer she needed to know where his mental state was at.

He grimaced. "No, not really. I think after that fuckery at the apartment I'm just assuming every interview is going to turn into the goddamn OK Corral, y'know?"

"Hey, at least Van Dad didn't pull a gun on you."

"That's true. We'll call that one a win."

They were dawdling, and it wasn't clear if the hesitation was due to fear that Savoy *was* their man, or fear he *wasn't* and the real shooter was still out there.

Margot took a breath and got out first, the night air cool and surprisingly bracing. She jogged across the street, not wanting to be out in the open longer than necessary. Pulling out her phone she dialed one of the officers parked further down the block to have them on the line since they were staying off the radio.

"Car 53 we are on the move, heading up to the front door. No motion, no sign of activity. Gonna just leave you guys on the line, move in if you hear the word."

She heard a muffled "10-4" as she lowered her phone hand and pulled out her gun. While they had no immediate threat, given what had happened that evening—not to mention what had happened during her last interview—Margot wasn't about to play it too safe. The gun's safety remained on, but having it in her hand made her feel better.

She knew Wes had done the same. Even though he'd gotten out after her, his long legs carried him ahead and put him through the wrought iron gate that surrounded the property first. He cleared the porch steps in two swift motions and then looked back at her. She gave a nod.

Her heart was in her throat, making it hard for her to swallow or breathe. Something about this didn't feel *wrong*, but it felt right in a way that was terrifying.

Wes stepped to the side of the front door, away from the window beside it, and rang the bell before quickly following that with a quick series of knocks. "John and Erica Savoy? This is the San Francisco Police Department. We need to speak with you both immediately."

Margot thought about Erica, about the tension in the woman's eyes and the earnest fear she had shown both times she appeared at the station. She hoped John had remained blissfully unaware of those visits, and of her call. She hoped that by being here she hadn't put Erica into her husband's crosshairs.

Wes knocked again when there was no sign of light or movement in the house.

"Let's try around back?" she suggested.

A sick, sinking feeling in her stomach was starting to creep in on top of the anxiety. In a house this small the knocking and the doorbell should have woken anyone asleep inside, no matter how deeply they normally slept. All around them the neighbors' lights were coming on, and already curious onlookers were sneaking out onto their front steps to see what was happening.

Margot and Wes skirted around the side of the house to the back door, where Wes repeated his knocking and again, there was no response. The back door had no curtain on it, offering a clear look into the kitchen, and when no one came to the door, Margot decided to risk it and looked through.

The kitchen was mostly dark, but there was a peninsula counter dividing the kitchen from the tiny dining room. On the floor, just beyond the peninsula, was a pair of bare feet sticking up. One still had a slipper half-on.

"Oh Jesus," Margot whispered. She took out her phone. "Car 53, we're requesting immediate backup. I'm entering the premises on grounds of exigent circumstances. I see a body on the floor. We're at the back door." Giving this explanation over the phone instead of over a radio broadcast was, she realized, pointless. But if they were later questioned about her reasons for smashing out the back window of the house without a warrant, she wanted someone *other* than Wes to be able to back her up.

Margot smashed in the window, then, covering her hand with her jacket sleeve, fumbled for the lock, pulling the door open to allow Wes to enter ahead of her. As she brought her arm back through she cut her nice leather jacket to bits. Better the jacket than her arm. Inside, Wes covered her as she made her way to the dining room, setting her phone on the peninsula to free up one hand.

Erica Savoy was already dead, Margot didn't need a medical degree to know that. Her skin was waxy and gray and her eyes had already taken on a milky whiteness. The blood pooled around her head had congealed hours ago, and a lazy fly buzzed around the bullet hole on the woman's forehead. Margot checked the pulse on Erica's wrist anyway, the skin so cold when she touched it that she jerked her hand back on instinct before actually being able to check.

No pulse.

She'd been dead at least a day, maybe longer.

Bootsteps clomped up the back stairs as the two officers from Car 53 appeared in the doorway. Margot felt bad, she hadn't even learned their names. One was a woman in her early fifties, her red hair going gray, pulled back in a severe bun. She didn't wear a lick of makeup, but her skin was impressively flawless. Her nametag read O'Connell.

Her partner was in his thirties, dark hair and a neatly trimmed beard. His expression was a bit higher key than his partner's as his eyes darted around the kitchen and beyond, half expecting a monster to jump out at him any moment. His nametag read Farrow.

Lights out front announced the arrival of the other cars. No sense in being subtle with their approach now.

"We need to check the whole house. She lived here with her husband. Former cop. Be careful, be attentive," Margot directed, standing over Erica is if protecting her from prying eyes.

She was just following O'Connell into the living room when she heard Wes's voice call out from a room just beyond. "Margot, I think I just found John Savoy."

Margot was sure when she walked into the bedroom she was going to find the husband with a handgun in his mouth, the sniper rifle lying at his side. So when she followed Wes's voice into the primary bedroom and found John lying still tucked into bed, wearing a pajama set in a matching fabric to the one Erica had been in, with an identical gunshot wound to the head, she was briefly stunned into silence.

John Savoy hadn't killed himself.

He'd been murdered.

Margot and Wes exchanged mutually shell-shocked expressions, and she was about to ask him if he had any ideas when one of the officers shouted from the room next door. "Hey Detectives, I think you're going to want to come have a look at this."

Still half in the hallway, Margot stepped next door, where O'Connell had continued her efforts to clear the house. The home had looked so small on the outside, Margot had assumed it was only a one bedroom, but here was an obvious second bedroom.

*Spartan* was the only word for the space.

At first, Margot thought it might just be a guest bedroom with no personality, but as she looked around, it became apparent in very subtle ways that the space was regularly used. The closet was filled with almost identical clothing, a few white dress shirts, charcoal trousers, plain Nike runners all lined up in perfect order.

On the dresser were a comb and a used tube of deodorant. The bed had been made with military precision, not a crease to be seen, and on the nightstand was a Bible and an empty glass of water.

O'Connell was standing next to the desk, shining her flashlight down on something.

The paper was the only thing in the room that showed signs of distress. It was wrinkled and re-smoothed, as if someone had crumpled it in their hands and then reconsidered.

The date on the top was from three weeks earlier. Margot recognized the letterhead immediately.

*Dear John,*

*We wanted to take a moment to thank you for your application to the San Francisco Police Department. We regret to inform you that after reviewing your written application and subsequent professional examinations, we will not be asking you to attend future interviews. We thank you for your time, but request you not submit any new applications going forward.*

*With our thanks,*

*Captain Tildon Marsh*

*Head of Recruitment*

Margot reread the letter several times, her gaze circling back to the date, to the wrinkles, the address that wasn't for this house but an apartment in the Tenderloin area of San Francisco, and then landing on the addressee's name at the top.

*John Savoy Jr.*

She looked around the room again, the minimalism suddenly taking on a more sinister overtone.

"We need to find—"

Margot didn't get to finish her sentence before the big glass window over John Jr's bed shattered. Margot grabbed O'Connell and yanked her to the floor as a volley of bullets peppered the interior of the house.

# THIRTY-NINE

Glass and drywall dust showered the room, and pieces of the broken window bit into Margot's skin as she covered her head. She had instinctively fallen across Officer O'Connell, who had also huddled into a ball, and they stayed together, tucked under the desk, until the shooting stopped.

The reprieve was short.

Shouts reverberated outside, and for the first time since the gunfire began, Margot remembered they weren't alone here.

The deep, masculine voice of one of the SWAT team members bellowed out through a loudspeaker, waking any of the neighborhood who had managed to sleep through the hail of bullets.

"We have your position surrounded. Come out with your hands up."

At first Margot thought they were directing this at the Savoy house, until a short *crackcrackcrack* of gunfire sounded from the house next to them, and she realized the truth.

John Savoy. Or more specifically, John Savoy Jr., was holed up next door and had been watching as they prowled through his house and found his parents dead. With the little bungalows so close together—and Margot and Wes announcing their presence when they knocked—he would have had no trouble knowing when they arrived.

Margot squeezed O'Connell's shoulder and when the older woman looked at her, Margot pointed toward the hallway. The pair of them moved across the carpet, crawling on elbows instead of hands to avoid the sparkling glass everywhere around them. In the hallway, Wes was on the ground, pressed up against the wall.

It looked like he had been coming their direction, and Margot saw the immediate flash of relief on his face when he spotted them.

Margot glanced around and saw one of the officers who had followed them into the house on the carpet halfway in and halfway out of the primary bedroom. He'd taken a shot through the throat.

There was nothing anyone could do for him.

Two more officers were down on the ground in the living room, but Margot could see that both were alive. One was holding her shoulder, a clear wince of pain pinching her features, though she appeared far more torn up about her fallen partner.

Margot crawled over to Wes, and leaned back against the wall, where bullets had punched holes into the drywall two feet over their heads, shattering framed family photos.

O'Connell sat across from them and Margot was impressed by her almost stoic countenance. The past few minutes had been a hell of a ride, but O'Connell only seemed focused on finding her partner once her gaze skimmed over the body on the floor a few feet away.

"Farrow," she whispered through clenched teeth. "You OK?"

"Yeah," came the answering call from the living room.

They couldn't risk much more beyond that, not without knowing where Savoy was.

O'Connell sat back, letting her head thump against the wall with a short sigh of relief.

Shouting continued from outside, escalated by the arrival of more sirens, more officers. Margot tried to figure out what was happening but being stuck on the floor and forced to avoid windows, she was basing everything she knew on little snippets coming in through the broken windows, and whatever the SWAT guy shouted on his loudspeaker.

Margot was kicking herself for leaving her phone on the counter in the kitchen, until she remembered that her call had been connected to Car 53. To O'Connell. She looked at the woman across from her with renewed interest.

"O'Connell, you still got your phone on you?"

The officer gave her a quizzical look, as if wondering who the hell she wanted to call at a time like this. The police were already here to give them backup. She didn't speak the question aloud, though, and instead offered Margot her phone, the call with Margot's own cell phone still connected.

Margot hung up on herself and dialed Leon's number from memory.

"Detective Leon Telly," he said formally, his voice tight with concern. "Make it quick."

"It's Margot."

"Oh, thank fucking Jesus! I've been trying to call you, but the line goes right to voicemail. Where are you?"

"We're inside the Savoy house. Can you let the officers outside know that the name of the sniper is John Savoy *Junior*. He killed his parents, not sure what he's done to the neighbors, but that's where he's holed up. Got rejected from the police department. Reading between the lines—and the bullet holes in the house—I'd say it was something on his psych eval. Not sure if knowing who he is will help talk him down. Guy seems to be hell-bent on playing suicide by cop."

Leon sighed but couldn't disagree. Savoy had to know that after killing multiple police officers there wasn't going to be much lenience for him. He would be going to jail for the rest of his life, likely joining Ed on Death Row. Given the choices between rotting in jail and going down in a storm of bullets, they both knew the likely outcome here.

"I'm on my way there right now, you stay put and stay safe. Don't think the captain had this in mind when he said you could go back on active duty."

That made Margot scoff out a laugh. "I might let him put me back behind the desk for a little while after this, not going to lie."

"You and me both," muttered Wes beside her, not getting Leon's side of the conversation, but obviously not needing it.

"See you soon, kid," Leon promised.

Margot handed the phone back to O'Connell, who pocketed it. "At least now they know who and why," Margot explained.

O'Connell sneered. "Naming the guy isn't going to help us much."

"It might help *them*"—Margot gestured toward the street— "and if anything happens to us, then at least they know who the guy is." That was the grimmest possibility, but considering the bullet holes torn through the entire house, it was an eventuality worth planning for.

Outside, the SWAT man was back on his loudspeaker. "John. John Savoy. We know what's going on and we want this to end peacefully. Please come out unarmed and this can all end peacefully."

*Peacefully* had been abandoned two dead parents and several rounds of ammunition earlier, but Margot was impressed with the SWAT guy's efforts.

"I'm not going to bow down to you *pigs*," came a shout from the house next door. With the bedroom windows all smashed open, it sounded as if John Savoy Jr was standing in the room with them. "If you had wanted me so bad, you wouldn't have sent that fucking letter. Guess you want me now, don't you?"

There was simply no arguing with someone who saw things that way.

Margot stared into the spartan emptiness of John Jr.'s room, a space completely devoid of personality. She saw a grown man who wanted to walk in his father's footsteps. Likely so that he could accomplish the things his father hadn't been able to—namely an acceptance to the SWAT team—and now it seemed the only end in sight for this was John Jr. dying at the hands of the very team his father had wanted to be a part of.

It wasn't poetic, it was just deeply, tragically sad.

The shouting on the street took on a new and frantic tenor, and Margot instinctively leaned forward, tucking her head between her knees, and covering her ears. There was a tension turning seconds into hours and causing her to feel her own pulse in her mouth. The threat of imminent danger came to a boil, and one of the cops in the living room said, "Is that nutcase going to do what I think he's going to do?"

Margot lifted her head enough to see that Farrow, O'Connell's partner, had crawled up to the front window and had raised up enough to peek outside.

"Christ, Farrow, *get down*," his partner warned.

In her imagination, Margot saw him die like she had seen so many others die at the hands of Savoy's single-minded mania. She pictured the pink haze of brain matter, the way his body would slump like a marionette whose strings had been cut.

Instead, he dropped back to the floor and scuttled safely away from the window. Margot almost breathed a sigh of relief when a chorus of voices on the front street started to shout the same instructions at different times, their words muddled and confusing.

"—down—"

"—drop your—"

"—don't shoo—"

"—last chance—"

The directions were lost under the sound of a shout, and then a barrage of gunfire. Margot had no idea who was firing. Wes grabbed her, shielding her body with his, and muffling the sound of the frenzy happening just outside.

A minute, maybe an hour, maybe a lifetime later, everything was quiet.

"*Clear, clear, clear,*" someone screamed outside, and a few moments later heavy footfalls pounded through the Savoy house. She looked up from her place on the ground to see a fully outfitted SWAT member standing over her, his rifle aimed to the floor. Someone behind him stooped to check the pulse of the dead police officer on the ground.

"He's gone," a feminine voice said. Over her shoulder-mounted radio she said, "We've got a deceased officer in the house." They already knew about the dead parents, thanks to Margot's call.

"Everyone else in here OK?" The lead SWAT officer lifted his tactical visor. While Margot couldn't see much of his face, he did have kind eyes.

"Lexington needs an ambulance," Farrow stated, reminding Margot of the female officer who had been holding it together remarkably well up to that point.

"Did you get him?" Wes asked.

"Not alive," the lead SWAT officer said grimly.

"Good," mumbled O'Connell under her breath, accepting a hand up from the female SWAT officer.

Margot didn't feel good about celebrating a death, but in this one instance, she was inclined to agree.

# FORTY

The story about the discovery of Marissa Loewen's body was relegated to a tiny corner of the front page of the *Sentinel* the next morning. Margot was just getting back to her apartment when a bundle of early editions hit the stoop, and the doorman handed her one as she shuffled zombie-like through the lobby.

She had a brief visit with an EMT at the scene of the Savoy shooting, and they had patched her up with little butterfly bandages—not cute children's bandages, but little white ones designed for minor injuries. And that was what her external injuries were: mild.

Her jacket had suffered more damage that night than her body.

Her mind, on the other hand, was going to take a little time to get right again.

Brody, the front desk attendant, gave her a questioning look as she made her way to the elevator, but she simply offered him a wave and a gentle smile, showing him the front page of the paper by way of explanation.

"Rough night at the office." She tried to keep her tone light, but her throat was scratchy, and she was so deeply exhausted that there wasn't any humor to be offered.

Safely locked in her apartment, she tossed her destroyed jacket on the couch, knowing it was a lost cause. Sometimes it felt lonely coming back to this place by herself, but tonight the mis-matched furniture and the TV set she'd left on earlier so she wouldn't come home to silence, were like a balm. It had been a long time since Margot had really felt *home* anywhere.

She realized now, she felt a sense of peace here, among the hideous old paintings she'd taken off a street corner, and the pilled crochet throw blanket from Grandma Pat. This was a space that was hers and hers alone, untouched by what she'd experienced as a child.

After the night she'd just had, she was grateful to have this to come back to. She ignored her growling stomach, downed a glass of water in one long draft, and threw herself fully clothed onto her bed, pulling the crochet throw over herself, because getting under the duvet was too much effort.

She woke up ten hours later to her phone ringing over and over again.

Groggily she pulled the phone to her ear, stunned she'd remembered to plug it in to charge before she fell asleep. She had thought it was impressive enough she remembered to take it from the Savoy house on their way out.

She was also grateful that she had texted Dr. Singh after the events of the previous day to bump their appointment a few days. He had been very understanding, given the outrageous circumstances.

"Unh." It was the best anyone was going to get from her.

"Good evening to you, too, sweetheart," crooned the all-too-chipper voice of Wes Fox.

Margot frowned. "Why do you sound like you just got laid? No one should be that cheerful after the night we had."

"Well, I was just wondering if, perhaps, you might feel

inclined to solve a murder case with me tonight? Van Dad's forty-eight-hour hold is going to be up soon and I think we're going to be up a creek on that one if we don't get him talking soon."

Margot flopped onto her back, staring up at the ceiling and wondering when the last time she cleaned her ceiling fan was. Had she ever done it? Maybe if she took a week off of work after all this, she could give the apartment a deep clean.

She was also, against her better judgment, planning to call her brother and tell him he should come for Christmas as he had suggested. While the idea didn't fill her with excitement, she was also feeling very aware of the fleeting nature of life right then. It might be nice to spend the holidays with the one living person in her family who didn't make her feel violently ill whenever she visited him.

"You want me to interrogate a suspect. Now?" The clock on her nightstand said it was almost five. Her curtains were closed but she knew it was probably already dark again. She'd missed the whole day.

"I think now is the *perfect* time for you to interview a suspect."

Margot wanted to argue that this was an insane perspective, given everything they'd gone through—everything *she* had gone through—in the last two days, but she also knew that Genesis deserved closure for her death just as Marissa did.

The newspaper was lying next to her on the pillow. The headline read, *Marissa Loewen recovered after twenty-nine years.* The sub-headline added, *The cold case has been tied to notorious Bay Area serial killer Ed Finch.*

Margot had no doubt Sebastian would soon be needling her for follow-up details, especially since he knew she'd been involved in the Theresa Milotti case that summer.

Perhaps what Margot needed right now was a win. Finding John Savoy Jr. hadn't felt like a win. Yes, the sniper case was closed, the city could breathe easier at night, but all Margot could think about were the dead civilians who had just wanted to see the ocean; the cops who had just been doing their jobs.

Mostly she thought about Erica Savoy, lingering outside the station.

Erica had thought it was her husband.

She might have thought that right up until the moment her son killed her.

The case might have been closed, but Margot didn't feel *good* about it.

"Give me an hour. I need to shower and consume my weight in coffee, and then I'll be there. Make him sit in the room. No lawyer. He doesn't need to talk. He can wait and he can listen."

"That's my girl."

Margot's leather jacket had fallen onto the floor in the living room. It and her entire current outfit were beyond saving, they'd all need to be tossed in the trash. She stripped down, checking her body for nicks and scrapes she hadn't seen while clothed, but was pleased to find that her injuries were minimal and entirely superficial.

She showered, peeling off the tiny white bandages as she did, and then applied light makeup, not attempting to hide the cuts and small bruises on her face. As she was getting dressed, her phone rang again.

"I'm almost out the door, Wes, I promise."

A long pause on the other end told her she had made a mistake. "Detective Phalen?" The voice was familiar but in her current state of brain fog Margot couldn't quite place it. "It's Wally Albright."

The old Muir Woods warden.

"Oh my goodness, Wally. How are you doing? Did you see the news?" He'd been tough through the shooting they'd witnessed, but it had to have shaken him. She hoped that it brought him some peace knowing the shooter was no longer out there.

"I did, it's hard to miss. Sounds like he was a very damaged individual."

"Yes, I think you're right."

"I didn't call because of that, though, and you're obviously in the middle of something so I won't keep you. The last time we spoke you asked me if I could think about any cases in my history at the park that might have stood out as suspicious. I didn't think much of it at the time—as you can imagine we would remember murders—but I was going through some of my old logs this week."

Margot glanced at the clock on her nightstand, continuing to dress while Wally talked. She didn't want to rush him, but she did need to go.

"And these were, you understand, my journals from then. In a sense. Anyway, I was looking back and there was an entry in there from 2001. I wasn't a warden anymore, but we had a bit of hullabaloo one day when a hiker came across a body. Now, we very quickly determined that the dead woman had likely fallen while hiking by herself and the case was ruled an accidental death. But my notes had something interesting in them."

"Oh?"

"I just wrote one line and it said, *Why would she go hiking in those shoes?* And I'm sorry to tell you that's it. But it stood out as interesting and made me wonder if perhaps that death might not have been so accidental after all."

"Do you remember what shoes she was wearing?" Margot wasn't sure if there was anything to this tidbit, but it didn't hurt to ask.

"I don't, unfortunately. I wasn't out there personally when they found her, but I was the one who waited for the medical examiner to arrive. I remember them taking her out and thinking the shoes she was wearing were probably what had caused her to fall."

"Was her name in your journal?"

"Yes, we had to do an official incident report. Natasha Everett. I believe she was in her twenties. Like I said, I'm not sure if any of that helps you, but I thought I'd pass it along."

Margot jotted down the name and year of the event, plus the note *shoes?* on a notepad on her dining room table.

"Thank you, Wally, really. It might be nothing, but then again it might be something. I'll look into it."

"You're most welcome, Detective. And hey." A pause. "Good job on that shooting case."

Margot thought back to being huddled in the hallway of the Savoy house while the SWAT team had turned John Jr. into a piece of Swiss cheese outside. But there was no sense in explaining to Wally what a Pyrrhic victory the man's death really felt like to her, and likely to many others.

"Thanks."

She stuffed the note with his tip into the pocket of a different jacket, the khaki green safari jacket that was probably years out of style, briefly mourning the loss of her favorite leather one, and headed out the door.

Wes was waiting for her at the station, her ever-dutiful partner, a cup of coffee in his hands. It wasn't *fancy* coffee, but it was better than whatever shit would be in the break room that time of night. She took it gratefully

"Is he in the interview room?" she asked.

"I'm confident his butt cheeks are completely asleep at this point. He's been pacing."

"Perfect." Margot handed off her jacket. "How do I look?"

Wes seemed perplexed by the question, his expression slightly bemused. "Like you just left a bar fight, if we're being honest with each other."

"Perfect."

He, on the other hand, looked like he had woken up in the pages of a Pottery Barn catalog, the kind of place where human worries don't exist. He'd been in that house with her, and yet looked entirely unscathed.

It was a front, she knew, but a convincing one.

Margot gave him a smile and sipped her coffee. It was bitter, and that suited her just fine.

The man waiting in the interrogation room was precisely what she was expecting him to be. Middling. Boring. An average-height, average-weight, brown-haired, brown-eyed suburban schlub. A dime a dozen.

Desperate.

Desperate for anything to make his average, boring, humdrum life just a little special.

Margot sat down across from him, and he stared, slack-jawed, as if she had appeared from the ether and not through a door.

"It's about fucking *time*," he snapped. "I've been in here for a fucking hour."

She suspected he was about to say more, but then his gaze passed over her face and froze. *She* knew that the wounds were minor. *She* knew the cuts were already starting to heal. But what mattered to her most in that moment was that to *him* it would look like she'd just had a one-on-one fight with a plate-glass window and had won.

"Holy shit, are you OK?" He couldn't seem to help himself. He was a dad, after all. Even her own dad might have asked the same question.

She pushed that thought away and sipped her coffee as if she had no idea what he was talking about and didn't have a single care in the world. "Hmm? Fine. Yes." She set her drink down and opened up the folder she'd come into the room with, then started to lay photos out on the table, all facing him. High-resolution photos of a young woman, first as she had been in life, smiling, laughing, pretty. Then as she was in death, her face destroyed, her life over.

"I asked for a lawyer," the man said, refusing to look down. The room was hot, yes, but the sweat on his brow hadn't been there a moment ago.

"I know, and that's fine. You don't need to say anything. Actually, it's better if you don't say anything. I think for once you're going to listen."

Whatever he'd been expecting her to say, this hadn't been it. His mouth hung open and his jaw seemed desperate to form words, but Margot just lifted her finger to her mouth and said, "Shhh."

He fell mute.

Margot lifted one of the photos, forcing him to look at it.

It was one of the pictures of Genesis from when she'd been alive. They'd found it on her social media, the Coach purse clearly visible slung over her shoulder, a cocktail in her hand, and a laugh parting her bright pink lips.

"I think you know this woman. I think you *knew* her, very well. I will go so far as to say I *know* you bought her the purse in this photo. It's OK, don't worry about agreeing with me. You don't need to speak right now." She set the photo down again, picking up another one; here Genesis's head was just a caved-in hole of gore. The man—who Margot realized in this moment she hadn't even bothered to ask the name of—looked away. His name was irrelevant at the moment anyway. He was just another killer.

"You know what we call this? No, I know you can't answer, don't worry. We call this *overkill*. This is what happens when a killer knows a victim and has a personal attachment to them. When their rage over some perceived wrongdoing, or jealousy, leads them to do more than just *kill* a victim, they must obliterate them. But see, what you don't know, because you didn't stick around, was that this didn't kill her."

That got his attention. Instead of trying to avoid looking at the photo, he instead looked past it, at Margot. "What?"

"Yeah, she was still alive after all this. She was broken, she was in agony, but she was still alive. It took probably another hour for her to die. Choking slowly. Drowning in her own blood. Can you *imagine* how that felt for her? How much time she had to think about you betraying her. The man she thought she had trusted, the man she thought might be able to take her away from the life she was living. The man whose baby she was carrying."

Margot put the photo on the table and slid it across the surface, so it was right in front of him. He was still staring at her.

"Slowly drowning. On dry land. With no one to save her."

"No," he said. He was now looking past Margot, staring at the wall behind her, so she tapped the photo, forcing his attention back down.

"I can't ask you questions, I know that, I'm just going to brainstorm here. Maybe you killed her because you saw her with someone else that night. Or perhaps you killed her because she told you about the baby? Maybe she wanted money. There's always the chance she was threatening to tell your wife. I'd have to bring your wife here to ask her about that, though."

Van Dad's jaw was tight. Suddenly he swiped his arm over the table, scattering the photos. If he had been trying to spook Margot, though, he had picked the wrong week. She'd recently been sitting across from a serial killer, and she had told *him* to stick his opinions up his ass. So she was in no mood to be intimidated by a man with a paunch and a Planet Fitness membership.

"Are you done?" she asked.

"Fuck you," he snarled.

"I don't think I'm your type. I don't accept payment for services rendered."

For a moment, he looked as if he might hit her, and she locked her gaze on him, challenging him to try it. *Go ahead,* her eyes said. *Give it your best shot.*

Instead, his hands trembled, and he slumped back into the chair again. Margot lifted her hand off the table a fraction of an inch, just the most subtle wave to Wes who was likely ready to knock the door down, to let him know she was OK.

"I didn't want to do it," he said, his body suddenly shaking with sobs. "She didn't give me a choice."

She had him. While she couldn't interrogate him into confessing after he asked for a lawyer, there was no rule that said she couldn't sit in the room and state facts. And while his lawyer *was* on the way, there was also nothing to stop him from confessing of his own free will without a lawyer present.

It was a fine line, but Margot knew the rules. She hadn't broken them, just pressed them to their limit.

Margot gave a smile that didn't reach her eyes. "Why don't you start from the beginning?" she cooed. "Tell me everything."

And so, he did.

# FORTY-ONE

## JANUARY 1989

Petaluma, California

It may have been winter, but the sun was high in the sky and the weather was too nice to stay indoors.

Kim, whose temper was still on a knife's edge with Ed these days, suggested it might be fun to get the kids out for some fresh air while it was so lovely out. Weather in Northern California could be temperamental, sunny and warm one day, wet and miserable the next. The kids had been cooped up in the house over Christmas thanks to a long run of chilly days, and it seemed a pity to keep them trapped indoors on a day like this.

Ed, too, felt as if he'd been trapped inside. Kim watched him like a hawk, questioning where he was going whenever he left the house. Calling to check on him at work if he was running late. She had told him if he fucked up again she would be done with him, and he needed to be careful to respect that.

He needed her.

As much as being with her rotted something inside him, made him more resentful day by day, he also knew that no one looked at happy family men to be responsible for heinous murders.

They *did* look at newly divorced men. Men who stank of desperation.

His marriage might not be a happy one behind closed doors, but he didn't care about the reality. He cared about the image.

It meant, however, he did need to play the part of the loving husband, the doting father, and he'd been letting his act slip lately. That was how Kim had caught him. And thank God she only caught him in a supposed moment of weakness, a fidelity slip-up.

Things would have been a lot more dire if she'd figured him out for real.

That was a contingency he'd have to plan for at some point. What if Kim *did* realize what was going on? Obviously he'd need to get rid of her, that was simple enough. It was what came after he didn't want to deal with.

TV cameras and police. Everyone monitoring him for the right amount of tears, the proper affectation of grief. Ed knew the role, he'd watched dozens of lesser men on news broadcasts try to fake their way through a sob story, only to be found guilty of it soon after.

They lacked the skill.

Ed just lacked the energy.

Killing Kim meant he'd be a single father, and how could you kill when you had toddlers? He missed the days when Megan was a baby and taking her for long nightly drives to get her to sleep had been the norm.

It was during those drives, away from the cloying presence of Kim, his imagination began to roam freely. He saw the way girls would just wait on the side of highways with their thumbs out, or stagger home from the clubs without a sense of decency or awareness.

Fodder.

There was so much fodder.

When Kim suggested they go to Helen Putnam Park, he thought it was a trick. He watched her face, trying to gauge what her motivations were. But there was nothing there. Nothing more than the usual exhaustion, spite, and dissatisfaction.

He wondered, sometimes, if she hated their life as much as he did.

They were both trapped. Both captives and captors, in the same boat. For better or for worse.

Ed drove the family to the park, Megan in the back talking a mile a minute about some cartoon she was fond of, and periodically taking a break to sing the *Care Bears* theme song on repeat. Ed was grateful he got to leave the house most weekdays, because it meant he didn't need to watch the drivel that kept his kids amused when Kim needed a break. Cartoons about ponies and magical bears couldn't possibly be teaching them anything useful. They were just going to turn into stupid spoon-fed puppets like the rest of the world.

Maybe not Megan, though. There was still hope for Megan.

They walked together through the park, and Ed hazarded putting his arm around Kim's shoulder. She resisted at first, a full-body tension that was powerful in its silent message of repulsion. But soon she softened, leaning against him. She let herself ease into the lie because it was comfortable. Simple.

Megan ran off to investigate a patch of clover, evidently dead set on finding a four-leaf one. Her red hair gleamed penny-bright in the sunshine, and she scrunched up her face tight with concentration.

Kim kneeled down to help Megan pick through the greenery, and Ed's gaze drifted. He followed a jogger running alone, a yellow Walkman clipped to her shorts, headphones in her ears.

He thought about how easy it would be to grab her when she wasn't paying attention.

They so rarely paid attention when it mattered the most.

His gaze continued to drift until it landed on the little copse of trees that hid the small pond. A lazy smile came to his lips as he thought about the girl. She was still down there. No one had found her. Maybe they'd never find her.

"I got one!" Megan squealed with delight, bounding over to show her father her proud discovery.

"Of course you did, Buddy. Because you're my lucky girl." He planted a kiss on the top of her head, gaze drifting back to the trees.

Luck ran in the family.

# FORTY-TWO

## TWO WEEKS LATER

"How are you feeling, Margot?" Dr. Singh was sipping a cup of tea, a serene expression on his face, and Margot wondered how it must feel to be that relaxed.

"I gotta say, Doc, if there was a Top Ten countdown of life-altering traumatic events, we might have to rearrange my rankings a little, but the top three don't have to worry about getting dethroned."

The reason she liked Dr. Singh was that he didn't waste time telling her she used humor as a defense mechanism.

He offered her a small smile. "Well as long as the top three are secure."

In truth, very little had changed for her since the sniper case was closed. She had already spent so much of her life peeking in her back seat, checking her locks, making sure she wasn't being followed, that it didn't *change* her paranoia. It had, perhaps, focused it more sharply, but it didn't have any real impact on her day-to-day life.

She'd been off work for almost two weeks since the shoot-out at the Savoy residence. So had Wes, and the other officers in the house. It was a mandated cooling-off period for them to get their heads right and make sure they weren't suffering any initial symptoms of PTSD.

In that time, Leon had passed along the details they had learned. Savoy was a night security guard for a company that offered services to several local office buildings. With his badge, he had twenty-four-hour access to a number of very prominent, very *tall* buildings. He had used that—and his ability to avoid the in-house cameras—to find prime locations, and then he would just wait for his moment.

The neighbor's house where he had taken his last stand had been blessedly vacant, the couple who lived there were on a short trip to Phoenix visiting their daughter who had just had a baby.

The officer who had been shot but survived was leaving the force, Leon told her, but everyone else seemed to be biding their time until they could return to duty. The officer and the driver who had survived the Broadway shooting had both been released from hospital, and the three officers who had died by the gunman's trigger had been given police funerals, which had cast a sober pall over the city for about a week, with them happening on back-to-back days.

Things in the outside world were returning to normal, though. Christmas was inching closer, and the arrival of December seemed to remind everyone that there was hot choco-late to drink and gifts to buy. The lurking terror that had chased citizens inside and kept tourists at bay had faded. Margot didn't think people had forgotten, but to look outside on any given day it certainly seemed like no one remembered. There was a collec-tive release of breath in knowing that the man who had done this was dead, a kind of justice had been served.

She knew the effects of the killings would never disappear entirely, but it *felt* like a ghost story from hundreds of years ago rather than something that had happened just weeks earlier.

Margot, meanwhile, was regretting her choice to invite Jus

— David to come for Christmas, because it meant pretending she cared about the holidays. Wes had promised to help her pick out a Christmas tree that afternoon, and she was certain that was just because he was *dying* to decorate her house.

Wes, as it turned out, really fucking loved Christmas.

Dr. Singh was patient, waiting for Margot to go on, and when she stayed quiet, he nudged her. "Do you think you're handling this all OK?"

She shrugged. "I don't know if there's a good way or a bad way to handle what happened. I think I'm accepting of it."

"Have you spoken to the FBI recently, have they asked if you want to go see Ed again?"

Margot couldn't hide the frown. "No. Since closing the Marissa Loewen case things have been pretty quiet on that front. I don't know if it's because they want to give me space after the shooting, or if it's because Ed has gone quiet and isn't taunting them with any other details. I'm not sure I care. It's been nice, to not think about it."

This was a lie, because there wasn't a day in her life that went by where Margot didn't think about Ed in some capacity. And now he wasn't just a ghoulish specter lurking in her history. He was present in her every waking moment, and she knew it was only a matter of time before she had to sit down across from him again and make another deal with the Devil.

"Do you feel ready to go back to work?" Dr. Singh set his cup down and watched her carefully.

"I feel as capable of doing my job as I did before all this happened."

She could tell he wanted to pick apart this statement, and ask why it wasn't just a *yes*, but instead he observed her silently a moment longer and then nodded.

"Do you want me to tell them you *aren't* ready to go back?" he asked softly.

She thought about that for a long moment, and then, for the

first time in the entire session, she smiled. A real genuine smile, that turned into a laugh, one that left tears in the corner of her eye.

"No, Doc. Thank you for the offer though."

A low *gong* sound through the ceiling-mounted speakers announced their session was over.

"Until next time," he said, rising to show her to the door. He always said this, and there was something comforting about the consistency of it.

Margot shook his hand at the door, before heading out into the chilly December air.

She tugged her winter coat around her, red strands of her hair pulling loose from her ponytail and sticking to her lashes. Work would start again tomorrow, and she already had a meeting on the calendar with Leon to review the Muir Woods case and some of the details that had come up before she took her break.

The new leads—Rebecca's bruises and Wally's hiker with mysterious footwear—might not break the investigation wide open, but they were a mild thaw in a cold case that refused to let her rest.

She climbed into her car and turned on the heater, chasing away the fog inside her windows. The city streets outside were decorated for the holiday, and it was surprisingly comforting to see garlands and Christmas lights everywhere she looked. A Christmas tree in her own home was a foreign concept, but one she might learn to enjoy, given time.

It had been years since Margot had put up a tree.

Maybe it was time to start new family traditions.

As she put her key in the ignition to start the car, her phone buzzed in her inside coat pocket. She was still technically on leave, so she wasn't expecting a work call, and it was probably Wes arranging where to meet later. She'd told him she had therapy today. Maybe he wanted to ask if she'd been given a shiny sticker that said *Sane* on it.

Instead, the caller ID read *Shitty Lawyer*.

She stared at the screen, debating whether or not to answer. She pictured the night she was supposed to have. Christmas trees. Eggnog. Wes in her apartment, singing off-tune carols as he told her how bad she was at distributing tinsel.

Whatever Rosenthal had to say, it was going to dampen whatever positivity she had started to feel toward the day. But she also couldn't just ignore it, no matter how badly she wanted to.

"Hello?"

"Good morning, Ms. Finch," he said formally. She was about to correct him, but something in her gut told her to be quiet. Ford had been good about using her correct name in recent months. Something was wrong. "Ms. Finch, I have your father on the line with me, and he has requested a conversation."

Bile rose at the back of her throat, and she considered hanging up the phone right then. What a tricky son of a bitch. He couldn't get to her but knew Rosenthal could. She couldn't believe the lawyer would let Ed manipulate him this way.

Her finger hovered over the *End Call* button for a heartbeat, but she couldn't bring herself to hit it.

Something inside her, something ugly and unnamed, had been waiting for this.

Margot leaned back in the driver's seat, her gaze drifting over the street, watching the people go about their lives, blissfully unaware of the threat that might exist around any corner, the eyes that might be watching their nighttime windows, the killer who might be out hunting at that very moment.

She sighed. At least this time she would remember to record it.

"Put him through."

A click announced that Ford had joined two separate calls. Margot didn't bother to give a greeting, and it seemed Ed wasn't expecting one.

"Megan, did I ever tell you about the summer you turned eight?"

Margot closed her eyes.

"No."

"I think you're really going to like this story."

She doubted that very much.

But she let him tell it.

# A LETTER FROM THE AUTHOR

First of all, let me say a huge "THANK YOU!" for reading *Her Father's Secret*. I hope you enjoyed the ongoing dramas of Detective Margot Phalen, and if this is your first book with Margot, don't miss out on reading *The Killer's Daughter*, where it all began.

If you want to join other readers in hearing all about my Storm new releases and bonus content, you can sign up for my newsletter:

www.stormpublishing.co/kate-wiley

And if you want to keep up to date with all my other publications, you can sign up to my mailing list:

eepurl.com/ASoIz

Reviews are enormously helpful to other readers looking for their next book, so if you enjoyed *Her Father's Secret*, and can spare a few moments to leave a review, it would be hugely appreciated. Even a short review can make all the difference in encouraging a reader to discover my books for the first time. Thank you so much!

The Margot Phalen books have been a huge labor of love for me. I know that's a strange thing to say about books where one of the main characters is a serial killer, but the idea for these books has been haunting me for years (in case you're wondering why they are randomly set in 2017, now you know). I'm so delighted to get to tell these stories over not just one book, but several, and I hope you'll stick around to see where Margot and Ed's journey ends up.

Thanks again for reading, and I hope you'll stay in touch—there's so much more to come!

Kate Wiley

www.katewiley.com

 facebook.com/SierraDeanAuthor

 x.com/sierradean

instagram.com/sierradeanauthor

# ACKNOWLEDGMENTS

No book is truly ever written alone.

Thanks for this go first to my editor, Vicky Blunden, for giving this series life and also being one of my most supportive cheerleaders. There's truly no gift quite like having someone who just *gets* your book, and I got very lucky. To the entire editorial team at Storm, thank you for making my books shine.

Second, to my mom. *Her Father's Secret* was finished in a crunch over Christmas break while I was off work, and I was most certainly a nightmare person existing on little sleep and even shorter patience that week. Not the most Christmassy, but she kept me in fresh coffee and baked goods and without her, this book likely never would have been finished on time.

To everyone who loved and reviewed *The Killer's Daughter*, thank you so much. That was my first thriller and it meant the world to me that people enjoyed it.

And to every aspiring writer out there with a story to tell, let this series be a beacon to you. I had multiple agents and publishers overlook these books until they found their perfect home with Storm. I believed so strongly in Margot's story I simply couldn't give up on her, and now you're here, reading the second book in her series. Persevere!